SHADOW GIRL

Also by Liana Liu:

The Memory Key

SHADOW GIRL

LIANA LIU

HARPER TEEN

An Imprint of HarperCollins Publishers

HarperTeen is an imprint of HarperCollins Publishers.

ISBN 978-0-06-230667-8

Typography by Ellice M. Lee

17 18 19 20 21   PC/LSCH   10 9 8 7 6 5 4 3 2 1

❖

First Edition

FOR MY SISTERS, KARINA AND KRISTEN

SHADOW GIRL

BEFORE

MY FIRST OFFICIAL JOB—ONE WITH TAX FORMS AND A PAY-
check, instead of the grungy wad of dollars I'd get for
babysitting or running neighbors' errands—was at a kids' day
camp. I was fifteen, and labor laws allowed me to work up to
forty hours a week when school was out of session. That summer I worked forty hours a week and would have worked more
if it had been possible. We needed the money. And I was glad
to be busy. It was the year my father left.

The camp was a twenty-minute walk from our apartment: first through crooked slimy streets and a fierce heat that
smelled of salt and herbs and rot; then, around the corner,
the buildings grew taller and wider, the sidewalks straighter,
the air softer; then another corner, and the buildings shrank
but became more ornate. On the next block was the redbrick
school building that housed Sunshine Day Camp.

From the beginning, I liked my job. I loved the kids,
most of them. And the ones I didn't love—the ones who mis-
behaved out of pure spite and felt no remorse when caught

and reprimanded—I still tried to love. If I could love them, I thought, maybe that would make them lovable. It took me half the summer to realize things didn't work like that.

But generally I loved the kids, my kids, my group of wiggly, giggly seven-year-olds. On a field trip to the aquarium, as the children crowded in front of the shark tank, I remembered that old saw about how sharks had to keep moving or they'd die, and it reminded me of my kids, especially the boys, who fidgeted when forced to sit in chairs, who fidgeted until they fell from chairs. The boys were always falling from their chairs.

Every night I would come home with stories to tell over dinner: this little boy cried at recess, this little girl played alone, this little boy hummed "Happy Birthday" all day long. My mother would listen intently, and when my older brother, Andy, was home he listened too, or pretended to. That summer, it was useful having something meaningless to talk about.

So when I was fifteen and working at Sunshine Day, I focused primarily on the children. But I also thought about what I would do once camp was over. Maybe I was like that shark, too—I had to keep my mind moving or else I'd die. So while I braided hair and sang songs and organized raucous rounds of math tournaments, I also studied everything happening around me.

And I realized that the most difficult part wasn't managing the children—it was managing the parents. Although the kids were exhausting, you always knew what they wanted: every thought came pouring from their little mouths; every feeling was finger painted across their little faces. You knew what they wanted: your attention, all of it.

The parents were more complicated because they also wanted your attention but pretended they didn't. So instead they complained, rationally and irrationally. "My Adeline came home upset because Spencer teased her." "How could you punish Kiki for kicking Benny? We told you she's extremely sensitive." Or, when particularly upset, they might criticize using compliments: "It's good you haven't fixed the swing set yet—it teaches the kids about delayed gratification." Although their complaints were always on behalf of their children, it often seemed like they were actually talking about themselves.

As the most junior of the junior counselors, however, I didn't have to deal with parental grievances. I watched and listened, though, and noticed that some counselors were much better than others at handling the parents. And I knew I could be better too. All this passive-aggression reminded me of high school.

Plus, the parents liked me. Partly because I adored their children; partly because I was exactly their idea of what I should be—kind but firm with their babies, and sweet and deferential to them. The things they knew about me, the things I told them (only when they inquired; I never presumed their interest), confirmed their assumptions.

They asked: Where are you from? Were you born here? Where do you live? Where do you go to high school?

And when I answered their questions—sweetly and deferentially—they smiled, thinking that they were right about me.

On the last day of camp, when parents came over to say thank you and good-bye and Adeline will miss you so much, I told them I would miss Adeline so much too. Then I said in a quiet voice, my eyes slightly averted, that if Adeline wanted to get ahead during the school year, I was starting an academic tutoring service. That was all I said. If they asked for my phone number, I gave them my phone number.

I might have done it differently. I might have confidently asserted myself, declaring my aptitude and experience. I might have phrased my offer in terms of Adeline needing help rather than getting ahead. I might have made cards with my name in bold letters on bright paper, and passed them out like flyers. I'd considered doing all these things but didn't do any of them. If parents asked for my phone number, I gave them my phone number. Then I hugged Adeline good-bye.

The first year I had two students during the fall and three during the spring. The second year I had three students during the fall and four during the spring. And this year I had five during the fall and five during the spring. More parents called, but I only had time for five students. Because there was also school. And homework. And planning, as I kept my shark mind moving, moving, moving.

Summers were different, though. Slower. Most of my students went away to the country or the shore or abroad. Sunshine Day asked me to come back, but I respectfully declined in order to spend a relaxing summer with Adeline, writing stories and reading books. The following summer I worked for another family, conducting science experiments with their twin boys.

Now for this summer—the summer after my high school graduation. Joan Pritchett is the first one to offer me a job. I thank her and tell her I'll let her know in a few days. Joan is one of my more difficult parents. She's demanding and gossipy and not very nice. However, I really like her son, who I've been tutoring these past two years. So I decide to accept the job.

But then I get another call.

Vanessa Morison is blond and beautiful and wearing a lacy silky peachy something that looks like a bathrobe. It's true that it is very early in the morning and we are sitting in a room she calls her boudoir, a room that looks like a bedroom without a bed (luminous walls, fleecy rugs, lots of candles and mirrors). It's true that she is confiding personal details to me in a breathy voice. It's true that I am the one who looks out of place here, trying not to fidget in my shirt buttoned up to the collar and the navy skirt I thoroughly ironed last night.

But this is a job interview, and our first time meeting, so it must be a dress she's wearing. Even if it looks exactly like a bathrobe.

"My husband thinks Ella isn't working to her full potential," Mrs. Morison says, her voice a long sigh. "I tell him I agree, yet somehow we still end up fighting. Though I know it's just because he's stressed out from work. He runs a hedge fund, a really big one."

"Impressive," I say, as if I hadn't known. But of course I'd known. I'd done my research; I always do. And I'd done extra research on her husband and his hedge fund.

"It's a lot of pressure, especially with the way the markets have been lately. So I try not to bother him with anything else, but it's hard . . . with Ella . . ."

"Sometimes smart kids underperform in school because they're bored. The great thing about academic tutoring is we can customize the curriculum to meet each student's needs and interests."

She nods. "You're right. Ella must be bored."

Then I feel a little guilty, because I don't actually know Ella, so I don't actually know how bored or smart she might be. I change the subject. "Here's my résumé and two letters of reference, Mrs. Morison. Would you like to see a sample lesson plan?"

"Sure—but please call me Vanessa." She flips through the stack of papers I hand her.

"Vanessa," I say. "I can't wait to meet your daughter."

"And she's excited to meet you. It's too bad she isn't home now."

"She isn't? Where is she?" I smile so that I don't frown. When we spoke on the phone, I specifically asked if Ella would be there, and Vanessa Morison said that she would. I never take on students without meeting them first.

"Her babysitter took her to the park. It's such a nice morning, you know." Vanessa tosses her golden hair behind her shoulder. She adjusts the belt holding her dress together. She looks nervous. Her nervousness makes me nervous.

But then she tells me how much she will pay me this summer. She names a figure twice the amount of my usual salary. "Is that all right?"

And all I can do is agree. Of course that's all right, it's more than all right; it's everything. I start thinking about what I'll do with the money: some to my mother, save most of the rest, of course, but I'd like a new pair of sneakers since mine have started pinching, and my mother could use a rice cooker that doesn't leak and—

"By the way," Vanessa says, "you aren't superstitious, are you?"

I stare at her.

"No?" I ask instead of say, startled by the randomness of her question. And because I want an explanation.

But she doesn't explain. Instead she says she'll email me directions to their house on the island.

"The island?"

"Yes, Arrow Island. We go there every summer. We have a house there, right on the beach, so don't forget your bathing suit. There's also a pool in the backyard, of course. And I have the perfect room picked out for you. You're going to love it."

"That sounds wonderful, but . . ." I pause to think about how I'm going to explain this misunderstanding to her, that I'm very sorry but I can't go away with them; I can't leave the city.

Then I ask myself: Why not? After all, it's only for two months. Not years.

"But what?" asks Vanessa.

I clear my throat and say: "I'm really looking forward to spending the summer with you and your family. By the way, how did you hear about my tutoring service?"

"Oh, my friend Joan told me how much you've helped her son." She smiles.

"Joan? You mean Joan Pritchett?" I hadn't even known the two women knew each other. Their children go to different schools. The Morisons live uptown and the Pritchetts downtown.

"That's right. She won't be pleased that I've stolen you away from her, will she?" Vanessa is still smiling; nothing about her expression has changed, yet she suddenly seems different. As if her face has come into focus. She looks sharper now.

"Something wrong?" she asks.

"Uh, no, uh . . . I like your dress."

"This?" She glances down at peachy silk and lace. "This is my bathrobe."

When I get home, my mother is in the kitchen stirring the pot of rice porridge on the stove. She comes out to watch as I take off my shoes, place them neatly on the rack, and tuck my purse into the closet. "Zěnme yang?" she asks. How was it?

"I got the job," I say.

"Hǎo." Good. She turns to go back into the kitchen.

"Mom. This summer is going to be different."

She turns around again.

"I'll be staying with them in their house," I tell her.

She stares at me. "Wèishéme?" Why?

I think: Why not?

I say: "The family spends their summer on an island several hours away. They have a house. On the beach. With a swimming pool. I'll have my own room. And they're going to pay me a lot of money. Almost double what I made last year. Anyway, it's only for two months. It'll be fine. It'll be great. Really. Great. They're going to pay me a lot."

My mother continues staring. Although she doesn't speak much English, she can understand it well enough. But now she stares at me as though she doesn't understand a word I'm saying.

My shirt collar feels tight around my neck. I unbutton the top button. "I should change my clothes," I say.

"Huàn hǎo, jiù chī fàn." All right, then come eat.

I go into the bedroom and shut the door. I know what I have to do, and I'm dreading doing it. But I call Joan Pritchett and tell her how grateful I am for the job offer, though unfortunately I'm unable to accept as I'll be going away for the summer.

"What a shame. Benny will be disappointed," she says. "He was so excited when I told him you were going to be tutoring him every day. I don't know what I'm going to tell him now."

"I'm sorry. Benny's a great kid, and I hope we can continue our tutoring sessions in the fall. He's been making amazing progress."

"We'll see," she says. "So where are you going?"

"I accepted a position with a family outside the city."

"Which family? Anyone I know?"

"It's, um, well, I don't feel comfortable—"

"You can tell me. Tell me."

I know I shouldn't tell her. It's my policy not to discuss students or their parents with other students or their parents. And I particularly don't want to get involved with whatever is going on between Vanessa and Joan. Yet I don't know how to avoid it. "I'll be tutoring Ella Morison," I say reluctantly.

Joan inhales sharply. "I know Ella. Vanessa and I are friends. So I probably shouldn't be telling you this," she says, lowering her voice as if whispering a secret is the same as keeping it. "But did you know that Vanessa used to be a stewardess—that is, a flight attendant? In fact, that's how she met Jeffrey. While he was still married to his first wife."

I don't say anything. I'm trying to think of a way to politely end this call.

"And it's too bad about that trouble Ella got into this year, isn't it?"

I tune my voice to its cheeriest tone. "Yes, well, have a great summer!"

"Good luck with Ella. You'll need it," Joan says, and hangs up.

I tell myself she is just trying to make trouble. I tell myself that no matter what the situation is with the Morisons, it'll be better than working for Joan Pritchett. I put my phone down with a sigh.

The room has gotten dark. Outside, the sky is a pallid gray; it looks like rain. I shut the open window. I take off my shirt and skirt and hang them in the closet. Then I put on an old tank top and a pair of sweatpants and go back to the kitchen. My mother is still at the stove. She ladles the steaming contents of the pot—pallid gray as the sky—into a bowl and hands it to me.

Then she tells me not to take the job.

My mother speaks softly, as if she's afraid of disturbing someone in the next room. Our apartment is small, the walls flimsy, but there isn't anyone in the next room. And I have to take the job. I've already taken it.

I sit down at the table and stir my bowl of rice porridge. "Smells good," I say.

"Nǐ zhù zài jiālǐ. Nǐ kěyǐ zài zhè zhǎo gōngzuò." You can stay home. You can get a job here.

I continue eating. I feel her watching me, her gaze pressing, prodding. And all of a sudden I can't stand it any longer. I snap: "We need the money."

My mother turns away. "Zhen de," she says. That's true.

Instantly, I'm ashamed. It is true that we need the money, but it's because of me. Because I'm starting college in the fall, and even though I have a tuition scholarship and I'll be living here, at home, there will still be textbook expenses and student fees and transportation costs and a hundred other small bills and charges.

"I'm sorry," I say, trying to make my voice as soft as hers. "I already told them I'd do it. I guess I shouldn't have without talking to you first. But the pay is really good."

My mother nods. She goes to the sink, rinses out a rag, and wrings it out. She wipes down the countertop with a few brisk strokes, and rinses the rag out again. My mother is a small woman, short and very slender, but she has strong arms. She can open stuck jar lids that I can't open. She can scrub every surface in the bathroom without pausing to rest.

"Aren't you going to eat?" I ask.

I'm not hungry. She goes into the living room. A moment later, the vacuum cleaner roars on. I track her location by the sound vrooming through the flimsy walls of our small apartment: now she is in the corner by the bookshelf, now she is behind the couch, now she is right near the bedroom, now she is in the bedroom.

The longest I've ever been away from home, away from her, was a weekend.

I finish eating my bowl of porridge. I wash the dishes. Then I take a grapefruit from the refrigerator and dissect it, meticulously removing all the skin and pith and seeds. I cut the fruit into bite-size chunks, arrange the chunks on a plate, and carry the plate out into the living room.

My mother is unplugging the vacuum. She looks up and smiles. She loves grapefruit, but it's painful for her to peel one because the juice stings her dry hands. We sit down on the plaid couch and eat the sour-sweet fruit together. She doesn't speak until we're halfway done with the plate.

"Shèng xià liú gěi nǐ gēgē. Tā shuō, tā jīntiān huí jiā," she says. The leftovers are for your older brother. He said he'll come by today.

I put down my fork. There's no point in arguing with her about Andy.

It begins to rain, hard. Drops crashing into the windows, wind rattling the glass. A slash of lightning quickly followed by a gunshot of thunder. The room becomes very dark, as dark as night.

"Anyway," I say, "I'll only be gone for two months."

My mother reaches over and switches on the table lamp. Yes, she says, then you'll come home. If she doesn't sound happy, at least she doesn't sound unhappy. Which should be enough to make me happy.

I'm not, not at all.

Because even though the storm is outside, it suddenly feels as though it's inside, inside me, bashing my bones and rattling my head, as lightning slashes the underside of my skin. My heart is thunder. I stand up, frightened, and at the same moment there is a loud crash.

I run toward the sound, to the bedroom, and find that the window is open and the carpet is soaked and the porcelain ballerina figurine that is usually balanced on the sill, one leg lifted high, is now on the floor snapped cleanly in half at the waist. I slam the window shut. I pick up the pieces. My father gave me the figurine for my sixth birthday. I loved her then. I wanted to be her then: small and graceful with pink cheeks and fair hair.

But that was a very long time ago.

"Shì shénme?" my mother asks from the doorway. What is it?

"Sorry. I thought I closed the window," I say.

Although it's still storming outside, that strange rage I felt a moment ago has gone, as quickly and completely as it came. I feel absolutely calm as I get a rag and press it into the wet carpet; as I bandage the ballerina figurine in newspaper, label it CAREFUL—BROKEN GLASS, and drop the package into the trash can.

"I'll wrap this for later." I pick up the plate of grapefruit.

For your brother, my mother says.

I nod. I know I'll be the one to eat it later, when Andy doesn't show up.

As I set the plate of fruit inside the refrigerator, I notice the drop of blood, a perfect dark red bead on my pale palm. I must have cut myself on the broken ballerina, despite handling the figurine carefully. But I don't remember feeling any pain. And when I wash the blood from my hand, I can't find any cuts or breaks in the skin.

For some reason, it reminds me of that strange question Vanessa Morison asked me this morning: "You aren't superstitious, are you?"

I'm not superstitious at all.

But why did she ask?

PART I
THE ISLAND

1

TRAVELING FROM THE CITY TO THE MORISONS' HOUSE ON ARROW Island requires taking the subway to the bus station, the bus to the ferry terminal, the ferry to the island port, and a taxi to the house. The trip takes seven hectic, stressful, sweaty hours. For me it takes a few extra minutes because my taxi driver, a white man with a white beard straggling to his chest, is more interested in talking than driving. He asks me where I'm from, then where my parents are from, then tells me about his time in Korea. Which is not where any of us are from.

But I'm used to this sort of thing. I smile and nod and watch the scenery. We are on a narrow road lined by giant trees and thick shrubs and tall grass. The greenery rustles and sways against the blue sky. It's cooler here than in the city, and the air is sweeter. And quieter—it's gotten quiet in the car. The driver has asked me a question.

"Sorry, what did you say?"

"What's it like it in China?"

"I've never been there."

"Really? How's that?"

"Why's the island named Arrow Island? Does it have to do with arrows?" I ask.

The driver scratches his beard. "Nah, it's named after this guy Godfrey Arrow who came here in the eighteen hundreds. He and his family owned most of the island for a while, but now they're all gone."

"Where'd they go?"

"Who knows? The house you're headed to was built for Godfrey's oldest son. Stayed in the family for only two generations, then there was no one left to inherit. Bill Morison bought the property about twenty years ago. It's quite a place. You'll see."

He makes a sharp turn and stops in front of an enormous metal gate. He rolls down his window and buzzes the intercom at the side of the road. "Got a delivery for you," he barks into the speaker. "A nice girl."

Someone laughs at the other end. The driver laughs too. I do not.

The gate slides open, and as we spiral up a steep hill, the man starts telling me about his feud with the local post office, but interrupts himself to announce: "There it is!" He waves his gnarled hand at the windshield.

I glance up. All I see is grass and tree and endless sky. Then we go around one more bend and suddenly, there it is.

"Wow," I say involuntarily.

I pay the driver, climb out of the car, and just stare. I barely notice when he sets my suitcase down next to me. I barely remember to say something polite as he gets back into his taxi and zooms away. I'm too busy looking at the house.

It's a pale gray structure three—no, four—stories high, with shingles and arches and pillars and balconies and a tower with a pointed roof. It looks like something out of a fantasy or fairy tale; it looks like nothing I've ever seen in real life.

But then the front door swings open and a guy strides through the open door, a guy who is clearly not out of a fairy tale: he's wearing a faded shirt and a pair of lime-green swim trunks; his dark hair is choppy and clumpy, as if it hasn't been combed today, or maybe ever. And he's frowning. He looks really angry. He walks straight over to me and announces, "You have to go."

"Excuse me?" I say.

"You're at the wrong place."

"Isn't this the Morisons' house?"

"Yeah, but you're at the wrong place," he says.

"No, I don't think so, I mean, no, I'm in the right place, definitely, I'm Ella's academic tutor and I was hired last month and Vanessa is expecting me, I just spoke to her yesterday. . . . Is Vanessa here? Can I talk to her? Vanessa Morison?" I hate how my voice is fluttering, but I'm hot and tired and nervous, and now I'm also panicking. It took me seven hectic, stressful, sweaty hours to get here.

"Listen," he says. "No nice girls allowed."

I stare at him. "Are you kidding?"

The guy starts laughing. "Totally kidding. Sorry, that was a dumb joke. The expression on your face, though! You were so freaked out."

I think: Yes, it was a dumb joke.

I think: What a jerk.

I say: "Ha! Very funny."

"Sorry," he says again, but his apology is undermined by how hard he's still laughing. "Is that your bag? I'll grab it for you."

"I've got it." I clutch the handle of my big suitcase. He tries to pull it away. I grip tighter. He tugs harder. I yank it back. He lets go. I stumble backward and nearly fall over.

"Okay," he says. "I'm Henry, Ella's brother. So you're her new babysitter."

I smile to hide my annoyance. "I'm her academic tutor."

"Same thing," he says. He smirks.

"No, actually—"

"Henry! Are you torturing her already? Stop it right now."

I'm relieved to see Vanessa Morison walking toward us.

"Hello, darling." She clasps my shoulders and kisses the air adjacent to my cheeks. She smells sweetly clean, like the air after a good rain, and I know it's just perfume, her expensive perfume, but it smells astonishingly real. Today she is wearing a floaty floral something that I'm almost certain is a dress, not a bathrobe. Almost, almost certain.

"Welcome! I'm so happy you're here," Vanessa says.

"I'm so happy to be here," I say.

"Sure you are, nice girl," Henry says. Still smirking.

Vanessa frowns at him. "Aren't you grounded? Shouldn't you be studying?"

"You're right, Ness. I'm going now," he says with mock meekness.

"Good boy." She doesn't seem to notice the mocking part of his meekness.

Once he's inside, I turn to Vanessa and say, "I didn't know you have a son."

"Oh, no, no, no. Henry is my husband's son from his first marriage. I'm definitely not old enough to have a son that old. Definitely not," she says, her tone wavering despite all those definitelys. "Henry's your age. He also just finished his senior year of high school, more or less."

I'm curious about what "more or less" means, and why he's grounded, and what he's supposed to be studying if he's done with school, but I don't ask. It would be impolite to ask. Anyway, it's obvious that Henry Morison is just some bratty kid who likes to make trouble. I hope his sister isn't the same. I'm really worried that his sister is the same.

"Where's Ella?" I ask.

"She's around here somewhere. Let's get you settled—then the two of you can finally meet," Vanessa says. "How was your trip?"

"Great!" I grip the handle of my suitcase and follow her inside the house.

Then I stop to stare. Though the exterior looks like a fairy tale, the interior is all brand-new. Everything is glass and stone and perfect angles and gleaming surfaces. The furniture is stylishly modern. The ceilings are high, the rooms spacious. The atmosphere utterly serene.

"You like it?" Vanessa asks.

"It's beautiful," I say. And it is. Yet the mismatch between inside and outside is somewhat unsettling. It makes the place seem almost fake—despite the fact that everything here, every stone countertop and mahogany cabinet and flat-screen television and antique rug and designer textile, is undoubtedly genuine.

Vanessa guides me around a long looping hallway. She points out the living room and dining room and front staircase and entertainment room and kitchen and back staircase and pantry. I cannot believe the size of the place. I cannot believe it all belongs to them. I try to memorize the layout, but there are so many rooms, too many rooms. Also, I'm distracted by the sound my suitcase is making as I pull it along behind me, a squeaky cry that echoes against the gleaming marble floors. At least Vanessa doesn't seem to notice.

She stops in front of a metal door and presses a button in the wall. "Here's the elevator. The house has four floors. You and Ella are on the second, and so is the library. My husband's office, my studio, and our bedroom is on the third. On the fourth floor are my father-in-law's rooms. When you meet him, don't take offense, he can be a bit . . ."

I wait for her to finish. The door slides open. We step into the elevator. It lifts us up. The door slides open again. We step out. I'm still waiting.

"Your room is right this way." Vanessa lifts her arms, hands slicing air, like—I can't help noticing—a flight attendant pointing out the emergency exits on an airplane. At the end of the corridor, she flings open a door.

"Here we are!" she announces.

The walls are light pink. A white fluff of rug sprawls across the floor. The bed has a ruffled canopy and a rose-print quilt. There is an ornate dressing table against one pink wall and a mirrored wardrobe against another pink wall. I would have loved it when I was eight; it would have been the pretty room of my dreams. But now that I'm eighteen, it's a little too little-girl.

Nonetheless, I say, "It's perfect. I love it."

Vanessa smiles. "I knew you would. I redecorated it for Ella this year—it used to be a guest room—but when it was done, she refused to sleep here."

"Really? Why?"

She shrugs. "You know Ella."

"Actually, I don't—"

"Here's the thermostat. Feel free to adjust the settings."

"Okay," I say. "Is Ella's room nearby? I'd like to say hello."

Vanessa takes me across the hall. She knocks briskly on the door and then opens it, revealing a blue room the same size as the pink room, with a striped duvet and paintings of ships on the walls. The room is impeccably tidy. There is no sign that a child sleeps here, no toys or games or crayoned drawings, and no sign of Ella herself.

"Well, I guess you'll have to wait to meet her at dinner—six thirty in the dining room," she says. "Why don't you relax till then. Is there anything I can get you?"

"No, this is great. Everything is great. Thank you."

"You can ask our housekeeper for some oil for your suitcase wheels. I noticed they're a little squeaky," Vanessa says. "See you later!"

"See you later," I say, blushing, and go back into the pink bedroom.

At home there is only the one bedroom, which I share with my mother, so to have my own room, to close my own door of my own room—what a relief it is. I lay my sad squeaky suitcase down on the fluffy rug. The bag is old, almost as old as I am, with a stuttering zipper and a small rip that I stuck together with duct tape. I used black tape so it wouldn't be noticeable, but in this light, in this room, it seems very noticeable. After unpacking my clothes, I push my suitcase into the back corner of the mirrored wardrobe.

Then I open the door to what I think is a closet and find, instead, a bathroom, my own bathroom, with shining silver fixtures and velvety towels and a tub like a porcelain boat. There is a new square of soap in the ceramic soap dish, still wrapped in delicate paper. It's lovely. It's all so lovely that even my reflection in the mirror is not too bad, even though my clothes are limp and my braid is prickly and my face is pale with fatigue. I could use a shower.

But first I have to call my mother.

Are you there? she asks when she answers. It took so long.

"I got here a little while ago. What are you doing?"

I'm cooking dinner for your brother.

"Andy's there?" I don't believe it.

"Hái méiyǒu." Not yet. When my mother talks about Andy, she always speaks in "yet." He's not home yet. He hasn't finished school yet. He doesn't have a job yet.

"Then why are you cooking for him?"

She says my brother called and said he would come home tonight around seven. This is new: my brother doesn't usually give a time. He usually says that he'll drop in sometime later, or tomorrow, or next week. I consider the possibility that this might be the time he actually shows. Then I feel dumb for even considering it.

It's too bad you aren't here, my mother says.

"Yeah, I have to go get ready for dinner, but I'll you call again tomorrow, okay? Tell Andy I say hi. If he gets there."

"Hǎo de." All right. She sounds distracted. In the background, the exhaust fan roars. I imagine her leaning over the stove in her grease-spattered shirt, juggling five pots on the four burners. I hope she isn't making too much food. I'm sure she is making too much food.

This is why I shouldn't have left. But what can I do now?

I go into my own bathroom, take off my tired clothing, and

step into the shower. I'm careful not to smudge the shining
fixtures. I'm careful not to splash the pristine floor. But I do
adjust the settings so that the water streams heavy and hot,
and I do lather lavishly with the lavender-scented soap. Then
I stand there, in a floral cloud of steam, and let myself forget
about my mother, my brother, my squeaky suitcase, annoying
Henry Morison, and the disconcerting fact that I still haven't
met Ella.

And as soon as I do, I start laughing. How unbelievable
that I'm taking a shower in this beautiful bathroom in this perfect house. How unbelievable that I'm being paid to be here.
How unbelievable that this is my life—if only for the summer.

2

ALTHOUGH THE HOUSE IS BIG, ALTHOUGH IT'S ENORMOUS, I don't think I can possibly get lost when I come downstairs for dinner. Then I get lost.

I walk the long looping hallway, peering into room after room. I find the living room and entertainment room and back staircase. I find a wooden deck with an expansive sofa shaded by a white awning. I find a large closet full of beach towels and chairs and umbrellas and inflatable rings and sand toys—these are the first toys I've seen in this house.

When I come back into the hallway, I smell butter and garlic. My stomach roars. I sniff my way to the kitchen. "Hello?" I say.

There's a woman standing at the sink, a middle-aged white woman in an apron, her brownish-grayish hair twisted into a tight bun. She is rinsing a colander.

"Hello?" I say again, louder.

The woman sets the colander in the dish drain. She washes her hands. She shuts off the water. She dries her hands on a towel. Then, finally, she turns around.

I smile at her. She does not smile back.

"You're Ella's new babysitter," the woman says.

"Actually, I'm her academic tutor."

"My daughter used to babysit Ella during the summers. But now you're here."

"Oh. I'm sorry, I didn't mean to . . ." I stop speaking. I don't know what to say.

The woman turns back to the sink and begins scrubbing a saucepan.

I decide I can find the dining room myself. I hurry back to the hallway, check the rooms on the left side, then the rooms on the right side, and there it is. I don't know how I could have missed it before. But at least I'm not late. There's only one person at the table so far.

The elderly man rises slowly from his chair. Despite the heat, he is wearing a collared shirt and suit jacket and a striped silk tie. "Good evening," he says. "You must be Ella's tutor. I'm her grandfather, Bill Morison. Welcome."

"It's nice to meet you," I say.

He shakes my hand. His grip is surprisingly, painfully firm. "Please have a seat. I'm afraid that punctuality is not this family's strength."

Vanessa appears in the doorway. "Where is everyone?"

"I was just saying that punctuality is not this family's strength," says Mr. Morison.

"I'm sorry if you think that's the case," she says coldly.

"It's not an opinion, it's an observation," he says calmly.

From the hallway comes a thunder of footsteps; then Henry bursts into the room. "I'm here!" he announces. "I was studying so hard, I lost track of time."

I manage, just barely, not to roll my eyes.

"Where's Ella?" Mr. Morison looks at Vanessa.

"Where's Ella?" Vanessa looks at Henry.

"Where's Ella?" Henry looks at me.

"Uh," I say.

"She's probably out on the deck," Henry says.

"Shouldn't someone fetch her?" Mr. Morison asks. He sounds perfectly cordial, but Vanessa glares at her father-in-law with narrowed eyes, her lips pressed into a line.

"I'll go," I say. "The deck with the white awning?"

"That's the one," Vanessa says. "Thank you, darling."

As I leave the dining room, I hear Mr. Morison say, "How could you make her go find your daughter? Can't you do anything yourself?"

I start walking faster, down the corridor to the deck, though it seems unlikely I could have missed seeing Ella there before. But I slide the glass door open and step outside anyway. There is no one sitting on the sofa. No one leaning against the wooden railing. Obviously she isn't here.

Yet I linger for a moment to look at the view. Past the steep slope of grass, past a glittering stretch of sand, is the ocean. As soon as I see it, I smell it: a sweet saltiness that is nothing like the festering saltiness of the fish markets in my neighborhood.

I gaze out at that infinite ripple of blue-gray-green. The sight is dazzling. I imagine diving right into that water. No matter that I don't know how to swim.

Suddenly I feel a slither across the back of my neck, get the vague sense there is someone behind me, watching me. I whirl around.

Of course there's no one there. Yet something compels me to make sure. I walk to the far end of the deck and find, crouched in the narrow space between the sofa and the wall, a girl. She isn't watching me. She doesn't seem to notice me at all. There is a sketch pad propped on her knees and a pencil in her hand. She is completely focused on her drawing.

"Ella?" I speak quietly, so as not to startle her.

She is startled anyway. She jumps up and clamps her pad shut.

"Hi! I'm here to tutor you this summer. Did your mom tell you?" I smile.

"Yes," she says. Her voice is soft. Her expression is solemn. Ella Morison is a small girl with dark brown hair and dark brown eyes and a pale round face. She looks younger than her age, eight, and nothing like her mother. Although the dress she's wearing is surely something Vanessa picked out. It's white and gauzy and embroidered. Another kid might have looked cute in it. But on Ella it's all wrong: the top too small, the bottom too big, the fabric too fussy. It makes her pale skin slightly sallow. And there are a few gray smudges on the skirt.

"Can I see what you're drawing?" I ask.

Ella clutches her sketch pad to her chest.

I understand. "Maybe later. It's time for dinner. Are you hungry?"

"Yeah. A little," she says.

"Great. You'll have to show me the way to the dining room, though. I'm still confused about where everything is around here."

Ella nods and leads me inside the house.

As we walk through the hallway, I ask if she's been enjoying her summer vacation and what she's been doing and whether she's excited for our lessons.

"Yes," she says, and "Not much," and "I guess so."

Ella Morison is not what I expected. After Joan Pritchett's gossip and the way Vanessa seemed to delay my meeting with her daughter, I had worried that Ella would be unruly or defiant or just plain mean. This quiet and solemn girl I hadn't expected at all. But I'm extremely relieved to be wrong.

When we come into the dining room, Vanessa leaps up from her chair. She kisses Ella's cheek and rests her hand on her daughter's dark head. "Ellie, how do you always manage to disappear right before dinner?" she asks.

"Sorry," says Ella. She looks at Mr. Morison. "Sorry, Granddad."

"It's not your fault, sweetheart. Someone should be keeping track of you," he says.

Vanessa grimaces. She bends down and examines her daughter's dress. Particularly the gray smudges on the skirt.

"Ellie! Did you get this dress dirty too?"

"Sorry," Ella says again.

"You need to be more careful."

"Sorry," Ella says again.

"It's all right." Vanessa sighs. "I'll ask Mrs. Tully to wash it out tonight."

"Come on, El, I saved you the best seat right over here," Henry says. "Will you please come sit down now so we can eat and I don't die of hunger?"

Ella smiles. It's not particularly big or bright, no teeth revealed, but it's the first time I've seen her smile. She goes to sit next to her brother.

The food is now on the table: grilled chicken speckled with herbs, a fresh-baked loaf of crusty bread, a salad in a rainbow assortment of lettuces, and roasted broccoli and zucchini. It's a lot, and it's all delicious.

As we eat, Vanessa asks her daughter what she was so busy doing that she almost missed dinner and Ella replies that she was reading, and Henry tells his grandfather about some bird he saw at the beach today and old Mr. Morison guesses it was either a black-bellied plover or a black skimmer. Vanessa remarks that Ella is such a little bookworm, and Henry says that he thought the bird might have been a ruddy turnstone.

"It doesn't sound like a ruddy turnstone," says Mr. Morison.

"True. I just like saying ruddy turnstone," says Henry.

I eat the delicious food and wonder why Ella told her mother she had been reading when she had actually been drawing. I notice that she still has her sketch pad with her, in her lap, half hidden in the folds of her dress.

"So how'd you get into academic tutoring?" Henry asks me.

"Well, my first job was at a summer camp, and I really liked working with the kids. And I've always enjoyed school and studying. Tutoring is a way of bringing my favorite things together," I say. I've given this exact explanation many times, but I've never felt so cheesy giving it as I do now, with Henry Morison staring at me.

"You've always **enjoyed** school and studying?" he says.

"Yes," I say.

"Tutoring brings your **favorite** things together?" he says.

"Two of my favorite things," I say.

The way Henry's looking at me makes me feel like a fake. Yet everything I said is true—I like kids, I like school—even if I'm exaggerating a little. But I'm not about to tell the Morison family how much I need the money. Their money.

"Well, I think it's terrific," says Mr. Morison.

"So do I," says Vanessa. "You see, Henry, not everyone wants to spend all day lazing around." It's the sort of comment that might be acceptable if said with enough affection and humor, but she does not say it that way. Her tone is reproachful.

But Henry merely grins. "I refuse to believe that."

The woman from the kitchen comes into the dining room. "Is everything all right? Can I get you anything else?" she asks,

and the Morisons sing a chorus of compliments about the dinner. I murmur along, feeling as though I don't quite know the
words.

"Oh, and let me introduce you," says Vanessa. "Mrs. Tully
keeps our little house here running and cooks us these amazing meals. And this is Ella's new academic tutor. We're so
happy to have her here with us this summer."

"Great to meet you," Mrs. Tully says in a friendly voice,
with a friendly smile, and it's all so friendly that it must have
been a different woman who was rude to me in the kitchen.
Except it wasn't.

"Thanks," I say. "Dinner was delicious."

"I'm glad you liked it," she says.

Mrs. Tully clears the table, carries the dirty dishes away,
and returns a few minutes later with dessert: a golden sponge
cake covered in cream and berries. I'm already full. I have a
slice anyway.

"When do lessons begin?" asks Mr. Morison.

"Tomorrow. We'll work two hours each morning and two
hours in the afternoon." I watch Ella for a reaction, but she is
placidly eating her cake.

"Poor Ella," says Henry.

"Actually, it's going to be fun!" I say. "Right, Ella?"

At the sound of her name, Ella looks at me blankly. Clearly
she hasn't been paying attention. But she nods anyway.

"I think I'll have another piece of cake," says Mr. Morison.

"Really, Bill? What would your doctor say?" asks Vanessa.

Mr. Morison replies in an icy tone, but I don't hear what he says because Henry leans toward me and whispers, "Maybe you have the right idea after all. This academic tutoring business is a good way to get away from your family, huh?"

"No! That's not it at all," I say before I can stop myself, my voice too loud, too harsh.

For a moment Henry looks startled. Then he smirks. "Ah, I get it now. And I thought you were such a nice girl," he says.

It is at this moment that my irritation with Henry Morison becomes dislike.

I return to the pink bedroom exhausted: from waking up so early and traveling most of the day and smiling my way through dinner. I brush my teeth, wash my face, and change into my pajamas. Then I get out my laptop and check my email. I have two new messages: one from my best friend, Doris Chang, and one from the parent of a student.

First I read the email from Sadie's father. He asks if I have any book recommendations for his daughter. I do; I have a spreadsheet of recommendations organized by reading level and genre. I select half a dozen titles that I think will appeal to Sadie and send them to her father.

Then I read the email from Doris. It's an I-miss-you-already-smiley-face-exclamation-mark kind of email. Typical Doris. I don't reply. I'm too tired to reply with the necessary cheer, and if I don't reply with the necessary cheer, Doris will immediately call to ask what's wrong. Because that's how sugar-and-spice nice she is.

I turn off my computer and get into the floral bed. The mattress is firm. The pillows are soft. The sheets are smooth. Outside, the crickets are shrieking, but I'm used to car alarms and ambulance sirens and garbage truck grumblings, so the noise doesn't bother me. I fall asleep almost instantly.

And wake up gasping. The room is dark, so densely dark that I cannot make out the ceiling or walls or the shape of the furniture or even my hand. I sit up. I was awakened by something: a sound and a voice. A thudding sound. A wailing voice.

Just a dream, I tell myself. Go back to sleep.

But then I hear it again. Clunk-clunk-clunk. Followed by a tuneless moan.

"Who is it?" I call out.

Immediately, all sound stops. Even the insects seem to quiet.

I wait. Nothing happens.

After a while, I lie down again and pull the blanket to my chin. Just a dream, I tell myself. Go back to sleep. But it is a very long time before I do.

3

ELLA MORISON SITS WITH A PENCIL IN HER HAND, GAZING AT the workbook open in front of her. Every few moments, she carefully marks something down. Every few minutes, she gently turns a page. Aside from these movements, she is very still. Her posture is impressively straight, though occasionally her shoulders begin to slump, but then she'll jolt back up, as if she's been chided by a voice that only she can hear.

She looks like the perfect student, serious and focused. However, this is our third day working together, so I now know better. Joan Pritchett was right when she implied I'd have trouble with Ella. But the trouble, like Ella, isn't what I expected.

"Done." She lays her pencil in the crease of the workbook.

I go sit next to her at the table. We're in the room Vanessa calls the library. Oddly, it contains no books, but it's a comfortable place to read or study, with its tall windows and high ceilings and leather-upholstered furniture drifting in a sea of antique rug. As long as you bring your own book.

"Let's see. Question one. 'Where does Dottie find the dog?'"

And you wrote, 'Dottie finds the dog at the pet store.' Will you show me where it says that?" I say.

Ella hovers her finger up and down and across the reading comprehension passage but doesn't stop on any particular line. Probably because Dottie finds the puppy in the school yard, not the pet store. There is no pet store in this story.

"Sorry." Ella picks up her gummy eraser and scrubs off her answer. She writes, "Dottie finds the dog at the school yard." Then we continue to the next question. It goes pretty much like the previous question. And so on, and so on, and so on.

Clearly, she can do the work.

Clearly, she is not doing the work.

I've never had a student like Ella before. The well-behaved kids are usually good students, not necessarily because they're smarter, but because they try. They want to please. I know from personal experience; I was always a well-behaved kid.

Ella is extremely well-behaved, yet she doesn't try at all, and she doesn't seem to care about pleasing—or, more accurately, she doesn't seem to care about pleasing me. Though she comes when I ask her to and does what I tell her to and responds politely to my questions, I get the impression that she does it all automatically, while her mind is somewhere else.

I know what to do with defiant children and shy children and rowdy children and whiny children and hyperactive children and crying children and rude children and anxious children and bullying children and bullied children.

I don't know what to do with Ella.

On the first day, I tried bribery. I showed her a sparkly silver pen I'd bought precisely for this purpose and told her it would be her reward when she got a 90 percent on any section of her workbook. Ella seemed interested in the pen, yet her performance did not improve.

On the second day I tried having a heart-to-heart. I said I understood how it could be frustrating to spend your summer vacation getting tutored, but we could make this fun, and if there was anything in particular she wanted to learn or study, she should tell me, because we were in this together. Ella replied, "I don't mind tutoring," yet her performance did not improve.

This morning I tried a stern speech. I told her this was important work we were doing and that she was a smart girl, but she needed to stay focused and try harder, and that we couldn't waste any more time. Ella nodded and said, "Okay. I'm sorry," yet her performance did not improve.

So when the grandfather clock in the corner chimes twelve, signaling that it's time for lunch, I'm relieved. I feel a little bad about how relieved I am.

Lunch is served outside. We sit by the swimming pool, a lapping blue rectangle, at a round table inside a large gazebo, surrounded by flowering shrubs, cooled by the ocean breeze. How unbelievable that this is my life—but just for now, I remind myself.

Today it's only Henry, Ella, and me eating turkey sandwiches with pesto aioli on whole wheat bread, with a side of baby carrots and homemade potato chips.

"Where is everyone?" I ask.

"Aren't we enough for you?" asks Henry.

"You're much more than enough!" I smile my best fake smile.

He grimaces. I'm pretty sure he dislikes me as much as I dislike him.

"Granddad is at his doctor's appointment," Ella says. "Where's Mom?"

Henry turns to his sister. "Guess."

"Did she go to town?" she asks.

"Warm," he says.

"Did she go to lunch at Frankie's?"

"Warmer, maybe even hot."

"Is she getting lunch at Frankie's and then getting her hair done?"

"Burning hot, you got it!" Henry holds up his hand so Ella can high-five it.

She high-fives. "Does that mean Daddy's coming tonight?"

"That's the rumor," he says.

"Goody." Ella looks happy.

"Yeah." Henry looks not happy.

Mrs. Tully comes outside to collect our empty plates.

"Thank you," says Ella.

"You're welcome, Ella," she says.

"Thanks, that was great," says Henry.

"You're welcome, Henry," she says.

"Yes, thanks, lunch was delicious," I say.

Mrs. Tully grunts. She walks back to the house with the dishes stacked in her arms. Even with her hands full, she somehow manages to slam the door.

Henry leans back in his chair and stretches out his arms. He yawns a lion's roar of a yawn, a face-contorting, wide-mouthed wail. I get up and step away from his thrashing limbs. It's amazing how even his tiredness is annoying.

"Hey, I've got a genius idea," he says when he's finally done yawning. "Now that we're free from all those parental people, let's take the rest of the day off and go to the beach."

I know he's talking to Ella, not me, but I instantly say, "No way!"

They both stare at me. I force myself to smile.

"I mean . . . that's a wonderful idea, Henry, and I wish we could, but Ella and I need to get back to work. We have a lot to do. Once we're done, you'll still have plenty of time for the beach this afternoon, and the whole weekend—no lessons on the weekend!"

"God, you're really no fun at all, are you?" says Henry.

I keep smiling, despite my aching cheeks, despite my straining lips, despite my hurt feelings. I know I'm right for taking my responsibilities seriously, and he's wrong. Yet he makes me feel like I'm wrong.

Still, I keep smiling. "I guess not," I say.

"At least you know," he says. He smirks.

"But I want to go to the beach now," Ella says.

We both turn to look at her. Her eyebrows have tensed into little dark hooks. Her bottom lip juts out a millimeter. This is the most belligerent I've ever seen her, the most animated, and part of me is tempted to give in. If only giving in to her didn't also mean giving in to him.

"Ella—" I say, but Henry interrupts.

"El, you know she's right," he says. "We can't possibly go to the beach now—what was I thinking? It's too hot and we just ate and I have to, uh, study. But as soon as you're done getting tutored, I'll race you to the ocean. Deal?"

"Deal," says Ella.

They shake on it. Ella's expression is solemn, as it often is. Henry's is too, which is more uncommon. I hadn't thought that the Morison siblings looked very much alike: he has tanned skin and sharp features; she is pale and soft faced. But with their palms pressed and faces somber, I notice the resemblance between them for the first time. It's something about their eyes.

Henry glances up and catches me watching them. But he doesn't smirk. He gives me an earnest look that could be an apology. Or maybe not. His attention returns to his sister. He lifts their joined hands and spins her around. He laughs. He seems unable to stay serious for longer than sixty seconds. But as she twirls, Ella starts laughing too.

I can't deny that I disapprove of Henry Morison. He is

thoughtless and immature and rude and more than a little irritating. However, I also can't deny that he's a good brother.

In the afternoon, we switch from reading comprehension to math. Ella gets a few questions right—not because she tries harder or is more interested in the subject, but because of chance. This section is multiple choice. I ask how she got to the right answer and her explanation is as incomplete as the one she gives to explain a wrong answer.

After nearly two hours of this, I say, "Close your workbook."

Ella obediently closes her workbook. "Are we done?"

"Not yet." I've tried bribery and heart-to-hearts and a stern speech. Now I try something else. "Let's take a little break and talk," I say.

"About what?" she asks.

"Anything. Tell me about the books you're reading."

"What books?" Ella stares at the cover of her workbook.

"Any books. Your mom said you love to read. What do you read?"

"Lots of stuff," she says warily.

"Like what?"

"Books."

"Books about what?"

"Kids doing stuff."

"What kind of stuff?"

"Different stuff."

I lean back in my chair. "What about school? What are your favorite subjects?"

"They're all okay," she says.

"But you must like some better than others."

"I don't really like gym that much," she says apologetically.

"I never liked gym either," I say. "What about art?"

"Art?"

"Do you like your art class?"

"It's okay."

"But you like drawing, right? What do you like to draw?"

Ella shrugs. "I don't like drawing that much."

I think of the day I found her on the deck with her sketch pad, how focused she was. But I don't press her. "What about your friends? Who are they? What are they like?"

There is a long pause. "They're nice."

"What are their names?" I ask.

There is a longer pause. "Becca. Lindsay. Gretchen. Ruby."

"Which one is your best friend?" I ask.

There is the longest pause. Finally she says, "I don't have a best friend right now." Her voice twinges with some emotion: regret, maybe, or anger. I can't quite tell.

"That's okay. It's good to have lots of good friends. You don't need a best friend. What's your favorite animal?"

"Elephant."

"And your favorite food?"

"Chocolate."

"How about your favorite color?"

"Um. Pink."

"Really? I thought you didn't like pink."

"I do."

"Then why don't you sleep in the pretty pink bedroom your mom decorated for you?"

Ella glances up from her workbook cover. Our eyes meet. She looks at me, really looks, and for the first time it feels like she is actually here with me, seeing me, and thinking over my question. "It's not because it's pink. It's because . . ."

I wait for her to finish.

"I can't tell you," she says.

"Why not?" I ask.

"I just can't."

"But why?"

"I can't."

"Why?"

Ella shakes her head.

At Sunshine Day, the other counselors often remarked how good I was with the campers, how patient. I never told them that I felt the same impatience that they did, a gradual prickle that quickly became an almost unbearable itch. The difference was, I never let myself scratch. But now I can't help it.

"Ella, just tell me!" I snap, and my voice is painfully loud in the quiet room, fingernails screeching over four days of accumulated impatience.

"I can't. Because you have to sleep there now." Ella looks away. She looks far away out the window, past the waving tree branches, past the faded blue sky and the cloud-cloaked sun, past all the things I'm able to see. A moment ago she was here with me; now she is gone.

The grandfather clock chimes. We're done for the day.

"I'm sorry for snapping at you," I say. I truly am. "Shall we clean up?"

"Okay, it's okay," Ella says, her voice soft.

We stand up, push in our chairs, gather our workbooks and notebooks and pencils and pens, and leave the library. We don't talk. Ella goes upstairs to look for her brother. I walk down the hallway to my bedroom.

Some kids just aren't talkers, and that's fine. The problem isn't Ella's reticence. The problem is that her actual self, her thinking, feeling, dreaming self, seems to live a million miles away. And I haven't found a way of reaching her.

But I tell myself not to be so negative. My best friend, Doris, scolds me for being negative. She says, "If you don't believe that things will turn out for the best, how can they turn out for the best?" Doris is a smart girl, but when she says this sort of stuff I can't help thinking that she's not so smart after all. Then I feel bad for being negative. Again.

Anyway, I've been here for less than a week. I have time. I'll keep trying.

And tonight I have something to look forward to: I will finally be meeting Jeffrey Morison. That was, after all, one of the main reasons I took this job.

4

LAST MONTH, WHEN I TOLD MY ECONOMICS TEACHER THAT I would be spending the summer tutoring the daughter of Jeffrey Morison of Morison Capital, Ms. Baldwin gave me the severe look she normally gave to students who weren't paying attention. A week later, she stopped me after class and handed me a hardcover book. "A graduation gift," she said.

I read half of it on my way to Arrow Island, and the other half over the past few days. The book is about the recent financial crisis—the greed, negligence, and corruption of the financial industry that led to the recent financial crisis. It was an interesting and upsetting and frustrating read. I know Ms. Baldwin gave it to me to try to change my mind about working on Wall Street one day. But it did not change my mind.

Nonetheless, I'm writing her a thank-you email when my phone rings.

It's my mother. But it's never my mother. She never calls me; I call her.

"Mom, are you okay? Is everything all right?"

"Hǎo de." Yes, fine, she says.

I analyze her voice. She sounds fine. "Okay. Good."

"Nǐ hǎo ma? Nǐ méi dǎ diànhuà." How are you doing? You haven't called.

I'm about to protest that I called her the day I got here, but then I realize that was four days ago. Four days was a long time for me not to call her. Four days was longer than the longest I'd ever been away from home. And I hadn't even noticed.

"I'm great," I say. "Sorry I haven't called. Things have been busy here."

I understand, she says. Then she tells me that my brother is back.

"What?" I say.

She tells me that Andy arrived the day I left—isn't that funny? She tells me he's looking for a job, he had an interview today—isn't it wonderful? She tells me it's wonderful. Then she waits for me to agree.

"I knew he was coming home. Remember? I called you, and you told me he was coming." Except I didn't believe it then. I barely believe it now.

"Wǒ jìdé, wǒ jìdé," she says. Yes, yes. I remember.

"What kind of job is he looking for? Where was his interview?"

"Deng yi xia." Wait a moment.

"Hold on, Mom, I don't—"

"Hello?" says my brother.

"Andy?" I say. "Hi. How are you?"

"Hey, guess who I saw yesterday," he says casually, as if it's been hours since the last time we talked. It's been months since the last time we talked.

"Who?"

"Doris."

"My friend Doris? Doris Chang?"

"Yeah, Doris. She's cute, huh?"

"You stay away from Doris."

"Why? You think I'm not good enough for her?" Andy sounds hurt. He's an expert at sounding hurt.

"I was kidding! Of course I don't think that."

"Whatever. Who cares about your stupid friends?"

Then my mother is back on the line, saying how nice it is that my brother is home, how she wishes I were home too, how she wishes I hadn't taken the job this summer. My mother is generally not a talker, yet she won't stop talking, and as she goes on, on and on and on, I start getting annoyed, more and more and more annoyed, to the point where I imagine hanging up.

The telephone line dies.

I did it. That's my first thought.

But no, of course I didn't do it. That's my second thought, the reasonable, rational one. It's a coincidence that the line cut off the moment I was imagining—merely imagining—hanging up. So why do I feel so guilty? I call back and apologize.

My mother says it's fine; besides, she has to go. Make dinner. For Andy.

We say good-bye, and I carefully disconnect the line.

Then I call Doris. Though I told Andy I was kidding about him staying away from her, I was not kidding. He definitely isn't good enough for her. Doris is sweet and kind and super smart. Last year she won second prize in a national science competition. In the fall she's going to a prestigious premed program. She volunteers at soup kitchens and hospitals. She's an excellent listener. People like her.

And my brother is a creep.

Doris doesn't answer the phone, so I leave a message: "Andy told me he ran into you. So I just wanted to tell you—oh, I don't know, never mind."

I hang up and finish writing my thank-you email to Ms. Baldwin. "I'm at the Morisons' house on Arrow Island," I write. "It's beautiful here."

That evening I dress carefully for dinner. I put on my best button-down shirt and my navy-blue skirt. I put on the earrings my mother gave me for my birthday this year. Her own mother gave them to her when she got married. She used to show them off to me, dots of gold in a red velvet box. But I'd never seen her actually wear them.

I examine my reflection in the mirror. My eyes are still too small and my lips too narrow, but at least my hair is nice, smooth black and straight to my waist. I consider wearing it down. But I twist it up into a neat knot. I want to look professional.

It's not that I expect this summer will get me a finance job or an internship or a letter of reference from Jeffrey Morison. But there's always a chance that it will. As Doris says, "If you don't believe that things will turn out for the best, how can they turn out for the best?"

Right now, at least, I try to believe her.

When I come down to the dining room, everyone is there, except for Jeffrey. This is unusual. Punctuality, as Mr. Morison said, is definitely not the family's strong suit. But tonight they are all already there, sitting in their usual seats, linen napkins unfolded across their laps, though they haven't started eating. I peek at my watch to see if I'm late. I'm early.

"Sorry I'm late," I say anyway.

"Don't worry, we're still waiting for my husband. He should be here any second," Vanessa says. She has also dressed carefully for dinner, in a blue dress that swirls around her like a wave. Her face gleams with makeup. Her hair is lighter and brighter than it was yesterday.

"Maybe he got caught in traffic," Ella says. She has also dressed carefully for dinner, in a ruffled pink dress that reminds me of the ruffled pink bedroom. It's a pretty dress. But she looks terrible in it. Possibly because she's uncomfortable; she tugs the sleeves as if they're biting her arms, yanks the neckline as if it's chewing her neck.

"Maybe he forgot the address," Henry mutters. He has also dressed carefully for dinner, or at least more carefully than usual. His normal raggedy tee has been replaced by a polo shirt. And although he's still wearing his usual swim trunks, this pair looks clean and dry.

"I wouldn't be surprised if he did," Mr. Morison grumbles. He has also dressed carefully, but he always dresses carefully.

"Sweetie, stop fidgeting," says Vanessa. "And sit up straight."

Ella folds her hands in her lap and bolts her spine against her chair.

"Granddad, how was your doctor's appointment?" Henry asks.

"Fine. I don't know why he makes me come in so often. I'm fine."

Mrs. Tully enters the room with a platter of steaks and a deep dish of mashed potatoes, but Vanessa sends the food back to the kitchen, telling her to keep it warm until her husband arrives, that he should be here any second. There is a bowl of salad on the table, but no one seems to dare touch it, or even look at it.

Though Henry does sigh and say, "I'm so hungry."

"Bill, how was your doctor's appointment today?" Vanessa asks.

"As I just told Henry, it was fine," says Mr. Morison.

"El, are you hungry?" says Henry.

"A little." She furtively pulls at a pink sleeve.

"Sorry," Vanessa says to her father-in-law. "I didn't hear you tell him that."

"No apologies necessary," Mr. Morison says, but his tone implies otherwise.

Vanessa blushes, though you can barely see it through her makeup.

We wait ten minutes. We wait another ten minutes.

"Ness, maybe you should call and see where he is?" says Henry.

"Well, he said he'd be here, so he'll be here," says Vanessa.

"Call him," says Mr. Morison.

Vanessa leaves the room. She returns almost immediately and sits back in her chair. "It went straight to voice mail. He must be on the ferry. He'll be here in fifteen minutes."

We wait fifteen minutes. We wait another minute after that.

Then there is the thud-thud-thud of footsteps in the hallway. Vanessa smiles triumphantly as she stands. Ella jumps up and runs to the doorway. They converge upon him as he comes into the room, engulfing him in a whirl of golden hair and pink ruffle.

"Daddy!" cries Ella.

"Jeffrey!" cries Vanessa.

"Girls, my beautiful girls!" And there he is, standing tall as he genially surveys the table. Jeffrey Morison.

He is not a handsome man. I saw photographs of him while doing my research, saw his ragged hairline, his bulging gray eyes, his slug of a nose, his stout frame. But what the photos didn't reveal was that even though Jeffrey Morison is not a handsome man, there is something immediately appealing about him. His smile is full of teeth and cheer. His gaze is tender. His voice deep and soothing.

"Dad," he says, "you're looking well."

"Thank you," Mr. Morison says stiffly.

"Son!" he says. "What a tan. I'm glad you've been enjoying the beach."

"Just an afternoon here and there," Henry mumbles.

"And you!" he says, directing his big smile toward me. "You must be my little girl's academic tutor."

"Yes, Mr. Morison." I smile back at him.

"Please call me Jeffrey. I'm thrilled you're here. We're all thrilled."

"I'm thrilled to be here."

"Sure you are," Henry says. For once he doesn't smirk.

Jeffrey glances around at the blank plates on the table. "You haven't started eating yet? Did you wait for me? You shouldn't have waited."

"Your wife insisted," Mr. Morison says.

"Well, I'm starving. What's for dinner?" Jeffrey sits down.

Instantly, Mrs. Tully appears with the asparagus soup, then the platter of steaks and dish of potatoes. Then roasted root vegetables, creamed spinach, fried oysters, and a garlic flat-bread.

"Mrs. Tully, you've truly outdone yourself," booms Jeffrey Morison.

I watch in disbelief as she flushes and flutters in reply.

But it's true that the spread is impressive tonight. Although there is only one additional person here, there is twice the regular amount of food, and all of it is as delicious as always. We eat, hungrily.

"Daddy, how was your week?" Ella asks in a breathless chirp that sounds nothing like her usual soft voice.

"Excellent, sweetheart. I worked hard for my girls." Her father, between chews of steak, chuckles.

I look at Henry, expecting him to make a snide or sarcastic comment, or roll his eyes at the very least. He doesn't. He is eating his food with what appears to be complete concentration.

"My wife tells me that you just graduated from high school. Congratulations," Jeffrey Morison says.

I'm still watching Henry, so I see him cringe. Then I realize Jeffrey is talking to me. I turn to him. "Yes, thank you," I say.

"What are your plans for the future?" he asks.

I tell him I'll be going to the honors program at the city university in the fall, where I plan to double major in mathematics and economics, and when I graduate I hope to attend business school.

"Very impressive." Jeffrey nods approvingly.

I try not to blush. I don't succeed.

"Daddy, how long are you staying?" Ella chirps.

"I'll be here until Sunday night," says Jeffrey.

Ella counts on her fingers. "That's only two days."

"No, sweetheart, it's three days. Today is Friday. Tomorrow is Saturday. And then Sunday. Three days," he says as he briskly butters his bread.

"Today doesn't count. It's almost over."

"Be a good girl—no whining. Daddy's working hard for you."

"I know." Ella's breathless chirp is no longer quite as breathless, quite as chirpy.

"We just miss you, that's all. Your family misses you," Vanessa says.

"And I miss you all too." Jeffrey moves his gaze around the dinner table, pausing to focus affectionately on each member of his family in turn.

Vanessa looks lovingly back at her husband.

Henry nods awkwardly at his father.

Mr. Morison eats his potatoes.

And Ella smiles. It's a shining grimace that stretches her mouth nearly beyond her face. I don't see how anyone could mistake her expression for happiness, and yet her father smiles back at her contentedly.

I notice I've stopped chewing. There is a hard lump of food stuck to my tongue. All flavor is suddenly gone. It takes my total concentration not to choke as I swallow it down.

That night I have trouble falling asleep.

I blame the tensions at dinner. I keep thinking about the hostility between Vanessa and old Mr. Morison. The friction between Jeffrey and Henry. The antagonism between Mr. Morison and Jeffrey. And Ella. Ella's breathless chirp. Ella's warped smile.

But I also blame the food; I blame myself for eating too much. I'm not used to such large portions of meat and dairy, and dessert served with every meal. At home we eat lots of plain rice and vegetables. Sometimes there are slivers of chicken or pork. More often there is bean curd, in one of its many forms. Occasionally we have noodles instead of rice. For dessert we eat fruit, if anything.

I miss my mother's cooking. I also love the food here. The hunky steaks, the velvety sauces, the buttery cakes and tarts and cookies. I only wish I could digest it better.

My stomach groans. I turn over in the floral bed.

Then something in the room groans too.

I open my eyes. I blink. I sit up and blink again. And again. Standing against my closed door is a dark shape, the slim shadow of a small figure I can just make out in the moonight.

"Hello?" I say.

Instantly, the shadow is gone.

I tell myself it was a figment of my imagination, a hallucination, a bad-digestion dream. Like the strange sounds I heard the other night. Nothing to be scared of. Nothing at all. I lie down again. I turn over again. Eventually I fall asleep.

And when I wake up to the morning, a clear blue morning, it does seem likely that it was all my imagination. Until I get out of bed and find my bedroom door wide open.

5

THE FAMILY IS OUT ON THEIR SAILBOAT. THEY WILL PROBABLY have lunch at a seafood shack on a neighboring island, almost certainly eat dinner at their favorite restaurant in town, and most likely return very late in the evening.

This is what Mrs. Tully tells me when I come down to breakfast. She smiles maliciously. Perhaps she thinks I'm hurt by this reminder that I am not one of the family, that despite sleeping in their pretty pink bedroom and eating at their sprawling dinner table and chatting with them about their days, I'm still a hired employee.

If that's what Mrs. Tully thinks, she's wrong.

I am not hurt. I am not even reminded.

Since my first job at the day camp, there has never been a time that I've forgotten my position. Not when the parents cook me lunch or invite me to dinner or give me gifts of silk scarves and fine chocolate at holiday time. Not when they gossip with me or confide in me or compliment the length and thickness of my hair. Not when they tell me to make myself at home. I never, ever forget their home isn't my home. My home is a one-bedroom apartment in a brown high-rise building with my mother.

But I smile back at Mrs. Tully with no malice. "That sounds like a fun day out for the family," I say.

She looks disappointed. Then she shrugs and goes back to ignoring me.

I spend the day working. At this point, I should be familiar enough with Ella's strengths and weaknesses and interests to make my lesson plans for next week. So I page through her workbooks, searching for patterns in her right and wrong answers. But the only pattern is that she answered nearly every question wrong. I'm ready to give up when Doris calls.

"What's wrong?" she asks after we say hello.

"What do you mean? Nothing's wrong," I say.

"You sound upset."

"I'm fine! Everything's fine."

"Are you sure?"

"Yes! The house is huge and I have my own bedroom and my own bathroom and there's a library and game room and wine cellar and a swimming pool and every day we eat lunch outside in a gazebo."

"Wow, that sounds amazing."

"It really is!" I say, but I don't say it right. My voice wobbles. There is somehow both too much enthusiasm and not enough.

"Come on," she says. "Tell me what's wrong."

I sigh. "Well . . . the tutoring isn't going so great."

"What do you mean?"

I describe the trouble I've been having with Ella. "I don't know what to do. She's so closed off."

"Poor girl," she says.

"You mean rich girl," I say.

Doris is disapprovingly silent.

"It's a joke," I say.

"You have to keep trying," she says. "You're a great tutor. I'm sure you'll get through to her eventually."

This is why I hesitated before telling Doris. Because I knew she would say something kind and optimistic. Then I would think how ridiculous she was for being so kind and optimistic. Then I would feel guilty for thinking my best friend was ridiculous. Especially since she is only being kind and optimistic. And I am not.

"Okay," I say. "Anyway, are you still volunteering at the hospital?"

"Yes, but only for another month. Then I want to get a head start on my reading for the fall. I ordered my textbooks today!" She gleefully tells me she's already gotten the syllabus for one of her classes and the first assignment is due the first day of class.

"Wow. Everything's happening so fast."

"I know," she says. "Sorry I missed your call yesterday. What were you going to say about your brother?"

"What?" I grimace. I was hoping she'd forgotten.

"You know. In your message you said that your brother said he ran into me, then you were going to say something else about him, but you didn't."

"Oh, I was just going to say . . . he's a creep."

Doris sighs. "Andy isn't a creep. He made some mistakes, but he's trying to change. He was really nice to me when I saw him the other day."

"Of course he was nice to you."

"You have to give your brother another chance. Family is important. It's the most important thing."

I think: You have no idea what you're talking about.

I say: "You're right. Well, I should get back to work now."

"Okay. Good luck. I miss you. Let's talk again soon, okay?"

"Yes. Thanks. Bye." I hang up.

Doris Chang and I have been best friends since the second grade. We have a lot in common: her parents, like my parents, are immigrants; we both study a lot and work hard and do well in school; we are responsible and polite; we like to plan and prepare. People sometimes ask if we're sisters, though I don't think we look alike, aside from the fact we're both skinny Chinese girls with long black hair.

But over the past few years something changed. Now when we're together—volunteering at the soup kitchen or studying for an exam or hanging out with our other nice friends—I sometimes feel uncomfortable, like I don't belong, like I'm not truly one of the girls, giggling girls who faithfully believe that family is the most important thing and that if you don't give up you'll eventually succeed. Because . . . I guess . . . I'm **not** one of them anymore.

I start pacing around the room, back and forth, back and forth, and the bedroom, this spacious bedroom, begins to feel small, pink walls closing in, the floral prints stifling as if they're pungently perfumed. Then I can't help thinking about what happened last night. The groan. The shadow. The open door.

I'd been trying not to think about it, but now I can't stop. I remember when I first met Vanessa and she asked if I was superstitious. I told her I wasn't, and I'm still not. Yet I suddenly need to get out of here. Out of this pretty room. Out of this perfect house. As far away as possible.

I go to the beach. It's my first time going, but it's not hard to find; there's a winding path that leads to a narrow set of stone steps that leads to the sand. Then there's the ocean, so clear and so blue, even clearer and bluer than it appears from the house. It's beautiful.

"Hello there!" someone bellows behind me.

I turn around to find old Mr. Morison. Even on the beach, he is neatly dressed, though his ironed pants are rolled up above his ankles. His bare feet are long and scrawny, speckled with sand and age.

"Oh! You're not on the boat!" I feel as though I've been caught misbehaving. I have to remind myself that this is my day off; I'm not doing anything wrong.

Mr. Morison shrugs. "Enjoying this lovely weather?" he asks.

"Very much. I'm just taking a break from working on lesson plans."

"Ah, yes. How is the tutoring progressing?"

"It's going great!" I say.

"Excellent. I'm glad to hear it. My granddaughter is a good girl, but she's had a tough time of it lately. There was some trouble at school this year."

"What happened?" I ask.

"Her friends got her into some mischief, then named her as the ringleader. Can you imagine? I love my granddaughter, but she is no ringleader." He frowns out at the ocean.

"What did they do?"

"It was just some schoolgirl nonsense." He turns his frown toward me. "Of course it's her parents' fault. Why Jeffrey married that woman, I'll never understand, though I suppose she's an improvement over his first wife, with her diets and her nerves. My son has terrible judgment. What he's doing to the family name . . . it's shameful!"

"Um. Is that a lighthouse?" I point to a distant structure that is clearly a lighthouse.

Mr. Morison looks. His expression relaxes. "Yes, that's the old lighthouse. It's no longer in use, hasn't been for decades. Our property includes an acre just beyond it."

"I heard your house originally belonged to the Arrow family."

"That's right. Lionel Arrow built this house for his family. He and his wife had five children, all boys, five troublemaking boys. Poor Lionel. If only he'd had a daughter. If only I'd had a daughter. They're different, you know. Daughters will always love you and take care of you. Like Ella. She's a good girl. And you, you're a good girl. I can tell. You love your father, don't you? You'll always take care of him."

I nod noncommittally. "The taxi driver said there aren't any Arrows here anymore. Is that true?"

"Indeed. Those troublemaking sons squandered the family fortune, and eventually they all left. I was able to get this property at a very good price. No more Arrows on Arrow Island. Except for the bodies, of course." He chuckles, or maybe coughs. Either way it's a creaky, phlegmy sound that goes on for too long.

"Are you all right?" I ask.

"Perfectly fine." He thumps his chest and says, "The Arrow family cemetery is up on the hill, just beyond the lighthouse. The place is quite neglected, but an interesting spot nonetheless. It's unfortunate you can't go have a look around."

"Why not?"

"You aren't afraid?"

"I'm not afraid."

"Well, perhaps you should be." Mr. Morison gazes at me disapprovingly, his eyes fierce, his eyebrows pinched together. "It's dangerous."

Then I feel a pang of fear. "What do you mean?"

"The path goes directly past the lighthouse, and because my son hasn't maintained it at all, the structure is extremely unsound. It could collapse at any time," he says. His voice is low. Raspy. Angry. A moment later, he excuses himself and heads back to the house.

That night I go to bed early. I take a hot shower in the beautiful bathroom, put on my pajamas, and climb into bed. I'm exhausted. But I don't fall asleep. After a while, I get up, go to the door, and check that it's firmly closed. It is. I climb back into bed. I still don't fall asleep. Not because I'm afraid. I just can't.

When the Morison family comes home, I hear Ella in the hallway, breathlessly chirping, "Daddy, Daddy! Come tuck me in!" I hear Jeffrey Morison's jovial reply: "Be there in a minute, sweetheart, after I make a couple of quick phone calls."

Several minutes later, he thuds down the hall. A minute later, he thuds back.

Hours pass. I still don't fall asleep. Finally I get up again, grab the chair behind the dressing table, carry it across the room, and wedge it in front of the door. I feel utterly ridiculous. But I tell myself I'm not afraid; I'm just being . . . cautious.

This time, as soon as I climb back into bed, stretch flat on the mattress, pull the floral quilt up to my chin, and turn my head against the pillow, I fall asleep.

In my dream I am sitting in the corner reading when the man comes over, takes the book from my hand, and snaps it shut.

He tells me I need to stop fooling around, wasting time, messing about. He tells me I need to study harder, help my mother more, get along with my brother better, be a good girl. The same things he always used to scold me about.

But then his voice changes into Mr. Morison's, and he says that I'm his daughter, and so I should be taking care of him. He says I have to promise to take care of him forever.

Before I can promise, he raises his arm, and for a moment I'm afraid he's going to hit me, but then his hand opens to show me what he's holding. It's the porcelain ballerina figurine he gave me for my sixth birthday. The one that broke. She lies in pieces on his palm.

My father screams: Look what you've done. It's all your fault! What's wrong with you? What's wrong with you?

I jolt awake. Heart thrumming. Eyes burning. I sit up and look across the room for my mother, for the comfortingly familiar sight of her in her narrow bed. But all I see is my own self in the mirror: black tangle of hair, face swollen with sleep, bony limbs in a garden of pink. For a moment I have no idea where I am.

Then I remember.

I'm at the Morisons' house on Arrow Island.

I'm Ella Morison's academic tutor for the summer.

I repeat these facts to myself as if they are lessons to be learned.

Then I get out of bed and go to the door. The chair is

wedged against it, precisely where I left it the night before. I return it to its place behind the dressing table. I go to the window and pull back the curtains. Sunshine pours into the room. It's a beautiful day.

I'm at the Morisons' house on Arrow Island.

I'm Ella Morison's academic tutor for the summer.

It has been three and a half years since I last saw my father.

And I have no idea if I'll ever see him again.

6

AT THE LAST MINUTE, SUNDAY-NIGHT DINNER BECOMES SUNDAY
afternoon dinner because Jeffrey Morison has to rush back to
the city to prepare for a meeting scheduled for the next morning. Consequently, the meal is not up to Mrs. Tully's usual
standards. The meat is dry and the vegetables are hard. The
bread crust is sallow and slightly soggy.

Mrs. Tully is very apologetic about the inferior food. She
is obviously embarrassed, so I tell her, "The asparagus is delicious."

She frowns at me as she leaves the dining room.

"Daddy!" chirps Ella. She's wearing another pink dress
tonight, even frillier than the first. "Who's your meeting with
tomorrow?"

"Well, sweetheart, I'm meeting with some people from the
SEC."

"What's the SEC?" she asks.

"The Securities and Exchange Commission. They're a gov-
ernmental agency that monitors finance and business—"

"Jeffrey, what's this meeting about?" Mr. Morison interrupts.

"Nothing to worry about." Jeffrey shrugs.

His father shakes his head. "That attitude is going to get you in trouble."

Jeffrey winks at Ella, who is listening to them with an anxious expression. "Really, sweetie. It's nothing to worry about," he says. "Trust me."

She nods solemnly. "I trust you, Daddy."

"Which reminds me," he says. "Henry."

Henry jolts up in his chair. "Yes, Dad?"

"I finally heard back from Vice Principal Kristoff. He's traveling this month, but he's willing to meet with you at the beginning of August. So you better email him as soon as possible if you want to graduate."

"Yes. Yes, I will. Thank you."

"Don't screw this up, Henry."

"I won't, Dad. I promise." Henry's face is calm and his voice is steady, but the fork in his hand is trembling. Apparently when Vanessa said he'd finished his senior year "more or less," she meant less.

"All right then." Jeffrey Morison consumes the last of his dinner in three big bites. He gulps down his glass of wine. He stands up.

"Really, darling? You can't stay until we're all done eating?" says Vanessa.

"I have to go. I want to beat the traffic."

"But Jeffrey," she says, her voice wavering.

"Daddy! When are you coming back?" chirps Ella.

"I'm going to Europe for some meetings next week, so it'll be the weekend after that." Jeffrey leans over to kiss her cheek.

Ella swivels in her chair and flings her arms around him. "Okay, Daddy. Next, next weekend," she chirps.

He tenderly disentangles himself from his daughter and walks around the table to say good-bye to his son, then his father. A pat on the back for Henry, a clap on the shoulder for Mr. Morison. Then he comes over to shake my hand. His grip is surprisingly, painfully firm, just like his father's.

Vanessa stands. "I'll walk you to the door," she says.

After they leave, the dining room is silent. But I am the only one who is actually eating. Ella is crumbling her bread into crumbs. Henry is sawing his broccoli into cubes. Mr. Morison is glaring at his chicken.

When Vanessa returns, she does not eat either. Her eyes are red. There is a smudge of mascara on her cheek. But her mouth is sculpted into an impeccable smile. "Well," she says, "I just had the most fantastic idea. When we finish our dinner, how about we go into town for some ice cream?"

"Great idea, Mom!" Ella chirps, her voice louder and higher than ever. "You'll come, right, Henry? And Granddad?"

"You know I don't say no to ice cream," says her brother.

"I'd be delighted, my dear," says Mr. Morison.

Then, to my surprise, Ella looks at me. "Will you come too?"

* * *

The town is only three adorable blocks long. All the businesses occupy two-story buildings, all the houses are shingled and shuttered, all the shingles are brightly painted, and all the windows gleam. Vanessa drives and Mr. Morison points out the sights: the fudge shop and the bookstore and the art gallery and the store that sells personalized painted seashells and the family's favorite seafood restaurant. Everything is picture-postcard perfect.

"Hello, Morison family!" sings the lady behind the counter as we enter the ice-cream parlor. She has silver hair and pink cheeks and a gingham apron, and is as picturesque as the rest of town.

She chatters merrily as she scoops cookies and cream for Ella, chocolate for Henry, espresso for Mr. Morison, and lemon sorbet for Vanessa. When I ask for a small cup of strawberry, the lady says she'll be with me in a second, as soon as she rings up their order.

"Actually, she's with us," says Vanessa.

"Sorry! One cup of strawberry coming up!" Her pink cheeks get pinker.

"It's all right," I say graciously.

"I know! You must be little Ella's new babysitter."

"Her academic tutor," I say, slightly less graciously.

"Wonderful! Enjoy your stay on Arrow Island."

We stroll along the three blocks of town with our ice cream, and when we get to the end we turn around and stroll through again. First I walk with Vanessa as she peers into shop windows and chatters about what she likes and what she doesn't.

Then the group rearranges itself, and I'm walking with Ella and her grandfather. Old Mr. Morison is focused on the changes that have been made since he first bought the house. He tells me, "That gourmet food shop used to be a saloon. That candy store used to be a tobacco store. That building used to be the firehouse." Ella licks her ice cream.

Then, somehow, I end up walking with Henry. I expect him to quickly make some excuse and rejoin his sister or grandfather, or even his stepmom. But he doesn't.

"How's your ice cream?" he asks.

"Delicious. How's yours?" I ask.

"Great. Can't go wrong with chocolate, you know?"

I nod, startled by his politeness. But Henry has been polite all weekend. Subdued by the presence of his father, I thought. But now his father is gone.

"Anyway, can I ask you something?" he says.

I'm instantly wary again. "What?"

"You don't like it when people call you a babysitter."

"That's not a question."

"Okay. Why don't you like it when people call you a babysitter?"

"What makes you think I don't like it?"

"You got so mad at the ice-cream lady when she called you a babysitter."

"I wasn't mad. It's just that I'm not a babysitter."

"What do you have against babysitters?"

"Nothing," I say. I know I should stop here. Yet the explanation comes rushing from my mouth: "It's a business thing. Babysitters get less pay and less respect. I know, because I've been a babysitter and a camp counselor, which is pretty much the same thing, and I have two aunts and a cousin who are nannies. But I'm an academic tutor now."

Immediately I regret telling him. I'm embarrassed to have revealed the mercenary machinery of my mind, and to jerky Henry Morison of all people. I don't know why I did it. I'm sure he's going to make fun of me.

But he merely says, "That makes sense."

"Can I ask you a question? What's the story with your graduation and how you're supposed to be studying all day?" I figure it's only fair for him to tell me something personal now.

"Whoa, you don't mess around." Henry grimaces.

Then I remember who I am. And who he is.

"Sorry, never mind. I didn't mean to pry," I say.

"I'll tell you. It's not like it's a secret, anyway." Henry looks uncomfortable but continues. "So my friend and I were studying for our last final, in American history, and when we were done, we decided to celebrate with a tequila shot. One shot turned into two, turned into, I don't know . . . ten? Somehow we made it to the exam the next morning, but we were both totally hungover, or maybe still drunk, and I, uh, fell asleep during the test."

"No!" I say.

"Yes. And because this wasn't exactly my first offense, they're still deciding whether they're going to let me take the exam again. And the college I'm supposed to go to is deciding whether they're going to rescind my admission. It's a mess. The sad thing is, I could have passed easily. I'm not an idiot."

I just look at him.

He grins. "Okay, maybe I am an idiot, but I promise you I could have passed that test. If I hadn't fallen asleep."

I grin right back. "I believe you. So what happens now?"

"Well, my father happens to be an acquaintance of the vice principal at my school and has kindly arranged a meeting so that I can plead my pathetic case. And coincidentally, my father also happens to know an administrator at my possible college, who has convinced them to hold off from making a final decision about my admission status until August. So, lucky me," he says, his voice suddenly bitter. He shoves the pointy end of his ice-cream cone into his mouth.

"You are lucky," I say.

"I know. That's why I said it." Henry scowls.

Vanessa comes over and asks if we're ready to go. She looks tired. And so sad.

"Sure! Thanks for the ice cream. This was a great idea." I smile at her.

She smiles vaguely in return before walking back to Ella and Mr. Morison.

I feel Henry watching me. I turn to look at him. "What?"

"You're such a suck-up," he says. He smirks.

Then I can't believe that there was a moment, when he was telling his stupid story about how stupid he is, that I felt bad for him. That I thought he might not be a total jerk. That I thought we could possibly be friends, or at least friendly.

Obviously I was deluded.

But I put on my brightest face and say in my brightest voice, "What a fascinating observation." Then I turn around and go join the others.

Although I'm tired that night, I spend an hour writing emails to my friends. The messages are the same, all bubble and bounce, yet I write each one individually. Then I reorganize my clothes. Then I cut my nails. I keep glancing at the clock. It gets later and later, and I still don't go to sleep.

My brother, when he lived with us, would do this same thing: he would complain that he was exhausted, but he wouldn't go to sleep. Through the flimsy walls of our apartment, I'd hear him creeping around the living room, watching television with the volume low, muttering on the phone. The next day he would complain again about being exhausted and I'd roll my eyes. I couldn't understand why he wouldn't just go to sleep.

Maybe I do now. Because tonight I find myself dreading it: the lying down, the closing of eyes, the darkness and the emptiness. The wilderness of dreams.

It's midnight. It's one. It's two. It's almost three.

I force myself into the bed. I lie down and close my eyes. I try to give in to the darkness. The emptiness. But I can't. Not that I'm afraid. I'm not. I know that nightmares can't actually hurt me.

Then the room begins to shake.

I sit up. Everything is still. I must have imagined it.

Then a voice cries out, a high-pitched wail, a song of heart-break.

I get out of bed. Everything is silent. I must have imagined it.

Then the room shakes and a voice cries and someone is pounding on the door.

I run over to the closed door and fling it open. All sound and movement abruptly cease. I gaze at the person standing in front of me and realize how foolish I've been. There was an obvious explanation for my midnight disturbances, and an obvious culprit, yet I never considered it or her until now. But now here she is.

"This has to stop," I say, as calmly as I can. "I don't know how you're doing it, but you have to stop. It's okay if you're not happy that I'm here, but please talk to me about it. We have to find a way to work together." I pause to take a deep breath. Inhale. Exhale.

Then I ask, "Okay, Ella?"

She looks at me. Face gray and eyes glinting in the shadows. Her expression is solemn. But when she speaks, her voice is small and wobbly. Frightened.

"It isn't me," Ella says. "It's the ghost."

7

I BRING ELLA BACK TO HER ROOM AND COAX HER INTO HER BED. It's a warm night, but she is shivering, her teeth chattering. I get another blanket from her closet and tuck it around her. Then I sit down at the edge of the mattress.

"Ella, ghosts aren't real," I say gently but firmly.

"I hear her. Not every night. But lots of nights. I hear her banging around. I hear her yelling." Ella's voice is equally gentle, equally firm.

"Her?" I ask.

"The ghost. She's a girl."

"How do you know that?"

Ella shakes her head. "It was worse in the pink room—that's why I couldn't sleep there. I'm sorry you have to. I heard her tonight, and she was so loud that I came to see if you were okay."

"Thanks, but I'm perfectly okay," I say. "Because there's no ghost. The noises were just the house settling."

"No, it wasn't. It was the ghost!"

This is the first time, I realize, that she's really argued with me. This is the first time, I realize, that she's cared enough about something to argue with me. But it's three o'clock in the morning and I'm tired and I can tell, despite the insistence in her voice, that Ella is tired too. Her head flops on her pillow. Body limp under the stack of blankets. Eyelids fluttering.

"We'll talk about it tomorrow. We need to get to sleep. It's late now, so late it's almost early." I smile at her.

Ella smiles, her smile small, back. She closes her eyes. Then she opens them again. "Will you stay here a little bit longer? If you don't mind?" she asks.

"I'll stay until you fall asleep," I tell her. And I do.

We are exhausted the next day, Ella and I; we yawn all through the morning. Yet somehow our lessons go better than before. For the first time, she answers more questions correctly than incorrectly, and when I explain what she got wrong, she actually listens. But in every pause between the end of one chapter and the beginning of the next, Ella starts talking about it. About her. The ghost.

"The pink bedroom used to be her bedroom," she says. "Back when, you know, she was alive. A long time ago. She was Lionel Arrow's daughter. He built this house."

"Lionel Arrow only had sons, five sons," I say. "Your grandfather told me."

Ella shakes her head. "He had a daughter too. She was the youngest one, but they didn't count her. You know, in the olden days, daughters didn't count. They couldn't even vote."

I look at her, half amazed, half amused, and unsure of how to respond.

"Well . . . that's not exactly true," I say. "I mean, yes, it's true that women couldn't vote back then and they didn't have as many rights as men, and even today there's lots of, uh, gender inequality. But families still loved and valued their daughters. Most families. I'm sure if Lionel Arrow and his wife had a daughter, they would have counted her."

"If they had, she wouldn't still be here, haunting us," Ella says matter-of-factly.

I'm relieved when the library door opens and Vanessa appears.

"Girls! How are we doing in here?" she asks.

Ella widens her eyes at me, a look of panic and appeal. It's an expression I've seen on many kids' faces, though this is the first time I've seen it on Ella. In general, I know it means "Don't tell my mom." In this specific case, I guess it means "Don't tell my mom about the ghost."

I nod at Ella and smile at Vanessa and say, "We're good. How are you?"

"Fantastic! Sorry to interrupt, but I couldn't wait. I just had the most fabulous idea. What if we throw a surprise party for Daddy's birthday this summer?"

"A surprise party?" Ella says. She sounds surprised.

"I'm thinking we'll have about a hundred people, get a brass band, turn the pool into a dance floor. What do you think, Ellie? You think Daddy will like that?"

"I don't know. Maybe," Ella says.

Vanessa's smile falters. She turns to me. "What do you think?"

I think: How do you turn a pool into a dance floor?

I say: "What a wonderful idea!"

Her smile revives. "Well, I'll let you girls get back to your work now."

After her mother leaves, the door clicking closed behind her, Ella says, in a voice so low it sounds as though she's talking to herself: "But Daddy hates surprises."

All though dinner that night, Vanessa talks about her plans for the party. She tells us she has already contacted several event planners but hasn't yet found one she really likes. She tells us her various ideas about birthday cake. She tells us she started making the guest list and that we should tell her if there is anyone we would like to invite.

Henry shrugs. He looks bored.

Ella shakes her head. She looks tired.

Old Mr. Morison mutters, "No, no one." He looks unwell. His complexion is ashen, his lips the same sallow shade as his skin.

Vanessa turns to me and asks if asking people to RSVP within three weeks is reasonable.

"Yes, that sounds good," I say. I don't mention that I've never been invited to a party that asked people to RSVP, much less planned a party that asked people to RSVP.

"Great." She looks truly relieved.

"You should give them four weeks. Though I suppose you don't have the time now," says Mr. Morison. He lifts his water glass—hand trembling, glass trembling, water trembling—and takes a trembling sip.

"Are you all right?" I ask him.

"Fine," he snaps.

I try not to take offense. He looks really unwell.

After dinner, the family promptly disperses: Vanessa eagerly to her office, Ella sleepily to her bed, Mr. Morison gingerly to his rooms, and Henry howeverly to wherever. I've successfully avoided talking to him or even looking at him all day. I'm still annoyed by how he called me a suck-up when I was just being nice to sad Vanessa. I'm still annoyed by everything about him.

Then I come out into the hallway and Henry is right there, leaning against the wall as if he's waiting for me. "Good night," I say, and keep walking.

"Hang on," he says. "Want to go for a swim?"

Of all the things I imagined he might say, this is the most unimaginable. I turn around. "Seriously?"

"I'm always serious about swimming. Pool or beach? Your choice."

"No, thank you. I don't swim."

"What?" he demands. "You don't or you can't?"

"Both. I don't know how to swim." I'm embarrassed to

admit it and annoyed he made me do it.

"Really? Why not?" He stares at me in disbelief.

"Believe it or not, Henry, not everyone has a summer house on an island, with a swimming pool in the backyard and the beach in walking distance."

"I didn't—"

"Good night! Have a wonderful swim, though you might want to wait a little while since we just ate dinner and it would be really terrible if you got a cramp and drowned," I say.

Then I walk away, and I don't stop, not even when he calls out after me, claiming that he was only kidding, asking if I'm mad about yesterday, telling me to come back, that he'll teach me to swim. I roll my eyes all the way up the stairs.

Once I reach the pink bedroom, however, I shut the door and get to work. All day long my shark mind has been moving, circling around this new problem: the problem of the ghost. Not that I believe in the ghost. But Ella believes in it and is try- ing to convince me to believe too. And in trying to convince me, she is opening up, and in opening up, her work is improv- ing. As her academic tutor, I really want her work to improve, so this shouldn't be a problem, except . . . I know I shouldn't encourage Ella's belief in the ghost.

Yet the ghost may be the only way I can get through to her. And Ella is a girl with so few enthusiasms, I hate the idea of crushing any one of them. So I open my laptop to search for information about hauntings and the history of Arrow Island and the Arrow family.

This is what my economics teacher, Ms. Baldwin, would do. In fact, this is what she's doing with me. It's obvious she wants to dissuade me from pursuing a finance career. I don't take it personally: Ms. Baldwin worked at the same investment bank for over a decade, until her company merged with another company and she was laid off. If I was her, I'd be bitter too—not that she'd ever admit to being bitter. She claims she's happier now than ever before.

But instead of trying to persuade me to change my goal, Ms. Baldwin gave me that book about the recent financial crisis in hopes that I would convince myself. So I decide to try a similar strategy with the ghost problem. I go online and order a few books that seem both relevant and appropriate. Even though Ms. Baldwin's approach didn't work with me, that doesn't mean it won't work with Ella.

I put away my laptop and get ready for bed. As I'm brushing my teeth, I suddenly remember Henry's startled expression when I told him how terrible it would be if he got a cramp and drowned. Then a strange thing happens. I start laughing.

8

NOTHING DISTURBS MY SLEEP THAT NIGHT, OR THE NIGHT AFTER that. I point this out to Ella the next time she mentions the ghost, but she is unfazed. She says, "Sometimes she's quiet, but that doesn't mean she isn't there."

"Maybe it **does** mean she isn't there," I say.

Ella shakes her head. "She's there. I can see her."

"What does she look like?" I ask, though I know I shouldn't be encouraging her belief in the ghost. But I can't help being curious.

"She's small, kind of skinny. Her hair is brownish, I think."

I look at Ella. Who is small and skinny with brown hair.

"But it's hard to see her clearly because she only comes out in the dark. Or maybe she's only visible in the dark. Those aren't the same thing, though some people might not realize the difference," she says in a matter-of-fact tone I've begun to recognize. It's the voice she uses to talk about the ghost.

The grandfather clock in the corner chimes. We're done for the afternoon.

"You did well today, Ella," I say, and it's true. Although she isn't performing to grade level, her work has been steadily improving all week.

She smiles her small smile. "Will you do something for me?" she asks.

"Sure, what is it?"

"Promise you won't tell anyone about her. She doesn't want anyone to know about her, except us," Ella says.

"Who are you talking about?"

"You know, the ghost. Promise?"

"Um . . ."

"Please?"

"Okay."

"Say you promise."

"I promise."

"Thank you."

Ella leaves to meet her brother; they're going down to the beach. I stay and clean up, collecting paper scraps, straightening the heavy chairs, piling the workbooks together. I've just finished when Vanessa comes into the library.

"Hello, darling!" She pulls out one of the heavy chairs I straightened and curls up in the seat, silky dress bunched around her knees, bare tanned feet twining together, pearly toenails flashing. "I have a teeny favor to ask of you."

"Yes?" I say noncommittally.

Although I am very careful about being an academic tutor, there is an ambiguity to the job description that encourages certain parents to take advantage. For example, Kiki's mom, who once interrupted our tutoring session to ask if I would load the dishwasher and make the bed when we were done, because she was expecting guests and her cleaning lady canceled.

I did it. But I don't tutor Kiki anymore.

Now Vanessa says, "Great news! I found a calligrapher for the party invitations! The problem is I need to get her everything right away. I have a guest list and most of the addresses in my address book, but the calligrapher wants it in a spreadsheet, and I'm clueless about spreadsheets, so I was hoping you could help me. It shouldn't take long. You're so organized and efficient! You'll do it, won't you?"

I should say no. I say, "Sure."

"You're a lifesaver. I'll email you the guest list right away. You might have to look up an address and zip code or two, though I'm sure you'll be done in no time! If you could finish it by tonight, that would be really helpful."

Vanessa goes to her office to send me the information for the spreadsheet. I straighten the heavy chairs again. It's not that I mind helping her. But I'm an academic tutor. Not a babysitter or nanny or cleaning lady. Not a spreadsheet maker. And ever since the incident with Kiki's mother, I have been very careful to make that clear. Until now.

So why did I agree? I guess because I feel bad for Vanessa—she's obviously unhappy that her husband is gone. And because she asked nicely. And because I really am good at making spreadsheets.

I know these are all just excuses. I can't let this happen again.

Anyway, it doesn't take me very long—no more than an hour or three—to make the spreadsheet. I email it to Vanessa, and a few minutes later, someone knocks on the door of the pink bedroom. I open it to find Mrs. Tully staring grimly at me. She thrusts a cardboard box into my arms and walks wordlessly away.

"Thanks, Mrs. Tully! Have a nice day!" I call out after her. She doesn't turn around, but I didn't expect her to. Which is why I'm making a face behind her back.

I open the package. It's the books I ordered for Ella. I page through the first one, a kid's book about a girl who moves into a house that seems haunted. There are noises in the night, doors mysteriously opening or closing, and a pale figure fluttering in corners. However, the girl discovers that it's just the work of the boy who lives next door, who is angry that his best friend's family moved out and the girl's family moved in. Everything ends happily, with the girl and boy becoming friends.

The story is silly and the illustrations are clumsy. But it gets the right message across: ghosts aren't real. I put it with my workbooks on the dressing table. The other two books I stack on my nightstand. They're both longer, and I want to read them before showing them to Ella.

I get out my phone and call my mother. I'm trying to be

better about calling regularly. "How are you? Has work been busy?" I ask.

"Bùcuò," she says. She tells me my brother got a job as a clerk in an insurance agency and it's only part-time for now but he's doing really well and they're talking about hiring him full-time, but Andy's not sure whether he wants to go full-time because he's thinking about enrolling in some college courses in the fall.

"Oh. That's great," I say.

He's working hard and doing very well.

"How about you? How have you been?"

I'm fine, she says. Your brother went out with his friends and Doris.

"My Doris? Doris Chang?"

"Tā shìgè hǎo nǚhái." She's a good girl.

"She is." Which is why it doesn't make sense that she's spending time with Andy.

Though my brother is a troublemaker, a loser, a creep, he constantly has girls hanging around him. I guess some girls, dumb girls, are attracted to jerky bad boys. The same kind of girls, I bet, who would date someone like Henry Morison.

But Doris isn't dumb. And Doris doesn't even date. Though many boys have had crushes on her, she always rebuffs their advances, gently. Doris has never had a boyfriend, and it seems like a point of pride for her, as though she's too pure for some fumbling teen romance.

My own lone experience with fumbling teen romance

proves that Doris isn't missing much. For three months last year I dated this guy Paul Lim, also a junior. Paul was cute and smart and cool. I liked him. I wanted to like him more, but it never happened; nothing much happened between us. There was one party where we slow danced with my head on his shoulder, his hands clamped around my waist. There was lots of hanging out together with our friends, because we had the same friends. Some hand-holding. A little kissing. That was all.

When we broke up, mutually and politely, I wasn't upset. Even when Paul started dating Mary Choi three weeks later.

No—that's not true. I was upset.

But it wasn't Paul I was upset about, or even Mary Choi, who I considered a friend. It was me. I thought there was something wrong with me. I knew I should have been upset. A nice, normal girl would have been upset. So I was upset that I wasn't upset. Though it sounds pretty stupid when I put it like that.

And now I'm stupidly upset about Andy and Doris.

Because even though I know Doris is too smart to fall for his tricks, I don't trust my brother. Not one bit. Not after everything he's done.

After I get off the phone with my mother, there's another knock on the door of the pink bedroom. This time it's Vanessa.

"I just wanted to let you know that I sent the spreadsheet to the calligrapher. Thanks a million," she says, and extends her arm. In her hand is a small white box. "This is for you. A little something to show my appreciation."

"Oh, no, I'm just happy to help."

"Please," she says. "I insist."

So I take the box. Inside is a pair of elaborate earrings with tiny crystals dangling from strands of silver. They are lovely. They are obviously expensive.

"It's too much. I can't accept these," I say.

"It's nothing. A friend gave them to me, but they're not my style at all. They'll be perfect on you, though. Put them on."

I nod. It makes me feel better that it's a recycled gift. And, also, kind of worse. I take the box into the bathroom and slide the earrings slowly in, first the right, then the left. They pull heavily on my earlobes. I gaze at my reflection. Silver strands glittering, stones flickering against the black backdrop of my hair.

"Come out! Let's see!" calls Vanessa.

But when I come out to show her, she doesn't look. She is paging through the book about the girl and the haunted house. "What's this?"

"It's for Ella. I thought she'd like it."

She studies the description on the back. She frowns.

"It's about making new friends," I say. "But if you think—"

"I'm sure it's fine." Vanessa puts the book down. She turns toward me and exclaims over the earrings in my ears. She smiles. But I can still see the strain in the corners of her lips, the creases on her brow.

I don't know what to do. I thank her again.

"How's the tutoring going?" she asks. "I know Ella can be a

handful. I hope she hasn't been giving you any trouble."

"No, no trouble. We're making good progress."

"She's so stubborn. Like her father."

I nod, though I don't think Ella is particularly stubborn. "She's a great kid."

"I know. I know. It's just sometimes I wish . . ."

"Yes?"

"Those earrings are really perfect on you. I knew they'd be." Vanessa reaches over and lightly touches my hair, smoothing it back, the way she sometimes does with her daughter. Her fingers are cool and nimble. The sweet, clean scent of her perfume drifts over me.

Then she gives my shoulder a pat and wishes me good night.

After Vanessa leaves, I go back to the mirror to look at the earrings. They're beautiful but definitely don't match the tank top and shorts I'm wearing. They don't match any of the clothes I own. But I still appreciate Vanessa's gift. Regift.

I pull the silver from my ears and lay the earrings neatly inside their box. I twist my hair into a knot and secure it with a few bobby pins. Then I pick up the book I bought for Ella. The cartoon cover is as silly as the story: a little girl looks alarmed as she enters a spooky house while glowing eyes watch her from a dark rectangle of window.

I put the book down, facedown to hide its silly cover. My earlobes are stinging, the skin swollen where the heavy earrings pierced and pulled. I rub my aching ears.

"You aren't superstitious, are you?" Vanessa asked the first time we met. My answer was no then, and it's no now, but I'm worried I've somehow contradicted myself by promising Ella I wouldn't tell anyone about the ghost. I shouldn't have promised. It was a rookie mistake: never promise a kid anything you're not absolutely positively sure you can deliver.

But I did it. Now I can only hope I don't end up regretting it.

9

THE NEXT TIME JEFFREY MORISON COMES TO THE ISLAND, HE brings guests—Greg and Lorraine Chamberlain. Greg is a tall and handsome white man with the straight strong features of a television news anchor. Lorraine is a short white woman with unnaturally red hair and a lot of makeup. Her eyebrows are drawn dramatically upward. Her mouth is colored the same vivid red as her hair. She looks ridiculous.

But then she speaks. "Jeffrey, tell your family about the cop who pulled us over because you were driving thirty miles over the speed limit. Then he saw it was you so he apologized and let us go. Are you sure this is Arrow Island and not Morison Island? I didn't know the feudal system was thriving in this country—well, this part of the country," Lorraine says, laughing.

Her voice is low, in both tone and volume. Her laughter is a tinkling melody. She is, I suddenly realize, strikingly attractive.

"Tell them, Jeffrey," she says, and though her words point

the attention toward Jeffrey, everyone continues watching Lorraine. Especially Jeffrey.

"Well, Lorry, you just told the whole story. I've got nothing to add," he says with a hearty chuckle.

"Thirty miles over the speed limit, honey?" Vanessa tries to sparkle the question at her husband, but her voice is brittle. She sounds disapproving, not flirtatious, and when Jeffrey looks at her, he looks exasperated.

Lorraine interjects, "It was probably only ten. You know I can't help exaggerating."

"I know." Vanessa smiles stiffly.

Jeffrey surveys the table. "Where's my father?"

"He's not feeling well. He's resting," says Henry.

Lorraine gasps. "Oh no! Is he all right?"

"He's fine," says Vanessa.

Mrs. Tully comes in with the appetizers: salad and an assortment of savory pastries.

"Mrs. Tully! I've been pestering Jeffrey for an invitation just so I could come back and eat your food." Lorraine smiles. Her smile is as irresistible as her voice.

Mrs. Tully smiles back. "I made the mushroom quiches because I remembered how much you liked them last time," she says.

Lorraine thanks her gravely, as if she has made a vast personal sacrifice and not a tart made of cheese and dough. Her excessive solemnity should be ridiculous, but it isn't. Instead, it makes everyone else also thank Mrs. Tully.

Then we eat. Jeffrey Morison and Lorraine talk. Apparently they've been friends for a long time, since college or high school or maybe even before that. And they have a lot to talk about: Fran Larson is getting divorced, **again**; and Jackson Roy is under investigation for insurance fraud; and Mina Bradley has some sort of illness and is starting a foundation. Their conversation pauses for a moment, out of respect for Mina's illness. Then they continue. Vic Samson is cheating on his wife with his secretary and the secretary actually thinks he's going to leave his wife for her.

"Such a cliché. But Vic was always unoriginal," says Lorraine.

"That's Vic, all right." Jeffrey laughs and takes a long drink of wine.

Meanwhile, Greg eats his food, grunting appreciatively.

Meanwhile, Henry and Ella are communicating in a secret sibling language of eye rolls and nose wiggles and elbow jabs. I recognize it instantly, though it's been years since my brother and I shared anything like that.

Meanwhile, Vanessa watches her husband talk to Lorraine. Her blue eyes unblinking. Her glossy lips tremulously parted. As if she's watching a movie, a sad one.

I feel bad for Vanessa. But I'm also fascinated by Lorraine. She exemplifies the lesson that school assemblies, health classes, and teen magazines are always preaching: that attractiveness is not merely about looks, but also speech and action. It's about confidence.

I was never persuaded before, but Lorraine is dazzlingly convincing. She speaks with quiet authority, and everyone leans in to listen. She laughs often, and her laugh is infectious. Her smile is alluring. In comparison, Vanessa's hair flipping and eyelash fluttering seem juvenile and contrived.

The worst part is that if I were a stranger guessing about the couples at this table, I'd guess wrong. Because they look **right** together, Jeffrey and Lorraine, a perfect match of wit and charm. Whereas Vanessa and Greg are similarly and conventionally beautiful. And also—at least in this moment—dull.

Greg says nothing other than hello, nice to meet you, thanks for having us, and please pass the pepper. Then he is silent until he finishes his dessert, a thick slice of chocolate cake with whipped cream. He eats it all, leaving not a smudge on his plate. Finally he speaks again. He tells Vanessa, "That was some great grub."

"Thank you." She doesn't look at him. She is busy looking elsewhere.

Greg either doesn't notice or doesn't care. He turns to the person seated on his other side. Which happens to be me. "So, you're the nanny? How do you like it?" he asks.

It's a friendly question, and it deserves a friendly answer. I bend my lips into a smile. But before I can correct him, politely, someone else does.

"Actually, Greg, she's an academic tutor. Ella's academic tutor." It's Henry. Henry says it. Then he looks at me and grins.

I'm too startled to do anything but grin right back.

Then Greg is asking me what exactly an academic tutor does, so I give him my standard explanation, full of words like "aptitude" and "individual attention" and "personalized curriculum." I've given this speech dozens of times, so it requires no thought. Which is good, because I suddenly don't know what to think.

I think something has changed. I think it all day Saturday while the family and their guests are out: sailing on Jeffrey's sailboat, eating dinner at the Morisons' favorite restaurant in town. I think it all morning Sunday and most of the afternoon. I'm still thinking it when I meet Henry in the hallway, on our way to dinner Sunday night.

"Hey," he says. "Where've you been hiding?"

"I've been in my room, but I haven't been hiding," I say.

"Sounds like hiding to me." Henry smirks.

I ignore his smirk and say, "That was nice what you did the other night."

"I did something nice? It was probably a mistake."

"When you told Greg I was an academic tutor," I persist. "I appreciated it."

"Oh, yeah. That. That was definitely a mistake. Better to keep that guy confused. Though it's not like he needs any help. Maybe you should academic tutor him." Henry is still smirking.

And I feel so foolish. But I smile brightly. "Forget it," I say.

"Uh-oh, it's the smile of doom. Now what did I do?" he asks.

"Nothing. You've done nothing. You do absolutely nothing."

Henry stops smirking. "What's that supposed to mean?"

"Exactly what it means," I say, and dart past him into the dining room.

The adults are all already there, and it appears they've been there for a while. Drinking. On the table are bottles of whiskey and vodka and wine. In their hands are glasses. Jeffrey's face is deeply flushed. Vanessa's dress is slipping off her shoulders, not intentionally. Greg's swoop of hair seems to be deflating. Old Mr. Morison looks half asleep.

Only Lorraine seems unaffected, her elaborately made-up face intact, her dark clothing securely fastened. But when she speaks, her voice is slightly huskier than usual. "Here come our dear young people, the brilliant tutor and the dashing Henry," she says. "But where is our sweet little Ella?"

"I'll get her," I say.

I hurry to the small deck at the side of the house where I found her the day I arrived. Today she is not crouched in the corner. She is sitting on the white sofa, dressed in a fancy floral dress, with a book in her hands. It's the book I bought for her. She closes it when she sees me.

"I finished reading it," Ella says accusingly.

"Already? What did you think?" I expect her to argue that the ghost was real.

But Ella says, "Why did he forget about his friend so fast?"

"Who forgets about his friend?" I ask.

"The neighbor boy. At the end of the book he forgets about

his friend who used to live in the house and becomes friends with the new girl. How can he forget his old friend?"

It takes me a moment to remember what she's talking about. I've been focused on the haunting part of the book. "Um, just because he makes a new friend doesn't mean he forgets about his old friend," I say.

Then Ella, quiet and modest and well-behaved Ella, flashes me a look of utter disdain. "The drawings weren't very good either," she says. "My drawings are better."

"I bet they are," I say. "I'd love to see your drawings."

She drops her gaze. "Is it time for dinner now?"

We go to the dining room.

"Ellie!" cries Vanessa. "Come give Mommy a kiss. How pretty you are in that dress!"

Ella goes to kiss her mother. Then she goes to kiss her father. He gives her his cheek and a pat on the shoulder while he continues talking to Lorraine. Tonight they are not gossiping about mutual acquaintances. They are discussing business.

Lorraine is telling him about a new microchip under development at the technology company where she works. "The announcement will be made next Wednesday. It's going to be huge," she says.

"Thanks for the tip. I can always count on you," says Jeffrey.

"And vice versa." Lorraine smiles her alluring smile.

"Jeffrey, this is not an appropriate conversation," chides

Mr. Morison. His voice is cold, but his face is hot with anger. I wonder how he would have reacted to the conversation of the other night, their talk of cancer, divorce, and secretaries.

"Don't blame him. It's my fault." Lorraine transfers her alluring smile to the old man.

"Yes. I expect better from you, at least." Mr. Morison's expression softens. No one is immune to Lorraine's charm.

Mrs. Tully brings in dinner and more bottles of wine. Everyone eats and the adults drink and drink. A lot. By the time dessert arrives, Greg's handsome face is sweaty and swollen and Mr. Morison is swaying sleepily in his chair. Jeffrey and Lorraine are sitting very close together. Vanessa watches them.

Jeffrey whispers something to Lorraine.

Lorraine bursts into laughter.

The pure sound of it, the twinkling of her joy, startles Mr. Morison out of his stupor. He looks at her. Then he looks at his son and says, "She's the one who got away, isn't she?"

"Oh, I was never handsome enough for her," says Jeffrey.

"That's not true. I was never pretty enough for you," says Lorraine.

They smile, affectionately, at each other.

I glance at Vanessa. She looks close to weeping.

I'm getting ready for bed when Ella knocks on the door. She is still wearing her fancy dinner dress, and the sight of her in flowers and ruffles, surrounded by the flowers and ruffles of the pink room, is almost comical. But I don't laugh. Ella's expression is too serious.

"What's wrong?" I ask.

"She's here."

"Who?"

"The ghost."

"Ella, there is no ghost," I say.

She stares at me.

"Ghosts don't actually exist," I say.

Her face puckers. "Also, I forgot your book outside. Come get it with me."

"Please ask nicely. And it's your book now. I bought it for you."

"Will you please come with me to get my book please?"

"Yes, of course."

It's not very late, but the house already seems to be sleeping. The hallways are dark. The rooms are silent and still. We walk carefully through the shadows, speaking only in whispers.

"Do you feel the cold air?" Ella whispers.

"No. I think it feels warm here," I whisper back.

I tug the sliding door open, and we both jump at the stuttering swish—not because it's loud, but because the night is so quiet. There is no breeze, no insect buzz. Only the distant rumble of the ocean.

Ella scurries out and snatches the book from the sofa. Then she stops. She straightens. She lifts her chin and tilts her head.

"Come on, Ella. Let's go," I whisper.

"Do you hear that?" she asks.

"I don't hear anything," I say. But then I do. A high-pitched wail. And I know there's no ghost here, ghosts don't exist, but I have to resist the urge to grab hold of Ella and run back inside. I force myself toward the mournful sound. I walk to the outer edge of the deck and peer over the railing.

It's Vanessa. Vanessa talking to her husband. Vanessa wailing at her husband. They are down in the backyard, their faces glowing blue in the swimming pool lights.

"Aren't I enough for you? Is there something wrong with me?" Vanessa cries.

"Honey, you're acting crazy. Lorraine's like my sister. Besides, don't you realize how much I make off her information?" Jeffrey says.

"You leave me here with your kids. You stick me in this impossible situation with your father. You don't come back for weeks. Then you bring her!"

"You know I'd rather be here. It's work that keeps me away. You should be happy. You certainly seem happy enough to spend my money."

"Your money?"

I suddenly realize that Ella is next to me, stretched up on her tiptoes so that she can see over the railing. I take hold of her small, cold hand. "Let's go inside," I say.

"Wait," she says.

I don't wait. And she doesn't resist as I pull her across the deck and into the house. I slide the door closed behind us. Then everything is silent again.

As we climb up the stairs, I say, "All couples fight. It's a way of expressing their feelings. It can make their relationship better."

Ella slides her hand out of my hand. I don't take offense. Eight-year-olds are unpredictable when it comes to hand-holding. "Okay," she says skeptically.

I don't blame her. I'm skeptical too. Before my father left, my parents fought often. Or, more accurately, my father would fight with my mother. She wouldn't fight back—she would reply in a soft and agreeable voice, saying soft and agreeable things. Which only made him attack harder, complain louder, criticize more harshly and unfairly. Their fights didn't make their relationship better. But I doubt anything could have made their relationship better.

When we reach her bedroom, Ella grabs my arm and grips it with startling strength. "Do you feel that?" she asks.

"Ella, that's enough. No more ghost stuff," I say.

But then I feel it. The floor trembling under our feet. The walls shivering around us. My heart shuddering in my body, my body shuddering as everything—the whole house, the whole world, and Ella and me inside it—shakes and shakes and shakes.

"An earthquake!" I say. I try to remember what you're supposed to do. Stand in doorways? Crouch under tables? Huddle in the bathtub? I can't remember. No one expects earthquakes around here.

"No! You have to stop! Stop it now!" shouts Ella.

And all at once, everything is still.

10

IN THE MORNING, THE FIRST THING I DO AFTER GETTING OUT OF bed is go online to search for any reports of nearby earthquakes, aftershocks, tremors, or vibrations caused by natural or man-made explosions. I find nothing. Apparently, Arrow Island is in a low-risk zone for seismic activity. But if that wasn't an earthquake last night, what could it have been?

"Can you believe how mad the ghost was last night? She was so mad!" Ella says as she closes her workbook.

I'm impressed by her restraint: she waited until we finished our lessons before bringing up the ghost. But I've been preparing for this moment all day. "No, the ghost wasn't mad. There is no ghost. Ghosts aren't real," I say calmly, sensibly, authoritatively.

"How do you know?" she asks.

"Science has debunked the existence of ghosts."

"What does debunk mean?"

"Debunk means prove that something is false. Look at

this." I hand her a stapled stack of papers, photocopied from the second book I bought for her: an academic study by a psychologist that examines the science behind fake psychics and haunting hoaxes and other so-called paranormal phenomena. Most of the book is too difficult or disturbing for eight-year-old Ella, but there are parts I decided she could read. For example, the chapter about how certain locations may seem haunted because of sound waves caused by rumbling traffic or rustling wind.

Ella looks down at the first page. She looks up at me with a glazed expression.

"It's interesting. We'll read it together," I say.

"Okay," she says.

We leave the library. Ella goes downstairs to look for her brother. And I go upstairs to talk to Vanessa about the earthquake. Because what else could it have been?

However, I'm a little apprehensive. Vanessa was quiet during lunch, in her gray satin robe with no makeup on. Her husband left early this morning, taking his guests with him, but she didn't say anything about that, or anything about him, or much of anything at all.

I knock lightly on her office door.

"Come in!" she calls, so I do. Vanessa is sitting at her desk. In some ways, she looks much better than she did at lunch. She has changed into a long lilac dress. Her cheeks are flushed. Her lips have been colored pink. But her eyes are wide and wild.

"Is everything okay?" I ask.

"Everything's great! Why?" she says.

"Oh, I was wondering because . . . of the earthquake."

"Earthquake? What are you talking about?"

"It happened last night. Around nine o'clock."

Vanessa shakes her head. "There wasn't an earthquake."

"I'm sure there was," I say.

"Maybe you dreamed it," she says. "I've been having this recurring dream that I look in the mirror and my skin is green, a moldy green, and it's starting to crumble off. I try to press it back on, but the more I do, the more comes off, and there's nothing underneath. Just a black hole."

"That sounds scary," I say. "But . . . I didn't dream the earthquake."

Vanessa starts to laugh. It is not her normal laugh; it is not a normal laugh. It's a strangled sound that goes on and on and on, until it turns into a sob. Then she's crying. Hard. For a second, I'm not sure how to respond. No parent has ever cried in front of me before.

But plenty of children have.

So I walk around the desk, hunch next to her, and put my arm around her shoulder. In a low, soothing voice, I say, "It's all right. Everything's going to be all right."

"What am I going to do?" she says.

"What's the problem?" I ask.

I expect her to talk about her husband or Lorraine.

She says, "I'm so stressed about this party. I can't find an event planner; all the good ones are already booked. Part of me wants to cancel the whole thing. But I'll feel like such a failure if I do. I already feel like a failure."

"You're not a failure. I know you're going to throw a great party."

"You really think so?"

"Yes. All your ideas are fantastic!"

"But there's so much to do."

"You can do it. And I can help you," I say. Even though I'm an academic tutor. Not a babysitter or nanny or cleaning lady or spreadsheet maker. Definitely not a party-planning assistant. But what else could I say?

Then Vanessa smiles at me with such gratitude that I can't regret it. Not exactly.

When Doris calls me this evening, I'm tempted not to answer. I'm not in the mood to talk to her. But as the phone rings and rings and rings, I start feeling guilty. She's my best friend. I don't want to be a bad friend. So I shine up my voice and answer.

"Doris! How are you? It's been so long! I miss you!"

"I miss you too! It feels like you've been gone forever," she says. "All this stuff is happening and I'm dying to talk to you about it."

"What stuff?" I immediately think of my brother.

"Well, I met with my college adviser today, and we had an amazing discussion about my future, and I'm now considering going into neurology instead of cardiology."

I exhale. "Well, you don't have to decide yet, do you?"

"You know how I am, though. I like to plan."

"Me too," I say. "That's why we're friends. Remember in second grade when I asked if I could use your red marker, and you said I could but only if I used it right away because you'd need it in exactly three minutes to color the flowers in your rainforest sketch?"

"Then you gave the marker back two minutes and fifty-eight seconds later. That's when I knew we'd be best friends forever," she says.

We both laugh, and I'm reminded of the way it used to be between us—so fun, so easy. I wish it could be that way again. But then Doris starts talking about my brother.

"Andy did the sweetest thing," she says. "My headphones broke last week, and you know what he did? He bought me a new pair. Isn't that sweet?"

"He probably stole them," I say.

Doris is quiet.

"I'm kidding," I say.

"That's not very nice," she says, her voice gently chiding. It's the same voice I use to discipline my students. "Andy cares about you. He misses you."

"He really said that?"

"Not exactly. But he did ask me how you were doing."

"What did you tell him?"

"I told him you're great! Aren't you?"

I try not to think about the fight between Vanessa and

Jeffrey. Or how cold Ella's hand felt when I held it last night. Or how I may be compromising my job description. Or the earthquake that no one else noticed. Especially not that.

"Yeah, I'm great," I say. And wish I hadn't answered the phone.

The next few days pass uneventfully. Vanessa finally hires an event planner. Old Mr. Morison recovers from his cold. Henry is his usual obnoxious self. Ella and I continue making slow progress during our tutoring sessions. We also spend a few hours reading the supernatural-study photocopies, but Ella isn't that interested. I can't tell whether it's because she disagrees with the content or because it's too difficult.

On Thursday afternoon I'm in the library, reviewing my lesson plan for the next day, when Vanessa appears and sits down next to me at the table.

"I need your help," she says. "The calligrapher will be finished with the invitations and envelopes for the party tomorrow, and they need to be picked up and mailed right away."

"Okay," I say. After all, I told her I'd help. "You want me to mail the invitations?"

"If you don't mind."

"I don't mind."

"Great! You'll have to leave early tomorrow morning so that you can get there in time. Then I thought you might like to spend the rest of the weekend with your family. I know you must miss them."

"My family?" I'm confused.

"Don't you miss them?" she says.

"Yes, but . . . you want me to go back to the city?"

"The calligrapher lives in the city. I didn't mention that?"

"No," I say.

"Yes, she works out of her home downtown. Don't you live downtown as well? Anyway, I'd go myself, except my husband is coming tomorrow. Wouldn't it be funny if I left the island to go to the city the same day Jeffrey left the city to come to the island?" Vanessa does something to her face—I think it's meant to be a smile. It looks like a convulsion.

"So you'll go?" she asks.

"Of course." Even though I'm an academic tutor.

"Thank you," she says. "I'll tell Henry."

I frown. "What does Henry have to do with it?"

"He's going to drive you. I didn't mention that? I'm so absentminded today. Henry has a meeting with his vice principal tomorrow afternoon, so he's driving to the city. He'll stay with his mom for the weekend, and the two of you can come back together on Sunday. It's perfect timing, isn't it?"

"Um. Are you sure Henry won't mind?" I'm sure he will. I certainly do.

"I'm sure Henry won't mind," says Vanessa.

"What won't I mind?" Henry saunters into the library, and for the first time ever I'm glad to see him. I want him to reject this carpool plan so I don't have to.

"She's going to the city to pick up the party invitations, and since you have your meeting tomorrow, I thought you could drive her," Vanessa explains.

"You don't have to. I don't mind taking the bus," I say. Or, more accurately, I don't mind taking the taxi to the ferry to the bus to the subway. In fact, I'd prefer it.

"I'm happy to drive you." Henry grins as if he knows exactly what I'm thinking.

"Really?" I stare at him in disbelief.

"The two of us in the car together for hours and hours and hours?" he says. "We're going to have so much fun."

PART II
THE CITY

1

IT'S A LOVELY MORNING, BLUE SKY AND GENTLE BREEZE, AND
we barely make it past the metal gate before we start bicker-
ing. It begins when Henry asks if I want to take a turn driving
later.

"I'm sorry, I can't," I say.

"Because you can't drive?" he asks.

"You don't have to drive when you live in the city."

"So you don't drive or you can't drive?"

"I don't know how to drive," I admit. "You don't have to in
the city."

"But are you always going to live in the city?"

"Probably."

"Why do you sound so sad?"

"I don't sound sad."

"You do. You sound totally depressed."

"Well, I'm not."

"If you say so," he says. "Anyway, this car is really fun to
drive."

"I bet. It's like when an old man has a midlife crisis and gets rid of his wife for some hot girl, and exchanges his minivan for a car like yours," I say.

Henry grimaces.

I shrug. What else can he expect with a car so ridiculously red and fast and fancy? So obviously expensive and extravagantly unnecessary?

We turn into the ferry terminal and park at the end of a long line of cars waiting for the boat to come. As I watch it chug toward us, I do some calculations: it takes approximately four hours to drive from the island to the city, and we've been in the car together for twenty minutes. Therefore we have three hours and forty minutes to go, and the probability of one of us murdering the other during that time is 98 percent.

The ferry docks. The cars roll on one by one. On the boat, in the car, we bob across the ocean in silence. I do some more calculations. If we don't speak during the rest of the ride, the probability of murder drops 33 percent.

Unfortunately, Henry does not seem to realize it. As we near the mainland, he starts talking again. "Are you excited to go home?" he asks.

"Of course I am."

"You sound depressed again."

"Are you ready to meet with your vice principal?"

"Why aren't you excited to go home?"

"How are you going to convince him to let you graduate?"

"Is it your family? Do you hate your family?"

"What will you do if he won't let you graduate?"

"Why do you hate your family?" he asks.

"I don't!" I say.

The ferry stops with an abrupt lurch. The cars roll off one by one. Three hours and fifteen minutes to go. And the probability of murder has increased a whole percent.

"Do you mind if . . ." I don't finish my question. I lean over and turn up the volume on the radio until the music is so loud it hurts, so loud that there's no possibility of conversation. Thus we make it safely through the next hour of our trip.

Then Henry stops for gas, and I go to use the bathroom. When I get back to the car, he's sitting in the front passenger seat. I knock on the window. He rolls it down. He's smirking. Of course. How I hate that smirk. I ask him what he's doing.

"I got a great idea! You're going to drive now," he says.

"Very funny."

"I'm not joking. I'm going to teach you."

"No, thank you."

"But everyone should know how to drive. What if there was a driving emergency one day? Wouldn't you want to be prepared? Get in the car."

"No, thank you."

"Come on, it'll be fun. Don't you like fun?" he says.

I don't understand his insistence. Though he claimed he wasn't joking, I can't help thinking that this is a joke and the punch line will be me—Henry Morison laughing at me. And suddenly I'm angry, angry about a thing that hasn't even happened yet, but too angry to care that it hasn't. I speak in a harsh voice that isn't my voice at all.

"Don't you remember telling me I'm no fun? And a suck-up? It's too bad you didn't manage to get rid of me that first day, but you didn't. So whatever game you're playing now, stop it. It's not funny. It's stupid. It's so stupid and we're stuck together for the next two hours and fifteen minutes and the only way we'll both survive this is if you shut up and get into the driver's seat."

Immediately I regret it. Not because it isn't true. Because it isn't nice. And I'm supposed to be nice. Especially to the son of my employers.

But before I can apologize, Henry gets out of the car. He waits for me to get in, then shuts the door. He walks around and slides back into the driver's seat. He clips in his seat belt and turns on the engine. But he doesn't start driving. Instead he says, "I'm an asshole. You shouldn't listen to anything I say. I'm sorry." His face is red.

I can't believe it: Henry Morison is apologizing and . . . blushing?

"It's okay," I say. "I shouldn't have—"

"No," he interrupts. "I'm a total asshole."

"Not a total asshole," I say.

He half smiles at me. "Thanks for that."

"Besides, you're right. I can kind of be a suck-up."

"Kind of?" Henry raises his eyebrows.

"Okay, a huge suck-up. And sometimes I'm not that fun.

And I did say that your car was an old man's car. I guess I've been totally mean to you too."

"Not totally mean," he says.

I half smile at him. "Thanks for that."

"Anyway, I kind of like it when you're mean."

"That's not possible," I say.

"Why not?" he asks.

"Nobody likes it when you're mean."

"Not true. I like it. I just said so."

"You're the exception that proves the rule."

"What does that even mean? People are always saying that, but it makes no sense. Don't exceptions disprove rules?" he says.

"It's a proverb from Latin. It means that if you exclude the exception, it makes the rule stronger in all other situations," I say.

Henry stares at me. "Do you know everything?"

"Except how to drive and how to swim," I say.

Then he laughs, face bright and eyes glinting and perfect teeth flashing, and I suddenly notice that Henry Morison is sort of cute. If you're into that preppy white-boy thing.

We get back on the highway with the music on loud, but not too loud for conversation.

"So how about we start over?" Henry says.

"You think starting over is possible?" I say.

"Maybe not. Maybe it's better if we just continue on. Onward and upward! Except now you know I'm not trying to be a jerk, and I know you aren't a fun-hating suck-up."

"And I'll be mean to you because I know how much you like it."

"And I'll try not to be such a smartass. Though I don't know if I can do it."

"I can tutor you," I say.

"Great," he says with the most tragic sigh.

"Lesson one," I say. "Don't ever sigh like that again."

Henry sighs like that again. "Seriously, though," he says. "This summer has been rough with the maybe-not-graduating, maybe-not-going-to-college, father-in-a-rage, mother-freaking-out stuff."

"I can imagine. What are you going to say to your vice principal?"

"I don't know. Apologize? Beg? Cry? What do you think?"

"Lesson two," I say. "When meeting with your high school vice principal to discuss how you passed out drunk during your final exam, apologize profusely, express sincere remorse, tell him how grateful you'd be for another chance to take the test. But don't beg. Don't cry, either, but do blink hard, like you're bravely holding back tears."

"Like this?" Henry winks.

"Lesson three," I say. "Never ever wink."

"As soon as you tell me not to do something, I feel compelled to do it."

"Yeah, you and all my students. But they have the excuse of being eight."

He winks. "Not my sister, though, right? How's the tutoring going?"

"It's getting better now that she's more comfortable with me."

"Good. Ella's had a rough year. The girls she'd been friends with forever suddenly kicked her out of their group," he says.

"What? Why?"

"She and her friends got caught doing some prank and they all blamed Ella, though it wasn't her fault. I've never been so angry at a bunch of little girls before."

"Your grandfather told me something about that," I say. "What was the prank?"

"They vandalized the girls' bathroom, drew all over the walls and threw toilet paper everywhere. Dumb stuff," he says.

"Weird. That doesn't seem like something Ella would do."

"I know. I can see her going along with it, but not being the ringleader. That's why it's especially messed up that they blamed her. She was suspended for two days."

"That sucks. I wish Vanessa had told me about it earlier."

"Are you really surprised? Ness likes to keep up a good front."

Then we are both quiet for a few minutes. I'm remembering Ella's reaction to that kid's book I gave her. "How can he forget his friend?" she'd asked. Poor Ella.

"So . . . ," Henry says. "What do you think I should say to my vice principal?"

"You want to practice? I'll be the vice principal. You be you."

"How about I be the vice principal and you be me?"

"You sure you want me to be you?" I say. I smirk.

"No, no, not sure. You be the vice principal. He has a big beard, by the way."

"Perfect." I put my hand up to my chin and wiggle my fingers.

"Wow, you look exactly like him," he says.

"So tell me why you deserve another chance," I boom in my deepest voice.

Henry makes a face, but he tells me. I give him some tips and make him tell me again. And again, so he gets it exactly right. And again, to annoy him. And again, to annoy him some more. And again, but then his explanations get so ridiculous (a rabid raccoon, an alien abduction) that we're both laughing too hard to do it again.

The city takes me by surprise.

One moment I'm telling the story of when my student Adeline's little brother asked me, worriedly, if it was true that eating too much put a baby in your belly. "Because then your stomach bulges out a lot, like this," he said, lifting his shirt to show me his bulging stomach. I explained it wasn't true, skimming over the concept of sex, and asked him how he came up with such an idea. It was, of course, Adeline.

The next moment, I'm gazing out the car window, my nose

nearly bumping the glass. For there in the distance looms the city, bigger and brighter and more overwhelming than I remember. Home.

We drive across the bridge and into the streets. There is a lot of traffic, lots of pedestrians, everyone rushing everywhere. I give Henry directions to my apartment, and the closer we get, the more crowded it gets, and the more crowded it gets, the more trouble I have breathing.

"Now where should I go?" he asks.

"Pull over at the next corner. That's my building." I point at the brown high-rise. Even with the car windows closed and the air conditioner on, I think I can smell the usual smells of salt and herbs and rot. The usual neighborhood people swarm around the sidewalk. Elderly women teetering with their bulging bags of groceries. Loitering men in grimy undershirts scowling and scratching and smoking and spitting. Little kids with sticky faces tangled up in their mothers' legs.

Then I notice that one of the loitering men—in a T-shirt, not an undershirt, that appears reasonably clean—is my brother. Scowling and smoking.

There is a sinking heaviness in my chest. I stop breathing completely.

"You want help bringing your stuff up?" Henry asks.

"No," I say sharply. "Thank you," I add belatedly. "And thanks for the ride. Good luck with your meeting, and I'll see you Sunday. You have my number, right? Great. Have a good weekend."

He looks at me skeptically. I can tell that our new friendliness is in danger, but all I want is to get Henry Morison away from here, from the sights and sounds and smells of my real life. I leap out of the car and grab my bag from the back. I wave at Henry until he finally drives away. Then I turn around slowly.

I know he's there; I feel him hovering behind me. "Hi, Andy."

"Nice ride," says my brother. "You dating white guys now?"

"That was the brother of the girl I'm tutoring this summer."

"You dating the brother of the rich girl you're tutoring? Even better."

I sigh. "I'm not. We're just friends. Barely friends."

He laughs. "Sounds like a lot of excuses to me."

"Stop it." I step around my brother and walk toward the building, elbowing past the loitering men, moving aside for the elderly women, darting around the little kids.

"You've got no sense of humor." Andy trails after me.

"I don't know why Doris thinks you've changed," I say.

"She said that?" He actually smiles.

I go inside. My brother can't follow because he's still smoking his cigarette. "Hold on," he calls out after me.

But I hurry past the security guard picking his teeth with a toothpick, get into the tiny elevator, press the sticky button, and tap my foot as it lumbers up. On the eleventh floor the door jerks open. The air is musty with cooking smells. I stride across stained carpet, past stained walls, to the end of the corridor. I pull the key from my pocket and twist it in the lock. I press my palm against the scuffed knob and turn.

Then I pause at the threshold.

It's all so familiar. This is where I've lived my entire life; of course it should be familiar. Of course I should recognize the scents and sounds and the freckles on the doorframe where the paint has chipped away.

Yet it's all so foreign. I've been away for only a month, yet it feels as if I'm seeing this place for the first time, this tiny, dingy place crammed full of stuff: old shoes, old clothes; used gift wrap and boxes and rubber bands and string; takeout containers meant to be thrown away, and plastic forks and spoons and knives and sporks; sticky roasting pans and a missing-handled pot; crumpled balls of tinfoil; all kinds of bags in all types of material: plastic, paper, cotton, canvas, polyester, nylon, leather, pleather; foil packs of mayonnaise; used twisty straws; a VCR and several stacks of videos; melted stubs of birthday candles; more than one leaky umbrella; a box made of Popsicle sticks; a mug in the shape of denim-clad hips; hot sauce blackened by age; photo albums with peeling covers; tins of stale crackers; time-stopped wristwatches; engraved goblets with fake-gold rims; teeny pots of strawberry jam and orange marmalade; a rusty watering can; yellowed notepads with cartoon covers; a shrill table fan; a lifetime supply of disposable chopsticks; an embroidered footstool; ancient bottles of spices that have probably lost their spice; old and very old phone books; remote controls that control nothing; a tattered floral rug; more than one plastic jack-o'-lantern; a mobile of origami swans; emptied egg cartons; a dead space heater; paper packets of sugar; a stack of out-of-date calendars; my father's old stuff, all the stuff he left behind; and more stuff.

I take a deep breath and step inside. I'm home.

2

THE APARTMENT IS QUIET. MY MOTHER IS AT WORK, BUT SHE must have rushed back during her lunch break, because there's a cardboard container on the table with my name written across the top in her careful lettering. It's my favorite takeout meal: rice noodles with bean sprouts in oyster sauce, and it's still warm. I sit down and eat.

The food tastes like comfort. And guilt.

I don't want to be here, but I'm ashamed for not wanting to be here. This is where my mother, the person who loves me most in the world, lives. This is where I eat and sleep and study and read and think and plan. This is where I grew up; this is where I'm from.

So it shouldn't matter that our apartment isn't a fairy-tale mansion with an immaculately modern interior. It shouldn't matter that it's dingy and stays dingy no matter how much we scrub. It shouldn't matter that it's tiny yet overstuffed. Besides, I understand why my mother keeps everything. It's what you do when you're used to having nothing.

I eat half the container of food because my mother will worry if I don't eat at least half the container. Then I wrap up my leftovers and put them in the refrigerator. I step into my sneakers, double-knot the laces, and go. When I get downstairs, I look for my brother. I don't see him. But I don't look very hard.

The calligrapher's studio is only a fifteen-minute walk away from our apartment, but in an entirely different neighborhood. Here the sidewalks are calm and uncrowded. The shops are so spare that they appear to be selling nothing. There are lots of trees, tall and solid, full green in summer bloom.

I ring the bell at the brownstone building, and the calligrapher comes out with two cardboard boxes. I thank her and carry the boxes to the public library a few blocks away. The only free seat is between a snoring old man and a disheveled woman who is whispering to herself. So there I sit.

"Don't worry," the woman whispers as I check the addresses against the guest list.

"You tried your best," she whispers as I slide an invitation into each envelope.

"They expected too much from you. You're only human," she whispers as I seal each envelope with a sponge I've brought for that purpose.

"Good-bye," she whispers when I get up to go.

"Bye," I whisper back.

I bring the box of invitations to the post office, wait in a very long and slow-moving line, and buy several packets of the stamps Vanessa selected, a simple floral design. I stick a stamp, precisely, in the upper right-hand corner of each envelope. Then I toss them all into the mail chute.

As I walk home, I call Vanessa to tell her I've sent the invitations.

"I'm eternally grateful!" she says. "Also, I was hoping you could pick up some things for me in the city, since you're there. It's only a couple of things. Do you have a pen handy?"

"Um. Hold on." I move to the side of the sidewalk and out of the sun. It's hot here, much hotter than Arrow Island with its ocean breezes and green expanses. I get a pen out of my bag. "Okay, I'm ready," I say.

Vanessa rattles off her list. It's nearly a dozen items, ranging from a specific brand of candle in a specific scent to a five-pound box of cookies from her local bakery to a tube of red lipstick. "If you can't get everything, though, it's all right," she says. "I'm out of the lipstick, so if you could get that first, it would be great. And the cookies, they're Jeffrey's favorite. I hope it isn't too much trouble. You don't mind, do you?"

It's easier the second time. I zigzag through the crowd, hopping over the murky puddles, easily sidestepping the garbage in the street. I barely notice the slow lurch of the elevator or the grimy walls and worn carpet. This time I do not pause at the threshold.

My mother is home now. She comes out of the kitchen. She holds out her hand. I take her outstretched hand and kiss her soft cheek. She smells like citrus soap and cooking oil and the pungent herbal medicine she uses for her muscle aches.

"Nǐ è ma?" she asks. **Are you hungry?**

"No, I ate the noodles. They were good. Thanks."

My mother nods.

"I brought you something." I take a small package out of my bag.

She opens it and peers inside. "Shì shénme?"

"Fudge."

"Fudge?"

"It's a kind of candy. They make it on the island. It's really good."

Thank you. It wasn't expensive, was it? my mother asks.

"Not at all," I say quickly.

She nods. I can tell she doesn't believe me.

My mother returns to the kitchen. I follow her, but since there isn't much room in that narrow space, I stand at the outer edge. There are three pots on the stove: a wok and a frying pan and a saucepan.

"Do you need any help?" I ask. I know she'll say no.

She tilts her head as if she's considering my question. She says no.

"Where's Andy? Is he eating with us?"

He went to his friend's. Don't worry, he'll be here tomorrow.

"How thoughtful of him," I say.

My mother nods.

Anyway, I'm used to it being just the two of us for dinner.

We sit in our usual seats with our usual bowls of white rice, using our regular blue-and-white dishes, our regular bamboo chopsticks. My mother has made stir-fried broccoli and battered chicken. They were my favorites when I was little, the foods I asked for on my birthday. And even if I don't love them now the way I loved them then, they're still delicious.

"Delicious," I tell my mother. "I missed your cooking so much."

She bobs her head and murmurs wordlessly in return.

"How's work? Anything new happening?"

She shakes her head. "Méiyǒu." Nothing.

"How's Auntie Jeanie? And the kids?"

"Hěn hǎo." They're good.

I give in and ask the question I know will get a lengthy response. "How's Andy doing at his new job?"

My mother looks up from her bowl of rice. She tells me that he is doing very well. That they like him a lot and asked him to go full-time, but he decided that since he's starting community college in the fall he should stay part-time for now. She sounds so proud.

What are you doing tomorrow? she asks.

"I have some errands to do for my boss."

But it's Saturday. And you're only here for the weekend.

"I'll come home as soon as I can."

She looks down into her bowl of rice and softly exhales.

After dinner we watch her favorite soap opera together, but my mother is having trouble staying awake: every time I look at her, her eyes are closing or closed. She's tired from her long day of work and delivering my lunch and making my dinner.

"Mom, you're practically asleep. Why don't you go to bed?" I say. I know she won't. Not until my brother gets home.

"Wǒ zài kàn." I'm watching the show. She straightens in her seat. Then a few minutes later she's slumped back in the cushions, her eyes closed, her breathing a steady huff.

Finally I stand up and loudly yawn.

My mother looks up, sleepily.

"I'm going to bed," I say. "Good night."

In the bedroom, as I draw down the blinds, I notice a porcelain ballerina figurine balanced on the windowsill, one leg lifted very high, arms framing her pretty face. It's the figurine my father gave me for my sixth birthday. The figurine that fell to the floor and snapped into two pieces. I threw it in the trash.

I remember it perfectly, even though it happened weeks ago. It happened, I remember, the day I met Vanessa Morison for the first time.

The figurine broke at her slender waist. I look for the seam but can't see it. I skim my finger gently around her middle. My skin snags on something sharp. Then I'm bleeding. A lot. I stare in amazement at all the red spilling out of me.

A drop drips on the floor. Only then do I take the necessary action: I raise my arm to stop the flow and run to the bathroom. I wash away the blood and compress my fingertip until the bleeding stops. I inspect the cut. It's long but shallow.

There was more blood than there should have been from such a shallow cut. I smear ointment on my finger and wrap it up.

What is it? My mother peers around the door I've left half open.

"I cut my finger. It's fine." I move past her to get to the kitchen. From the cabinet under the sink I get out the bottle of carpet cleaner and a rag.

"Gěi wǒ kàn." Let me see.

"I've already bandaged it. It's fine." I go back into the bedroom and kneel on the floor. My blood is a black spot on the brown carpet. I spray the carpet cleaner. I scrub until the rag begins disintegrating into grayish flecks. The stain fades, but not completely.

"Zěnme zìjǐ shāng?" How did you cut yourself?

I look up. My mother is watching me scrub. I stop scrubbing. I carefully pick up the figurine and show it to her. I try not to throw it at her. I try to keep my voice calm as I say, "Mom, did you glue this back together?"

I knew you'd want it.

"It was broken. I threw it away."

It was easy to fix, only two pieces.

"I threw it away."

Your father gave it to you.

"I remember." I turn around and walk to the window. I replace the figurine on the windowsill. With my bandaged finger I flick her gently, so she gives a single twirl.

Then I tell my mother that I'm going to sleep. After she

goes back to the living room, I turn out the light and get into bed. I shut my eyes tightly. I do not sleep.

A few hours later, I'm still awake when the front door opens with a creak and shuts with a bang. Andy speaks, the sound thudding against the walls. I don't hear my mother's response at all. Though I can't make out what they're saying, I listen to them talking: the deep boom of my brother's voice, followed by silence.

My mother comes into the room. I lie very still. Even with my eyes closed, I sense her looking at me in my narrow bed. Then she moves quietly across the room to her own narrow bed. The mattress groans softly as she adjusts her position. Then, almost immediately, her breathing steadies and slows. She is asleep.

I turn my head to gaze at her, the shadow of her, curled up against the wall.

For weeks after my dad left, my mother was distraught. For months. For years. It didn't show in the obvious ways: she didn't weep, she didn't wail, she didn't make changes to her hair or wardrobe or life. Perhaps because she had to keep working. She had to keep cleaning and cooking and penny-pinching. She had to collect my brother from the police station when he was arrested for shoplifting a six-pack of beer from a deli. I went with her, to translate. That was a month after my father left. That was the first time Andy was arrested.

My mother did everything she needed to do. She did

it efficiently and without complaint, so you might not have noticed her unhappiness if you didn't know where to look. I knew where. It showed in slivers of stillness. For example, she would be peeling a potato and suddenly she would stop, clutching the peeler in one hand, clutching the potato in the other hand, peel dangling. Her eyes would go empty. Then she would resume peeling with renewed vigor.

In that second of stillness, I recognized her distress.

But I didn't really understand it.

My father was a difficult man to live with, critical and demanding. He reprimanded my mother when dinner was late or she forgot to buy his newspaper or for no reason at all. He scolded me when I was doing anything other than homework or housework. He screamed at customer service representatives on the phone. The only person he wasn't constantly rebuking was Andy, his son, his favorite.

So I didn't understand my mother's unhappiness.

It's true that after he left there was less money—much less money—and more worry and no one to fix the toilet when it stopped flushing, but we managed. My mother got a part-time cleaning job in addition to her full-time job at the factory. I took over the bill paying and discovered a few ways we could pay less and get more. My brother found a plumber, his friend's brother, who gave us a big discount.

And there was no more shouting around the apartment.

So I didn't understand my mother's unhappiness, even though I should have. I was supposed to be respectful of my elders: my parents, my aunts and uncles, my grandparents, my ancestors. My teachers, my librarian, my mailman, the butcher, the bakery cashiers, any grown-up anywhere. And, of course, him. My father. He was the one entitled to my greatest respect.

But my disgraceful, disobedient bad-daughter secret was that I didn't care that he was gone. I was glad. And despite my mother's sadness, my brother's acting out, and our worry over our bills, I hoped he would never, ever come back.

3

THE NOISE WAKES ME. HONKING HORNS, CLATTERING METAL grates, the zoom of a motorcycle, the screech of car brakes, the jingle-jangle-bang of street construction, screaming sirens, screaming babies, screaming people. The sun burns through my eyelids. I roll away from the bright light. And fall out of bed.

I cry out in surprise more than pain. No one comes in response. My mother must have already left to do her week-end grocery shopping. My brother must be ignoring me. For a minute I stay sprawled on the floor. I have never fallen out of bed before. But all night, my narrow mattress has felt too small. I've foolishly gotten accustomed to the big pink bed at the Morisons' house.

The carpet starts getting scratchy. I roll over and get up.

In the living room, I discover that Andy wasn't ignoring me. He is still asleep on the couch: breathing deeply, almost snoring, mummy-wrapped in a sheet. I've forgotten this, how my brother sleeps with his blanket pulled over his head so I can't see any part of him. It occurs to me, for the first time, that

that might be the reason he does it. To hide.

But there are other, more visible signs of his presence: a razor on the edge of the bathroom sink, a rumpled sock under the coffee table, a pair of sneakers pigeon-toed by the door. I resist the urge to find a better location for that razor, to pick up that rumpled sock and correct the stance of those sneakers. They look brand-new. I wonder how much they cost and who paid for them.

In the kitchen, I eat a custard bun while sorting through the mail. I look for the electricity and gas bills, but I don't find them. So I clean up, wash up, get dressed, and put on my most comfortable shoes. My brother is still asleep when I hurry out the door with Vanessa's shopping list.

I take the subway uptown to buy handmade soap wrapped in handmade paper and a box of fragile almond cookies. I take the bus to the west side to buy her tube of red lipstick and a bottle of sweetly clean perfume. I take the subway downtown to buy a pair of creamy candles. Every item is lovely, beautifully packaged, and expensive. But I remind myself it's just stuff, more stuff.

I'm in a fancy cheese shop, ordering two pounds of the Gruyère with pronunciation difficulty, when someone taps on my shoulder. I turn around.

"I thought it was you!" says Ms. Baldwin, my economics teacher. She is a tall black woman with impeccable style. Today she is wearing a blue sleeveless blouse with a bow-tied collar and white pants and gold sandals. She has a wheel of Brie tucked into the crook of her arm.

"And you were right." I smile.

"Big shopping day?" She points at my bags.

"No," I say. "I mean yes, but none of this stuff is for me. I'm getting some things for my boss while I'm in the city."

"That's right. You're tutoring the daughter of . . . what's his name again?"

"Jeffrey Morison."

"Of Morison Capital. How could I forget?" She grimaces.

I smile. "It's going really well."

"Does tutoring involve grocery shopping?"

I stop smiling. "No, but . . ."

The man behind the counter holds out a brown-paper package tied up in string. "Two pounds of Gruyère?" he asks.

"Thank you!" I'm grateful for the interruption. I pay for my cheese—Vanessa's cheese—and carefully tuck the receipt into my wallet.

Ms. Baldwin pays for her own wheel of brie and two loaves of bread. "My partner and I are having a dinner party tonight," she tells me. "But I have a little time before I have to get back home. Shall we go have a coffee?"

"I'd love to," I say, though I know I shouldn't—I still have two more stores to go to and three more items to purchase, and I promised my mother I would come home as soon as I could. But Ms. Baldwin was one of my favorite teachers.

"Great. Then you can tell me more about the duties of an academic tutor."

I wince. I should have known better than to think I could get away without answering her. Ms. Baldwin never let any of her students get away with anything.

We find a café across the street, a cavernous space with perfectly battered surfaces and cool baristas scowling in their black outfits. Ms. Baldwin orders a coffee, and I order an iced tea. I try to pay, but she swats away my wallet.

"Please," I say. "After everything you've done for me."

"What have I done for you?"

"You wrote my college recommendations **and** you gave me that interesting book about the financial crisis **and** you taught me a lot about economics."

She laughs. "When you put it like that . . . all right, you can buy my coffee."

I find us a small table in a cramped back corner, but Ms. Baldwin shakes her head. She leads me to a large table near the only window in the whole place. There are still people sitting there, but with empty mugs and crumpled napkins on their crumby plates.

"Excuse me," she says. "Will you be leaving soon?"

"Oh, uh, yes," they say, and stand right up.

Ms. Baldwin sits right down. She waves to a busboy, and he comes over to clear the table. Then she smiles at me. "You've got to be more aggressive. Don't be afraid to take up space."

I nod. It is more comfortable sitting here.

"And don't be afraid to tell your bosses no if they ask you

to do something that is clearly outside your job description," she adds.

"Well, I'm usually not, but Vanessa Morison is going through a rough time and—"

"No excuses," Ms. Baldwin says sternly, as if I'm trying to explain away some missing homework. "You're a smart and hardworking young woman. I want you to have the bright future that you deserve."

"Thank you." I blush.

"No blushing. If you really want to work in the finance industry, you can't be this modest. They'll trample all over you. Believe me, I speak from experience. As a woman, and a woman of color, you'll have to fight twice as hard to be heard."

I force myself to meet her gaze. "All right," I say.

Ms. Baldwin sighs. "So working for Jeffrey Morison hasn't changed your mind? I hoped it might. The stories I've heard about that man—he's ruthless, if not completely unethical."

"He's been very nice to me," I say.

"They're always nice . . . until they don't need you any-more."

"Well, I don't see much of Jeffrey anyway. He works a lot."

"I'm sure he does," she says, and takes a deep sip of her coffee. "Wall Street may seem very glamorous to you right now, but I want you to be prepared for what it entails. It's a world devoted to the pursuit of money."

"I don't care about glamour," I say. But I cannot deny that I need the money. That I want the money. Not because I want creamy candles or expensive perfumes or a beautiful summer house on the beach. But I do want to live somewhere larger than our tiny apartment. I want my mother not to have to work so hard. I want my life to be different. I want to be different. That's all.

Ms. Baldwin sets her mug down with a thud. "All I ask is that you keep an open mind when you go to college. Take classes in a variety of subjects. Please don't limit yourself."

"I won't."

"Good," she says. "Though I still wish you were going to Waltman College."

The pain is sudden and crushing. I'm as shocked as if she'd struck me; perhaps that's why I admit what I've never admitted aloud, or even admitted to myself: "I wish I were going there too."

Then immediately I shake my head at my teacher. At myself. I correct myself. "Actually, I'm happy to be staying here. There are so many opportunities at the city university. The class catalog is huge! Besides, this is my home.

"Anyway," I continue, "speaking of home, I should probably go. I'm only here for the weekend, and I should spend some time with my family. My brother's back, and I haven't seen him in ages! But it was so nice running into you. Thanks again, for everything!"

"Wait, please wait. I'm sorry if I've upset you. Let's talk about this." Ms. Baldwin places her hand on my wrist and grips lightly. Her fingers are cool. Her smile is warm.

"It's fine. I'm fine. I have to go." I pull my arm away and gather my shopping bags. I smile and tell her good-bye, cheerfully.

The sun is excruciatingly bright when I emerge from the darkness of the café. I blink and blink, trying to adjust to the light. My eyes are watering. I don't know why I'm upset. I shouldn't be upset. I tell myself not to be upset. It doesn't work.

Waltman College, a small, private liberal arts college, is one of the three schools I applied to and the only one of the three that isn't in the city. In fact, it is more than two thousand miles away from the city. A four-hour flight. A two-day drive. Half a week on the train.

Ms. Baldwin encouraged me to apply: it was where she went to school and the professors were inspiring and the other students were great and the campus was beautiful and she had loved it. And though the tuition costs are extremely high, my teacher assured me the college was generous with financial aid.

So I applied. And was accepted. With a decent scholarship.

Ms. Baldwin was thrilled. She was so thrilled that I didn't tell her I wasn't going until after I had turned down their offer. I knew it was cowardly of me. But I also knew I couldn't bear it if she tried to change my mind.

"Why?" she asked, her forehead furrowed with frustration.

"It's too expensive," I said.

"What about your scholarship?"

"It's not enough. Plus there are housing costs and food

costs and travel costs. I'd have to take out a lot of loans. So I'm going to stay here. I got a full scholarship to the honors program at the city university. I'll live at home and continue tutoring to cover my other expenses. It just makes more sense," I told her. I'd rehearsed this speech a few times. A few dozen times.

Ms. Baldwin eyed me skeptically. "What do your parents think?"

"It's my decision. Completely," I said. I hadn't even told my mother I got into Waltman College. I hadn't even told her I'd applied.

"Well. If that's what you want, then I'm happy for you." She didn't sound happy at all.

Nonetheless, I was relieved that she hadn't tried to change my mind. Even though it was already too late to change my mind, Ms. Baldwin was the kind of teacher who never gave up, not even on her most impossible students. It's why I liked and respected her so much. It's why I felt guilty about disappointing her.

But not as guilty as I would have felt if I had decided to go.

Now I'm walking east, toward the shoe store where they're holding a pair of sandals for Vanessa Morison. The shopping bags are heavy and jostling, my hands are cramped from carefully carrying the box of delicate almond cookies, and the tip of my finger is throbbing where I cut it on the ballerina figurine last night. Also, it's hot out. Also, I've had enough. I go home after picking up the sandals, even though there are a couple of items on Vanessa's list.

My mother is already in the kitchen preparing dinner, chopping a chicken apart with her cleaver. I lean against the refrigerator and watch her small hands, slimy and reddened, deftly handle the raw meat.

"What are you making?" I say.

"Gālí jī." Chicken curry. My brother's favorite.

I go sit on the couch in the living room. Andy is gone, his sheets and blanket folded in the basket under the coffee table, so neatly folded that I guess it was my mother who put them away. I take out Vanessa's purchases and organize the contents of the many shopping bags into a single shopping bag. I flatten the empty bags, wedge them into a stack under my arm, and walk to the door.

"Nǐ qù nǎlǐ?" Where are you going?

"I'm taking these to the garbage room. I'll be right back."

My mother comes out of the kitchen, drying her washed hands on a worn dish towel. She bends over to inspect the stack of fancy shopping bags. She fingers the ribbon handle of one bag, strokes the glossy surface of another. These are nice, she says.

"No, Mom. We don't need them," I say.

She reaches to take the bags.

I grip them hard under my arm.

She looks at me with confusion.

"It's more garbage. There's no room in here for any more

garbage," I say much louder than necessary. I don't know what's wrong with me. But I don't let go of the shopping bags.

She lets go. She is still looking at me with confusion. And hurt.

I know I'm wrong. I don't care. My finger is throbbing where I cut it last night. All I want to do is hurl the bags—sharp corners and dense cardboard and ropy straps—right at her. My mother.

Of course I don't do it.

Instead, I apologize. I tell her that she's right, the shopping bags are very nice and we should keep them. I lay them gently on the kitchen table. I announce that I have to go buy a few more things for Vanessa Morison, but I'll be back soon. Somehow, I smile.

Then I leave. I shut the front door with the softest possible thump and walk down the narrow hallway. I'm walking fast. I don't pause to wait for the elevator. I continue to the stairwell and sprint down the stairs, all ten flights of them. I race past the security guard snoring over his newspaper, past the elderly women and loitering men, past the women with groceries in one hand and their snot-faced kids in the other, past the steaming heat and putrid smells and I don't slow down, can't slow down, not until my surroundings become cleaner, clearer, and completely unknown.

Finally I stop. I have to because my lungs are swollen tight so I can't breathe and my legs ache and my heart hurts. I have to because I have no idea where I am. I have no idea where I'm going.

"Get the hell out of the way!" screams someone behind me.

"Sorry, I'm so sorry." I dart over to the side of the sidewalk. I wipe my sweaty face on my shirt. My braid is unraveling. I'm panting. I stand there until I stop panting.

Then I comb my hair with my fingers and secure it into a tight ponytail. I blot my face on my arm. There is nothing I can do about my streaky-soggy shirt. I look up the address of Vanessa Morison's coffee shop. I walk there slowly. I buy two pounds of premium espresso beans and a box of licorice tea.

"Are you all right?" the cashier asks me. She is my age, or a little older. A white girl with thick purple eyeliner and a pierced eyebrow, nose, and lip.

"I'm fine. It's just so hot out there."

"It really is. You have to be careful." She turns around. From the refrigerator behind the counter, she gets out a can of soda. "Here," she says. "Drink this."

"Oh, no, thank you. I'm all right, but thanks."

As I walk home I lecture myself, as if I'm my own student. Be patient, be nice, be happy to be here. Remember that your mother loves you. Don't let your brother get to you. I wipe my sweaty face on my sweaty shirt and think longingly of the cold can of soda the girl offered me. It was foolish of me not to accept it. But I didn't deserve it.

* * *

I'm taken aback by the chorus that greets me when I unlock the door of our apartment and step inside. There is my mother, of course, and my brother—even after seeing him yesterday, I'm still kind of surprised he's around. But what surprises me most is my best friend, Doris Chang, crying out a happy welcome. I hadn't told her I was coming home.

"I missed you so much!" Doris squeals.

"I missed you too!" I squeal.

"I'm so happy to see you!"

"I'm so happy to see you too!"

"Why didn't you tell me you were coming?"

"I . . . wanted it to be a surprise?"

"Hey, sis." Andy comes over and slings an arm around my shoulder. It's the most affectionate he's been toward me in the past three years. I doubt it's because of me.

"Hi, uh, **bro**. How are you?" I say.

"Awesome." He actually smiles. And I notice that he looks different—not just because he's smiling for once. He's put on some weight and it's an improvement. My brother was always too skinny, spiked elbows and stick legs, but he's filled out a little. He looks healthier now.

But that, in my opinion, is the only way he has changed. The rest of it is just acting: acting glad to see me and acting glad to be here and acting glad we're having dinner together. Clearly, it's all a show for Doris. I see it in the way his gaze slides toward her whenever there's a pause in the conversation. In the way he sits motionless when she speaks, giving her his complete attention. In the way he says her name, "Doris," and how frequently he says it, "Doris," and how gently.

"Doris," he says. "Will you please pass the vegetables?"

She smiles sweetly at him as she does. Then she notices me watching and smiles sweetly at me. Then, so no one feels left out, she smiles sweetly at my mother. That's Doris.

"How's the job going?" I ask Andy.

"It's cool. My boss is a control freak, but the work is easy," he says.

"Nǐ gēge qiūtiān shàng dàxué," says my mother. Your brother is going to school in the fall.

I think: You already told me that.

I say: "That's great."

"Yeah, I enrolled in some classes at the community college." Andy shrugs.

He's taking three classes. My mother gazes at him proudly.

"He's taking biology! We're going to study together," Doris says.

My brother scoffs. "You mean you're going to tutor me. I'm taking biology for idiots, you're taking biology for doctors."

"Biology is biology," Doris says serenely.

My mother says that if they study here, she'll cook for them.

Doris thanks her and says that she would love to come over for more of my mother's cooking—especially this curry, it's delicious. "Nǐ zěnme zuò?" she asks. How do you make it?

Unlike me, she speaks to my mother in Mandarin. Because her Chinese is better than mine. Because my accent is terrible.

Because I almost never speak it.

While my mom describes her ingredients and methods, Doris murmurs small sounds of approval and my brother nods benevolently. The three of them look so comfortable. I wonder if they've had dinner together while I was gone.

I stand and start clearing the table. As soon as I do, Doris stands and starts helping. As soon as she does, Andy stands and starts helping too. My mother stands, but we shoo her away, telling her to go sit on the couch, relax. She agrees reluctantly, but I can tell she is pleased.

While Doris and I wash the dishes, we talk about our other friends. Patty likes her job at her church's day camp. Tiff has moved upstate for school and is settling in well. Janine and her annoying boyfriend have finally broken up. Most of this information comes from Doris. As she tells me about Tiff's weird roommate, I realize I haven't stayed much in touch with the other girls this summer.

"What are you doing tonight?" Doris asks. "Andy and I are going to watch a movie here. You should watch with us."

I glance at my brother, who is hovering just outside the kitchen. I expect him to be scowling. But he is nodding. Perhaps not enthusiastically, but still nodding.

"What movie?" I ask.

"An action movie," he says.

"A romantic comedy," she says.

Andy gazes at her. "Fine, we can watch your stupid rom-com," he says, the sharpness of his words softened by the tenderness in his voice.

"Thanks. Though I know you secretly want to too." She smiles.

"Whatever you say, **Doris**." He smiles.

Another minute of this and I'm going to be sick.

Doris turns to me. "So you'll watch with us?"

"I'm not really in the mood for a rom-com," I say.

"What are you in the mood for?"

"Actually, I already have plans."

"What plans? With whom?"

"A friend you don't know," I say.

She looks doubtfully at me but doesn't ask any more questions.

I get my phone and go into the bedroom. I try to think of who there is to call. Obviously not my best friend, Doris. Probably not any of our other similarly sweet girlfriends who I've barely talked to since graduation. Possibly no one.

Except . . . maybe . . .

I dial before I can change my mind. The phone rings and rings and I decide he's not going to answer and part of me is relieved. Then he answers.

"Who is this and how'd you get this number?" says Henry Morison.

"Hi, yeah, it's, uh—"

"I'm kidding. Of course I know who you are."

"Yeah?" I say. "Who am I?"

"Academic tutor by day, party animal by night."

I laugh. "That sounds extremely wrong. How'd your meeting go yesterday?"

"Thanks to all our practice, it went okay," he says. "Kristoff let me retake the exam, and I'm pretty sure I aced it."

"That's great! I'm so glad."

"Now you have to come celebrate with me. What are you doing tonight? My friend is having a birthday party for his girlfriend, pretty close to where you live. You want to come?"

"Okay," I say.

"So I was right. Party animal at night. You'll fit right in."

I think: What have I gotten myself into?

I say: "What have I gotten myself into?"

And it doesn't reassure me when Henry just laughs.

4

IT'S STILL LIGHT OUTSIDE AND IT'S STILL HOT. I'M WALKING slowly now, though I left our apartment in a rush—without explaining to Doris and my brother why I couldn't watch the movie with them, without telling my mother where I was going or when I would be home. I didn't even change my clothes. Though I wish I had. My shorts are creased and my tank top is rumpled. My sandals could use a dusting. But I don't go back.

I stroll to the river and stare out at the waves. It's easy to forget that this is also an island, like Arrow Island. Yet completely unlike Arrow Island. Here the water is murky with shadow. The salt air smells off, old, a little rancid. But I admire the glittering skyline. And I appreciate that there are people, people of all ages and races and sizes and styles, walking and running and talking and laughing along the waterfront. I'd miss this—I tell myself—if I ever left.

"Hey! Check out how early I am."

I turn around. "Yeah, but I was earlier."

"Is this a competition?" Henry grins. I'm relieved to see

that he's wearing a ratty gray shirt and his hair is as uncombed as ever. His outfit makes my outfit look almost fancy.

"Everything is a competition," I tell him.

"Hmm. That perspective explains a lot about you."

"I'm joking."

"Are you?"

"I don't know. Where's this party?"

The party is on the top floor of something that looks more like an enormous sculpture than a building. It's glass and metal spliced together and rising, writhing, into the clouds. There is a man at the door who I don't realize is a doorman until he opens the door for us. He has slicked hair and tailored pants; he looks like he should live here, not work here.

"Going to Shelby's? Penthouse floor," he says.

"Yeah, man. Thanks." Henry high-fives him while I watch, fascinated. I didn't know this was correct doorman etiquette. But probably only for certain people.

The elevator zooms up so quickly that my ears pop and my stomach wobbles. I trip out when the doors open. Henry catches my elbow and steadies me. "Careful," he says. "We're not even there yet."

"Ha," I say. "Ha. Ha." I shove him.

Henry flails and falls exaggeratedly to the carpeted floor. He gazes up at me with the saddest, most pitiful expression. This time my laughter is genuine.

"Come on." I bend forward and reach out to him.

He grips my fingers. "Your hands are so cold."

"Cold hands, cold heart," I say.

"That's not how the saying goes." Henry jumps up.

I shrug. I tug my cold hands from his warm ones and twine them behind my back.

A door opens, and the hallway fills with banging music. "Henry!" someone shouts through the open door. Then there are more voices: "Henry!" they shout. "Henry! Henry! Hey, man! Get over here!"

He turns away from me and walks toward the shouting voices.

I follow him into the apartment. Then I stop. The living room is the size of a hotel lobby. The ceiling is so high, it strains your neck to gaze up at it. A chandelier like fireworks. Walls painted a glossy black. Leopard-print furniture. I realize I'm gawking and force myself look away. I look for Henry. He has disappeared into the crowd.

It's crowded. Almost everyone is dressed up. Especially the girls. Girls wearing short floaty dresses or long floaty dresses, and wedge sandals or high heels, and dangling earrings or delicate necklaces or gold bangles. Their mouths are red, their eyelashes are thick, their legs are long and shiny. Their hair is perfectly curled or straightened or tousled. They glitter and gleam, and every one of them is pretty, or at least gives that impression.

Some of the guys are dressed up too, in button-downs and nice pants, but not all of them. Henry isn't out of place in his old shirt and worn jeans.

I am completely out of place. I stand there alone, feeling that everyone can see how alone and out of place I am, like it's a smear on my face. My cold hands are still twined behind my back. I unhook my fingers and straighten my arms against my sides. Then I'm afraid I look too stiff. I bend my elbows slightly. I soften my knees. It's uncomfortable. I stay in that position. I wish I'd changed my clothes. I wish a lot of things.

"Amber! It's so good to see you again!" says a girl walking by, and when she stops I realize she is saying it to me.

"No, um, sorry. I'm not Amber," I say.

The girl frowns, as if I'm accusing her of lying to me. Or as if I'm lying to her. "Whatever, Amber. You're so weird," she says, and teeters away in her very high heels.

Henry reappears. "There you are! Where'd you go?"

"Nowhere," I say.

"Come on, I'll introduce you to some people." He brings me over to a group standing in a cluster and tells me their names: Franklin and Neal and Kenzie and Daisy and Emma Rose. They are all nice, impeccably nice and polite, smiling their clean, straight white smiles in my direction.

Emma Rose—glimmering green dress, auburn hair in loose waves, lovely like a mermaid—is next to me, so after the introductions are over and conversation resumes, she is the one who gets the job of talking to me. "How do you know Henry?" she asks.

"I'm tutoring his sister this summer." I shouldn't be

embarrassed to admit it; I'm proud of my work, proud of all I've accomplished.

"Cool! I love Ella, though I haven't seen her in ages. Is she all grown up now?"

"Not really," I say. "She's only eight."

Emma Rose giggles. "Yeah, but kids these days. My cousin is nine and she's already stealing her mother's lipstick and sneaking it to school."

"Ella's not like that, though. She's still a little kid."

"That's good, I guess."

"How do you know Henry?" I ask.

"We went to kindergarten together. And grade school. And high school. Henry was my first boyfriend. Can you believe it? Actually, since you know him, you probably can. Henry's practically every girl's first boyfriend. He was also Daisy's first boyfriend. And, oh my god I can't believe I forgot, Tina Dorsey. All this was in, like, fifth grade. Ridiculous, huh?"

I nod and laugh on cue. But why does my laughter sting my throat?

"Emma Rose, I heard my name. What lies are you telling about me?" Henry bumps his way between us. He smiles at me. He smiles at her.

"Remember when we broke up? Then three seconds later you asked Tina Dorsey out?" She slaps his arm, her palm loudly smacking against his skin.

"Tina Dorsey. I forgot about her. Poor Tina," Henry says.

"Yeah, I wonder what she's up to now," Emma Rose says.

Henry turns to me. "Tina's father is Mick Dorsey. You know who he is?"

I shake my head.

"He was arrested for embezzlement our sophomore year. It was a huge deal. On the front page of the newspaper and everything. He went to jail," says Emma Rose.

"Then Tina stopped coming to school. I think she and her mom eventually moved to . . . uh, I can't remember. Somewhere far away."

The two of them grimace. Then they change the subject.

"Congrats—I heard you convinced Kristoff to let you graduate," says Emma Rose. "You're lucky. I hear he's been super happy lately because he has a new young girlfriend."

"What? No way," he says.

"She's a mail-order bride or something. They met on the internet and he flew out to wherever to meet her, then bring her back. She's like forty years younger than him. Gross, huh?" she says.

"Hey, if Kristoff is happy, then I'm happy," he says.

"Yeah, you're happy he's letting you graduate," she says.

Henry turns to me. "Kristoff isn't a bad guy. He's had a rough couple of years. He and his wife got divorced and his son went to rehab."

"Actually, it was his daughter," says Emma Rose. "She had an eating disorder."

"But didn't his son have that drug problem?" he says.

"No, no. That was Barker's son," she says.

They keep talking and I have nothing to add, no gossip, no insight, no joke. They keep talking and I stop listening. They keep talking and I take a step backward. Another step. Another and another, until I've slipped away.

The party has expanded to fill the cavernous space. I drift around the edges of the crowd, snagging on bits of chatter about people I don't know and places I haven't been to and things I don't understand: "I can't believe Patrick John is hooking up with Kerry. . . ." "No, no, this August we're going to the Riviera. . . ." "I found the Chloé at Barney's but in peach not cream. . . ."

"Hey!" Someone grabs my shoulder. It's a stranger, a skinny white guy with glasses. He's smiling, but I expect him to ask me what I'm doing here, who invited me here, and why.

The stranger asks me where the kitchen is.

"I'm sorry, I don't know," I say.

"That's okay. I haven't met you yet. I'm Glenn," he says. "Want to help me find the kitchen? Looks like you need a drink too."

"Sure," I say. It's something to do.

Though it's obvious that he doesn't need my help. The lights are on in the kitchen, a blazing beacon leading us from the dark living room. On the stone countertop there are bottles of liquor, dozens of bottles lined up and gleaming. My new acquaintance, Glenn, swings open the stainless-steel refrigerator to reveal more bottles, beer and soda and beer and juice and beer.

"What do you want?" he asks.

"I'm fine," I say.

"I can mix you something, anything. Just name it."

"No, thanks. I'm not a big drinker." I've only had a total of three alcoholic beverages in my life. The first and most fun was a strawberry wine cooler I drank at Patty's birthday party our freshman year of high school, before Patty got seriously religious. It was six girls and we all got warm and giggly and talked about how we would be friends forever. The second and most disgusting was a beer I drank because Paul Lim, my then-boyfriend, handed it to me. It tasted bitter and felt bristly; I finished it anyway and immediately got nauseous. The third and most unexceptional was a vodka orange juice I drank at Shirley Yang's graduation party. There probably wasn't much vodka in it because it tasted entirely of sugary fake orange and afterward I felt no different at all.

Glenn pulls something out of the refrigerator. It's another bottle, this one a deep green with a silver foil wrapper and a red seal. "Champagne," he says. "Do you like champagne?"

And I don't know if it's because of the handsome bottle, or because I have nothing better to do, or because I feel out of place and I'm tired of feeling out of place, but I say, "Yes. I love champagne."

He untwists the wire, and the cork pops out with that heart-thrilling sound I've heard so many times in the movies. Except now this is my real life. I laugh and take the glass he offers me, a tall, slender wine glass—I know there's a specific name for it, and I remind myself to look it up later—and study the glittering gold inside. It smells sweet. I bring the glass to my lips.

"Wait," says Glenn. "We have to toast."

"Right." I've half forgotten he's there. I lift my arm obligingly and Glenn says something about new friends as I watch the tiny bubbles in my glass sparkle to the surface. We clink. Then we drink.

It tastes as sweet as it smells. Not too sweet. Perfectly sweet. And I'm pleased to discover that I haven't lied: I do love champagne. I drink the whole slender glass in five easy gulps. Glenn pours me a refill teetering to the brim.

"Are you Japanese?" he asks.

"Are you Korean?" he asks.

"Are you Filipino?" he asks. "I mean Filipina?"

I shake my head as I drink, drink, drink. Then I tell myself to slow down. Too late; it's all gone. Glenn raises the green bottle again, but I shake my head and cover my glass. "I think I've had enough," I say.

"You think?" he says, tilting the bottle over my hand over my glass.

"I've had enough." I try to say it firmly, but my voice is much too soft.

He tilts the bottle higher and splashes my hand. I recoil from the cold wet. I dash to the sink to wash off the sticky sweetness. I come back to find that Glenn has refilled my glass. And I'm furious. But when I open my mouth to shout, someone else shouts:

"Who opened that? We were saving the champagne for midnight!"

A group of girls comes tumbling into the kitchen, and one of them grabs the bottle from Glenn's hand. "Oh, Glenn. Of course it's you," she says, rolling her eyes. She slings the bottle to her lips and drinks deeply.

It's the girl who called me Amber. She is drunk, drunker than before, and she seemed rather drunk before. Though her blond hair is still perfectly curled, her floaty floral dress now has a dark blotch on the chest and her red lipstick is a crooked smear with a faded center. And her dishevelment makes something inside me relax. Because she looks the way I feel.

Maybe that's why, when the girl glances up and sees me and smiles and bounces over to give me a hug and cries, "Amber! There you are!" I don't resist and I don't correct her. I hug her back.

She whispers, "We have to get away from Glenn. He's disgusting."

I whisper back, "Agreed. Don't forget the champagne, though."

She laughs uproariously and declares, "I knew there was a reason I liked you."

Then she instructs her friends to grab more champagne from the refrigerator, links her arm through mine, and pulls me out the door. Glenn trails after us, speaking in a plaintive tone, but his words are trampled over by the girls rushing to catch up with us, cradling green bottles in their bare arms.

The first girl, the drunk girl, introduces me to the others. "Vera, Molly, and Deidre, this is my amazing friend Amber. Amazing Amber," she says.

"Nice to meet you!" I say, and suddenly find a green bottle in my hand, uncorked, so I lift it to my lips and swallow fizzy mouthful after fizzy mouthful as we skip down the long hallway.

We don't return to the living room. We dash up a flight of stairs. A door opens and we burst out into the warm night. The rooftop is covered in greenery, thick grass and curling vines and small trees, and in the center is an oval-shaped swimming pool. The only reminders that we are high off the ground are the tops of the tall buildings surrounding us, lighting the real sky with thousands of artificial stars.

Next to the swimming pool, there's a group of guys lounging on some cushioned chairs and the girls run to them, so I do too. Deidre slides in next to one of the boys, her head leaning into his neck, his arm dropping around her waist. Vera and Molly sit on an empty chair, kick off their heeled sandals, and lean together, talking quietly.

The drunk girl, my friend whose name I still don't know, pops open all the unpopped champagne and passes the bottles around. She introduces me to the guys as Amber, and I tell everyone how happy I am to meet them. I'm so happy. A cute boy thanks me for wearing such a casual outfit because it makes him feel better about being underdressed (he's also in a shirt with shorts), and I tell him that's why I did it—just so he'd feel comfortable. He laughs and holds up the green bottle in his hand. There's a green bottle in my hand, so I lift it up and tap it to his. The sound rings clear as a bell and then we both laugh and then we both drink.

"How do you know Annelise?" asks the cute boy.

I realize he is talking about my drunk friend, and I say, "Oh, Annelise and I have known each other for years and years, practically forever."

"I've known her for years too. Why haven't met before now?"

"It wasn't the right time yet." I wink. I can't believe I just winked. I am, I notice, drunk, very drunk, extremely drunk, wonderfully drunk. I didn't know it could be like this, so easy and confident and comfortable and free. I didn't know I could be like this.

How strange to think that less than a mile away, my brother and Doris Chang are sitting on the lumpy plaid couch in our small living room, watching some ridiculous romantic comedy on our old TV, while my mother dozes in the corner. I feel so far away from them, from home, from everything and everyone I know, as if I'm in some glorious foreign city.

Except I'm not.

Then all at once I'm crushed by sadness. Because I realize none of this is actually me or permanent or real. I don't belong here; I can't belong. It was only the alcohol that made me believe—for a brief moment—that I could.

"Are you all right?" The cute boy looks alarmed.

"I don't know." I scrub at my eyes.

"Okay." He quickly gets up and goes and I'm ashamed to have scared him away, why do I scare everyone away? I'm so ashamed and sad and my father, I can't believe my fucking father, and I'm so angry and mortified and hopelessly and uselessly drunk. I want to go home. I never want to go home.

"Amber, what's wrong? Why are you crying?" Annelise comes to sit next to me. She wraps her arm around my shoulder. She sways slightly, and she sways me along with her.

"I'm not crying," I say. "It's nothing."

"It's obviously not nothing," she says.

"It's just life. Life is so sad," I say.

"Oh, yeah. I know." Annelise hums a soft tune, pausing occasionally to swig from her green bottle. She offers it to me and I take one small, careful sip. For some reason I'm expecting it to suddenly taste bad, sour, harsh. But the champagne is as sweet as ever.

"You know what will cheer you up? Let's go for a swim." She puts the bottle down and swivels around so her back is facing me. "Unzip, please?"

"Really?"

"Really. Unzip!"

As soon as I do, she cannonballs in. The splash is enormous. Everyone stands up, first squealing because of the splatter, then cheering because Annelise is swimming a smooth stroke through the blue. Everyone begins unbuttoning and untying and unzipping their own clothes. Everyone leaps into the water. Except for me. Annelise's dress is a floral puddle on the ground. I pick it up, shake it out, and hang it on the chair.

"Amber! Get in here!" shouts Annelise.

I smile at her but shake my head.

"Amber!" someone else shouts from the pool. Then there are more voices. "Amber!" they shout. "Amber! Amber!" they all shout. "Amber, get in here! Now!"

Then I can't help laughing at the sight of their wet faces and soaked hair and the slurp of the water and the fervor of their voices as they shout my name, which isn't even my name, but it doesn't matter. They're calling for me. I take off my shirt; I step out of my shorts. For a moment I'm self-conscious about my cotton underwear, but I tell myself that the shadows hide its plainness. I step to the edge of the pool. I take a deep breath. I jump. It's what Amber would do.

The water is as warm as a bath, a sunny day, a mug of cooled hot chocolate. It's warm as my champagne-warmed skin and my sadness dissolves, most of my sadness, as I slosh in the shallow end with everyone else, just one more wet-faced, soaked-hair body among bodies in this oval of ocean. We dip and lunge and play games with no apparent rules and no apparent object, other than to splash and be splashed. We tease and stagger and scream.

Annelise climbs out of the pool and cannonballs back in, water flies and shrieks echo and limbs flail perilously close to heads and a voice in my head is babbling about safety and caution and danger, but I can hardly hear it over the sound of laughter, my laughter. The boy grabs my ankle under the water. I send a wave into his face when he surfaces.

Then suddenly the pool gets crowded.

I no longer recognize everyone I'm splashing, or who's splashing me. I lose track of Annelise. I lose track of Vera and Molly. I lose track of the cute boy. I get trapped behind a couple who are either making out or wrestling or both. I try edging around them and get elbowed in the shoulder. I try edging again and get kneed in the hip.

Finally I try paddling right into them and it works—they untangle themselves, cursing, to allow me through. It works until I've thrashed past them and then I start sinking, and when I set down my leg to steady myself on the floor my foot stretches and searches and finds nothing because I have somehow thrashed my way to the deep end of the pool where I cannot reach the floor to steady myself, and so I sink.

I panic. I struggle against the water, clawing, punching, kicking, and the water fights back, burning my nose, stinging my eyes, choking down my throat and into my lungs. I struggle harder, but what chance do I have against an opponent that is so much bigger and stronger and doesn't care about winning or losing? I sink.

Then I feel a sudden pressure behind me. A person. I twist around to try to grab hold of them, but they have their arms anchored under my arms and are pulling me up, pulling me through the pool, back to the shallow end. With their assistance, I prop myself up on the steps.

I cough out water. It runs out of my mouth, out of my nose. It drips from my ears. I inhale. I can't remember it ever feeling so good to inhale air. I exhale just so I can inhale again. I rub my stinging eyes.

"I'd have thought you would know better than to drink and swim. Especially since you can't swim and refuse to learn how," says my rescuer.

My vision is blurry. I have an excruciating headache. My heart is wild. My stomach churning. I'm worried I might throw up. And I feel amazing. I feel so alive. I grin at Henry Morison, throw my arms around his neck, and kiss him right on the mouth.

5

WHEN I STUMBLE INTO THE LIVING ROOM THE NEXT MORNING, my brother takes one look at me, snickers, and says: "You're so hungover."

"For your information, I almost drowned last night."

"Almost drowned in some vodka?"

"Actually . . . ," I say. Then I remember that I don't care what my brother thinks. Besides, I suppose it's possible that my pounding head and dried-up mouth are symptoms of a hangover and not a near drowning. "Never mind. Where's Mom?"

"She's watching the kids while Auntie Jeanie goes shoe shopping," he says.

I make a face. Andy makes a face. Here is something we can agree on, perhaps the only thing: Auntie Jeanie takes advantage of our mother's kindness; our mother lets herself be taken advantage of by Auntie Jeanie's bossiness.

A flood of dizziness overtakes me, and I nearly fall over a basket of magazines. I steady myself against the bookcase, but I lean too hard and set the shelves shuddering. "Why is there so much stuff in here?" I grumble.

"Don't blame the stuff for the fact you're hungover," my brother says.

I try frowning at him, but my mouth spasms uncooperatively. I must look pretty bad, because Andy says, "Drink a bunch of water and eat something greasy. It may be hard to get down, but you'll feel better afterward. It always works for me."

"Oh. Okay. Thanks."

"How'd you like keeping Mom up all night worrying?"

"I didn't keep her up all night!"

"You sure?" Andy smiles.

I stomp into the kitchen. I was fairly certain I had come home before midnight. But I can't remember exactly when. Or how. In fact, I can't remember most of the party. Except that I almost drowned. And that people were calling me Amber and I, for some unfathomable reason, responded. When I try to remember more, my head hammers in protest. So I stop trying.

I drink a glass of water and then another. I heat up the leftover rice noodles in the refrigerator and gag them down. I drink another glass of water. I almost throw up. I manage not to throw up.

Andy goes out to play basketball, or so he claims. He's still laughing at me when he leaves. "Now who's the bad one?" he says.

I ignore him and stumble back to the bedroom. I'm about to collapse into bed when I notice my bra and underwear on a hanger by the window. They're dry but still smell of chlorine. I didn't hang them there. I vaguely remember putting my soggy clothes in the laundry basket when I got home last night. So it must have been my mother.

I cringe. I hate that she had to pick up after me the way she always picks up after my brother . . . the way she always used to pick up after my father.

The front door creaks open. All I want to do is to collapse into bed. I go out to the living room. My mother's face crinkles with concern when she sees me. "Nǐ zěnme yàng?"

"Hi, Mom! I'm great!" I smile broadly.

You got home so late last night. Almost two in the morning.

"Oh. Um. I'm so sorry. You shouldn't have stayed up."

You didn't tell me you would be home so late.

"I'm so sorry," I say again.

"Méiguānxì," she says. It's okay.

I wait for her to ask about my underwear, so I can explain about the swimming pool. She goes into the kitchen and starts putting the groceries away. When are you leaving? she asks.

"Soon. In about half an hour."

"Wǒ xiànzài kāishǐ zuò." I better start lunch right away then.

"No, it's okay. I ate the leftover chǎofěn," I tell her.

Nonetheless, my mother starts chopping and peeling, and soon the air thickens with the smell of hot oil. There's a stormy crackle when she throws the garlic into the wok. A pungent aroma fills our apartment. I go into the bedroom and shut the door and sit on my bed, my fingers clamped over my nose and mouth. I gag. I am never, ever, ever going to drink again. Never. Ever.

Henry texts me to say he's on his way. I force myself up. I grab my underthings dangling in the window and throw them into the laundry basket. I stuff my clothes back into my duffel bag. I gag.

There's a gentle tap on the door, and my mother comes into the room. "Lái chīfàn," she says. Come eat lunch.

"I told you I already ate. Anyway, I have to go now," I say.

All right. She goes back into the living room.

I hang my bag on one shoulder and the bag of Vanessa's purchases on the other. When I walk out, my mother swings another bag toward me. I know what it is without asking: fried noodles with slivers of roast pork and leafy green vegetables with hard stems. It's the lunch she made for me.

She tells me there are two containers, one for me and one for the boss's son.

"Thanks." I loop the plastic bag around my wrist. "Mom, I looked through the mail, but I didn't see the electricity or gas bills. Do you know where they are?"

"Nǐ gēgē zuòle." Your brother already paid them.

"Oh. Um, good. Well, I guess tell Andy I said bye." I kiss her soft cheek. I place my arms around her delicate frame. I breathe in her scent of citrus soap and cooking oil and the medicine she uses for her muscle aches.

Then, as quickly as I can, I leave.

Henry is already there when I get downstairs. He gets out of his ridiculous red car when he sees me hobbling over. The sun on his glowing face, it's too much brightness, and I can't look at him directly. He takes my two heavy bags, and I'm too woozy to refuse his help.

"How're you doing? Moving a little slower than usual?" he asks.

"Yeah, sorry. I hope you haven't been waiting long."

"It's fine. I'm just happy I got to win this time."

"What?" I hold my hand over my eyes to block out the light.

"Remember? Last night you said everything's a competition."

"I can't remember much about last night."

"No way," he says. "You're not getting out of this that easy."

"Getting out of what?" I ask.

Henry grins. "You remember."

"No," I say. Then a memory flutters in my mind. "No."

"Yes," he says.

"No, no, no," I say.

Because suddenly I remember. My arms around his neck. My lips against his lips. Did he kiss me back? Maybe yes. Maybe no. Maybe just enough to be polite. I can't remember. Though I remember him laughing afterward. Laughing exactly like he's laughing right now.

"Oh no," I say, covering my face with both hands.

"Oh yes," Henry says. Laughing.

"I was extremely drunk. I'm sorry," I mumble through my palms.

"Don't apologize."

"I'm so embarrassed."

"Don't be."

"That's impossible." I walk to his car, open the door, and get into the passenger seat. Then I cover my face back up with my hands.

Henry gets in. Laughing.

"I'm sorry," I say.

"You have to stop apologizing," he says.

"I can't. I'm sorry."

"Well, can you explain what you're apologizing for?"

"Um, because, um, totally drunk and embarrassing and uh, almost drowned. And then I did. That thing. Why. I don't know. You must think. Oh god." I groan.

I still have my palms over my eyes so I feel him, don't see him, grip one of my wrists and then the other. His fingers are very warm. He gently tugs. When I resist, he tugs with slightly more force. My hands come down one at a time. I force myself to look at him.

Henry is no longer laughing. He's not even smiling or grinning or smirking. His expression is serious, and this serious expression is so unnatural on him I almost want to giggle. But I don't. I gaze back with equal seriousness.

"I know all about getting drunk and doing things you wouldn't normally do. You know I know," he says. "So don't be embarrassed, okay? Stop apologizing. All you did was kiss me. And I didn't mind. So you don't have to apologize for that. Please don't."

It requires all my effort not to apologize again. I nod.

His face relaxes, and Henry looks like himself again. He smirks like himself again. "Besides, I'm used to it. It's a tough job being irresistible, but someone's got to do it."

"Yuck. You're the worst," I say.

"Thank you."

"You're welcome."

Henry turns on the car engine and pulls out of the parking space. There isn't much traffic, so we're soon speeding across the bridge, leaving the city. I don't look back. I recline in my seat and close my eyes.

"What's that smell?" Henry asks.

I open my eyes. Vanessa's scented soaps and candles are packed in the trunk, so I know he's asking about my mother's cooking. A greasy perfume oozes from the plastic bag.

"My mom made food for us," I say. "But you don't have to eat yours."

"Why not? What is it?"

"Fried noodles with pork and vegetables."

"Yum. Can I have it now?"

"Can you drive and eat?"

"Yeah."

"Noodles?"

"Maybe not," he says sadly. "I'll wait until we stop."

"And I'm going to take a nap."

"But who will entertain me then?"

"You have to learn to entertain yourself."

"Never," he declares.

"Good night." I close my eyes. Then I'm asleep.

In my dream I'm looking for Ella. I search room after room, down long corridors, through narrow hallways, opening door after door after door in the Morisons' enormous summer home. I circle around, I backtrack—or I think I do—but the house keeps shifting, growing, changing. A door appears in a place where there is no door. I knock, calling her name. I think I hear her calling out in return. I try pushing into the room, but I am pushed out by a mountain of stuff. A jumbled, towering confusion of objects. I take a tentative step toward it. Immediately it begins avalanching down and I fall and fall and—

"Wake up," a voice says into my ear. "Wake up, please, I'm so hungry. Soooooooooo huuuuuuuuuuuuungry."

"Are we home?" I mumble.

"No, home's the other way."

"Oh. Right." I force my eyes open.

"You were muttering in your sleep," Henry says. "Was it a nightmare?"

"I dreamed I was looking for Ella and I couldn't find her."

"Sounds scary."

"Yeah. It was." I yawn and stretch and glance around. We are parked in a parking lot, facing a cluster of trees, sunshine flooding through the green. "So, you're hungry? Or did I dream that too?"

"Starving," he says. "My mom is always on some new diet, so she barely has any food in her house, only these green . . . shakes? Smoothies? I'm not sure what to call them. I don't know how my stepdad survives. I barely had any breakfast. I mean, she did get us some bagels, but nothing other than that bagel. With cream cheese. And lox."

"Sounds terrible." I try unknotting the bag of food, but I've knotted it too tightly. I rip the thin plastic apart and pass Henry his container of noodles, and the plastic fork and napkin that my mother had also supplied.

"Organization runs in the family," Henry says.

"I guess so." I lean back in my seat.

"Aren't you going to eat?"

I shake my head. I feel better after my nap, but I'm still a little queasy.

He takes a huge bite. "Yum. Your mom's a great cook."

And though she really is, I have trouble believing that Henry really believes she is. But he slurps his food with apparent delight. And eats every last squiggle of noodle, every crumb of pork, every leaf and stalk of vegetable.

Then we get back on the road. Henry puts on some music, I turn the volume up, and we bop along as we race down the highway, then chug across the water on the ferry, then cruise along the narrow roads of Arrow Island.

But at the exact moment that we pass through the metal gate, the music is replaced by a fuzzy buzzing. I look quizzically at Henry.

"It does that. We're out of range now," he says.

"As soon as we get on Morison land," I say.

"I still think of this as Arrow land. You know our house originally belonged to Lionel Arrow, the son of the first Arrow on the island."

"Yup, your grandfather told me." I reach over and turn off the buzzing radio.

We spiral up the hill. Round and round we go as the road grows narrower and narrower, and the trees taller and taller, and the shadows darker and darker. Then the forest suddenly falls away, and we drive into a burst of light. The sun is bright above the house, shining sharply on its many windows so that it appears almost as if the whole place is burning, from the inside out. I drop my gaze into my lap. Henry parks the car and we get out.

Vanessa comes out of the house, waving both her hands at us. Then Ella darts past her mother. She runs over and hurls herself onto her brother. She whispers something to him that makes him laugh. He whispers something to her that makes her laugh. When they are done laughing, Ella comes over to me.

"I missed you," I tell her. I open my arms to see if she'll hug me and she does, though with more restraint than when she hugged her brother.

She doesn't tell me that she missed me too, though. What she tells me, in a very low voice, is "The ghost was mad you were gone. The first night she kept knocking on the walls. Last night I heard her crying."

I step back so quickly that we both almost fall. I catch myself, then I catch her. "Sorry, Ella," I say.

"Sorry for what?" Vanessa asks as she strolls toward us.

"I tripped. I'm a little clumsy after being in the car for so long," I say.

She nods and flings her arms around me with none of her daughter's restraint. "I'm so happy you're back. It felt like you were gone for ages!"

I inhale the sweet clean of her perfume, the same smell as in the bottle in the trunk of the car. "I bought all the things on your list," I say.

"I appreciate it," she says. "And I'm sorry to have asked you—I was thinking about it and it really wasn't fair of me. It's not the job you were hired to do."

I'm startled. I'm touched. "It's all right," I say.

Vanessa pats my shoulder, then turns to Henry and kisses him hello. "Your father just left," she tells him. "He told me to tell you he's sorry he missed you, but he had an urgent dinner meeting tonight."

"On Sunday?" he asks.

"Apparently," she says.

Together the four of us go into the house, into glass and stone and perfect angles and gleaming surfaces. Past the stylishly modern furniture, past the spacious rooms. Up the solid, polished stairs. Then Henry goes to his room with his bags and Vanessa goes to her room with her purchases. Ella goes with her brother. And I go to the pink bedroom.

As I twist the knob, I feel strangely apprehensive. But then I open the door and the room is immaculate, just as I left it. The rosy walls warm with afternoon light. The white rug perfectly fluffy. The floral quilt smooth and straight on the bed. I don't know why I expected anything would be different.

I go into my own bathroom to wash my hands and face. I smile at my reflection, even though my reflection is still a little hangover gray around the edges. Then I unpack: put away my toothbrush, fold my clean clothes and stack them in the mirrored wardrobe, squash my dirty clothes into the laundry basket.

When I dip my hand into the bottom of my duffel bag, it touches something unexpectedly hard and cold. I recoil. I pull the bag wide open to look inside. And flinch. I know I didn't put that hard, cold thing there. I know my mother didn't either; she couldn't have. Yet somehow there it is, there she is, nestled in my gray sweater.

The porcelain ballerina figurine.

PART III
THE ISLAND

1

THE NEXT MORNING, ELLA STARTS AS SOON AS I GET TO THE library: "The ghost was crying so I told her not to cry. Then I asked what her name was and she said Eleanor Arrow. She's Lionel's daughter, like I said."

"Eleanor?" I say. "Ella-nor?"

"Yes," Ella says. "Eleanor."

The worst thing would be if I laughed. I manage not to by chewing my lip and twisting my eyebrows and trying to look as if I'm thinking hard. Which I am. "But I didn't hear anything last night. Did you?" I ask.

"I think she was quiet because you're here again."

"Why would I make her quiet?"

"I don't know."

"All right. How about we work on our reading now?"

"Okay." She opens her book but continues looking at me.

"Yes, Ella?" I say.

"I'm glad you came back," she says.

"Of course I did." I smile at her, touched, but now she is gazing down at her work.

While Ella reads, I walk around the room. I pause at the window and glance outside. Henry is lying by the pool: shirt off, neon swim trunks on, sunglasses over his eyes. The sun brightens his hair into the same golden tan of his chest.

I realize I'm staring. I jump backward, feeling as if he's caught me. Which he hasn't—Henry looks more asleep than awake down there. I remind myself that he didn't think it was a big deal that I kissed him.

"Done," Ella announces.

"That was fast!" I rush back to the table.

We go over the questions and answers together. She got nine out of ten right, and the tenth was tricky. "That's amazing. You did a really excellent job," I say as I stick a cluster of gold stars into her workbook.

She blushes and fidgets and stares down at the stickers. And I feel a wave of frustration. I want Ella to be happy about her accomplishments. I want her to recognize how great she's doing. I want her to recognize how great she is.

"Ella," I say, "think of how much you've improved."

"Because you taught me."

I shake my head. "You did all the hard work. I just helped. I'm really proud of you, and I hope you're proud of yourself too."

Ella keeps staring into her workbook. But then she says, "I guess I'm proud."

"I'm glad. Now give me your hand," I say.

"Why?" She slides her arm across the table.

"You'll see." I stick a star sticker on the back of her hand, and another one, and another one. Stars down her fingers, stars up her thumb. Stars around her wrist. When there's only one sticker left, I lean forward and stick the final star to the center of her forehead.

"There," I say. "You're a star."

Ella is laughing. She lifts her hand and waves it around so that the stars shimmer. Then she peels a single sticker from her wrist. She wriggles across the table and sticks it to the center of my forehead.

"Now we're both stars!" she says.

I smile at her. "Yes," I say. "We are."

One afternoon, I start reading the last of the three books I bought for Ella. It's a history of the Arrow family, starting with Godfrey's arrival on the island. The author is M. R. Arrow, Godfrey's great-great-grandson, and I had my doubts about it from the beginning: the title is Family Cursed: A History of Arrow Island. My doubts doubled when it arrived: it looked photocopied more than printed, a booklet more than a book. But it was the only information on the family I could find, and if there was something in it that could help Ella, it was worth a look.

I'm just a few pages in when there is thunderous pounding on the door. I think briefly—very briefly—about Eleanor the ghost, but the day is bright and I'm pretty sure I hear giggling behind the pounding.

I yank open the door, and the Morison siblings come tumbling into the room.

"Yes, how can I help you?" I say with mock sternness.

"We're . . . ha . . . here . . . ha . . . to—haha!" Ella is laughing too hard to talk.

"We're here because it's time for your first swim lesson," Henry announces.

"No!" I say with actual sternness.

"Yes!" say Henry and Ella.

"No way," I say.

"How can you say no after what happened this weekend?" Henry asks.

"What happened this weekend?" Ella asks.

Henry smirks at me. "Why don't you tell her."

I glare at him. Then I turn to Ella. "Well, um, I was in a swimming pool and, um, since I don't know how to swim I had a moment when I, um, got a little scared. But your brother helped me out."

"You have to learn to swim. It's dangerous if you don't know," Ella says solemnly.

"From now on I'm going to stay away from all bodies of water. So I'll be fine," I say.

"But you're always telling me how important learning new stuff is," she argues.

It's a good point. I glance at Henry. "Did you tell her to say that?"

"Nope." He grins. "She came up with that all on her own."

Ella looks at me pleadingly.

I sigh. "Fine."

Ten minutes later, I am sitting awkwardly at the edge of the swimming pool, wearing my plain one-piece bathing suit that was once slightly too big and is now slightly too small.

"Ready?" Henry is already in the water.

"Not yet," I say. I'm trying not to remember the feeling of water in my mouth, in my throat, in my lungs. My flailing arms. My fear.

"Want to hold my hand?" Ella asks. She is sitting next to me.

"Yes." I tuck my hand around her hand. And feel surprisingly better.

"Now hop in," says Henry.

"Don't rush me," I say.

"I'm not rushing you," he says.

"I feel like you're rushing me," I say.

"All right, all right." Henry plunges underwater and swims a fast lap across the pool.

"Now he's showing off," I say.

"No, Henry's just really good at swimming." Ella wrinkles her nose at me—no jokes about her adored brother allowed. But she doesn't let go of my hand.

Henry swims over to us. "I'm not rushing you, but the water's nice and warm."

"It's nice and warm out here too," I say.

"Right." He flops backward and backstrokes another lap across.

"You can get in," I tell Ella. "You don't have to stay here with me."

"I don't mind," she says.

"Thanks."

"You're welcome."

Henry swims back over to us.

"Not yet," I say.

He swims to the other side.

"Maybe now," I say.

"Okay, we can use the stairs," Ella suggests.

I follow her to the side of the pool. She steps down one step. I step down one step. She steps down another. I step down another. I feel equal parts scared and foolish. But Ella keeps going. So I do too. The water gently laps around my ankles. My knees. My hips. My waist. Then I'm submerged to my chest, my feet bouncing on the bottom.

I'm breathing hard. I lurch to the side and cling to the concrete ledge. I tell myself not to be so scared; I am safe here, secure with my hand clenched to the ledge. I tell myself it's okay to be nervous; it's only natural after my traumatic experience.

"You made it!" Henry shouts from the deep end of the pool.

"Sort of!" I shout back.

Ella paddles next to me. "Try holding on to the side while kicking. That's what my swimming teacher taught me," she says.

"What do you mean?"

"Like this. Make some big splashes with your legs." She demonstrates.

I copy her movements. My splashes are not as impressive. I keep sinking. But I also keep kicking. At least until my hands start aching because I'm gripping the ledge so desperately. Then I stop. "I'm going to get out now," I tell them.

"Already?" says Henry.

"Okay," says Ella.

It's a relief to be back on solid ground. I sit on a lounge chair and watch the Morison siblings drift effortlessly around the pool. And I try to imagine that one day I'll swim with such ease. It's hard to imagine.

A shadow moves across my feet. I look up.

Old Mr. Morison looms above me, his white hair fluttering with the breeze. "May I join you?" he asks, and slowly lowers himself into the chair next to mine. He lifts his legs one at a time, a grimace twisting his face as he straightens his torso. He does not look well. But I now know better than to ask him any questions about his health.

"Are you enjoying your day?" I ask.

"It's lovely out, isn't it," he says as he watches his grand-children laughing and splashing in the blue water. It is lovely out, yet he seems unhappy.

I try to think of something that will cheer him up, or at least distract him. "I'm reading a book about the Arrow family," I tell him.

"I wasn't aware there was a book about the family."

"It's by someone named M. R. Arrow, Godfrey's great-great-grandson. I'm only at the beginning, but it starts with Godfrey leaving his home in Boston after the girl he loved turned down his marriage proposal."

"Nonsense," Mr. Morison sputters, his thick eyebrows bristling. "First of all, Godfrey Arrow was from a city outside Boston. Second of all, although he was quite the young idiot, he didn't leave because of a **girl**. He left because of a business deal gone bad."

I suppose sputtering is better than sadness. Also, it's good to have my doubts about the book—booklet—confirmed. "Interesting," I say.

"I hope you didn't spend much on that drivel."

"A couple of dollars."

"Well, young lady, I'm afraid that's a couple of dollars wasted. You should write to the publishers and demand your money back," he says.

Vanessa wanders through the backyard. She is on her phone. "Yes, we'll want a full ice setup for the oyster bar. Will you send me some photos?" she says.

Mr. Morison stiffens as she walks by. His hands clench, his shoulders hunch. "It's ridiculous," he mutters.

"What's ridiculous?" I ask.

He doesn't seem to hear me. His annoyance over the Arrow book has transformed into something darker. His eyes are rheumy and unfocused. His mouth is trembling. His sudden shift in mood is startling, and a little frightening.

"She's a fool if she thinks this party will change anything," he says in a raspy whisper. "He won't change. What's going to happen will happen."

I don't say anything. He seems to be talking to himself, more than to me.

"Look what came in the mail today!" Vanessa comes over waving a few familiar cream-colored envelopes at us.

"RSVPs?" I ask.

"Three yesses already," she says.

"That's great!" I say.

"Isn't it?" Vanessa smiles and walks back toward the house.

Mr. Morison watches her go. "This party," he says, "is going to be a disaster."

And although I know he is just a sick and grumpy old man who despises his daughter-in-law and disapproves of his son, I can't help wondering if he's right.

2

DESPITE OLD MR. MORISON'S PREDICTIONS, THINGS PROGRESS smoothly over the next week. With the assistance of her new event planner, Vanessa hires a band and orders a birthday cake: two tiers, six layers, chocolate with vanilla buttercream. Ella keeps making steady progress during our tutoring sessions. Henry relaxes after he finds out he passed his exam and will graduate. And Mr. Morison's health improves, then so does his mood, and then he stops making such pessimistic predictions.

My swim lessons progress . . . less smoothly. I manage to advance from clutching the ledge and kicking to clutching a foam board and kicking. With the foam board I can make short laps across the shallow end of the pool. But that's the end of my accomplishments, because, to Henry's frustration, I refuse to put my face into the water.

"I can't. I just can't. I'm trying," I tell him.

"Try harder," he commands.

This afternoon it's only the two of us at the house. Mr. Morison took Ella into town. Vanessa went to meet a friend for lunch and shopping. Mrs. Tully is out running errands or something.

"I'm trying as hard as I can." I dip my chin down. But as soon as the water licks my lips, I jolt back up, legs thrashing, arms flapping. Henry gets thoroughly splashed.

"Sorry," I say. "Or is this one of the things I don't need to apologize for?"

"No, this apology is accepted." He wipes his face with the back of his arm. Even though I can't see most of him, the part I can see is grinning. I find myself grinning back. And I feel a wave of something—at first I think it's the pool, but then I realize it's inside me. A wave of emotion.

It panics me more than getting my face wet.

A moment later, Henry drops his arm and looks up. He looks around. He looks puzzled. Because I'm no longer next to him. I'm no longer anywhere in the water.

"Hey," I say from the ledge next to the pool.

"Whoa, how'd you get out so fast?"

"I swam," I tell him.

He laughs. "Get back in and show me."

"If I show you I'll have to kill you."

"That seems worth it to me."

"But it's not worth it to me."

"Because you don't want me to be dead?"

"Because I don't want to go to jail for murder."

Henry swims toward me, and when he gets to the side of the pool, he pushes himself up and out. His arms muscle from the effort. Water streams down his shoulders. I fiddle with the straps of my too-tight bathing suit and go sit at the end of a lounge chair. He comes over and sits on the same chair, at the same end. He is close enough that I sense the damp warmth of his skin on mine. He is close enough that I can feel him breathing. We are as close as two people can be without touching.

I jump up. "It's getting cold. Don't you think?"

"Nope," he says. "I think it's hot, even hotter than yesterday."

"Well, I've had enough. I'm going in to shower."

I hurry inside the house, propelled by an inexplicable pressure in my stomach, an intense straining pain that is not exactly painful, but I don't know how else to describe it. I walk quickly up the stairs, trying to outwalk this uncomfortable sensation, and as soon as I get to the pink bedroom, I peel off my bathing suit. It helps. I take a hot shower and that helps too.

Then I sprawl across the floral bed and finish reading **Family Cursed**. The conclusion is as dramatic as the beginning. According to the author, four of Lionel Arrow's five sons owned a real estate company but were eventually accused of fraud. The four brothers disappeared. The fifth, although he had no involvement with the family business, became the scapegoat. Despite the lack of evidence against him personally, he was sent to jail. He came out a broke and broken man who was convinced that his family was cursed. A few years after getting out of jail, he got married and had one child. A few years after that, he died of liver disease. His only child's only child was M. R. Arrow, the author of this very book and possibly the last living descendent of Godfrey Arrow. The end.

I'm not sure what to think. The story is sad, but I'm skeptical after what Mr. Morison said. Still, there's one section I want to show to Ella. Since I definitely shouldn't give her a book called Family Cursed, I go to make a photocopy of the chapter.

As I walk upstairs, the only noise is the soft slap of my shoes on the steps. But when I reach the landing, I hear something behind me. I spin around.

No one is there.

I continue walking. As soon as I do, I hear something behind me again. Then I realize that it's just the echo of my shoes on the floor. I laugh at myself, and the sound bounces down the hallway, seeming to grow louder, bolder, almost hysterical. I stop laughing. I stop moving. Instantly, everything is silent.

Part of me wants to run back to the pink bedroom. Most of me knows I'm being silly. It's just that the house is so big. It's just that I'm the only one around. I force myself to keep going, all the way to the end of the corridor.

Vanessa told me I was free to use the photocopier anytime, but I still get nervous coming here, to this large room filled with light and not much else. Though there is a desk and a swivel chair and a filing cabinet and one potted plant, these items do not take up very much of the expansive space. Maybe it's the emptiness that makes the space feel neglected, even though there's not a dot of dust or a smudgy surface anywhere, and the plant has recently been watered. Obviously someone takes care of this room. After all, it's Jeffrey Morison's office.

The photocopier is in an alcove in the back corner. I copy the relevant chapter from Family Cursed and turn off the machine.

A sudden bang shakes the walls.

I jump farther into the alcove, into the shadows. Footsteps tap toward me across the bare hardwood. Then stop. Then they tap in the opposite direction. Then stop. Then a voice, a startlingly deep rumble, a man's voice, says, "Yes, hello, are you there?"

It takes me a second to recognize the voice. It's Jeffrey Morison.

Of course it's Jeffrey Morison. This is his house. This is his office. Today is Friday, the day he comes, if he comes—though he usually doesn't arrive until much later. I'm about to emerge, to respond to his greeting and explain that I was startled by the slamming door. But then Jeffrey speaks again, and I realize he is on the phone.

"Lorraine," he says, "calm down. Tell me exactly what he said."

There's a long silence. I have no idea what to do. I don't want to eavesdrop, but it would be awkward to come out now. And I seem unable to move.

"So he doesn't have any proof," Jeffrey says. "And you didn't give him anything, right? You denied it all."

A pause.

"We should be safe then," he says.

Another pause.

"It's only suspicion," he says.

Another pause.

"Lorry, sweetheart, have I ever failed you?" he says.

A shorter pause.

"And I won't fail you now. Sit tight and I'll figure out what we can do. We're going to find our way out of this. I promise," he says.

A moment later there is a thud, presumably the sound of Jeffrey Morison putting down his phone. Then he starts cursing. Goddamn motherfucker bullshit. Fuck. Fuck. Fuck. A pause. And then a giant crash.

I bump into the photocopier, thump it hard, making a noise that I can't believe Jeffrey Morison doesn't hear, but he doesn't seem to. Probably because he is cursing again: "Fuck. Fuck. Fuck," he says as he stomps out of the room. The door slams and the walls shake.

Though I can now freely move, breathe, leave, I don't. I stay perfectly still, trying to make sense of what I just overheard. I stand there for a minute, two minutes, three, but I make no sense and figure out nothing.

Finally I pick up my photocopies and book. My body moves stiffly, as if I've just awakened from a long sleep. I step out from the alcove. I stop to stare at the swivel chair. It's now on the floor, on its back, and there is a deep crack in on one of the armrests.

I'm still staring at the overturned swivel chair when the door opens and Jeffrey Morison barrels back into the room. His face is red and shiny with sweat. He jolts when he sees me. He looks at me with none of his usual friendly charm. He looks at me with pure rage.

"What are you doing in here?" he demands.

"I was making photographs. I mean photocopies. For Ella. Vanessa told me I could. Anytime." My voice is sluggish. I sound stupid. I feel stupid.

"How long have you been in here?"

"Just a minute."

"You sure about that?"

"Yes. Is something wrong?" I stumble over the last word. Wrong.

His gray eyes darken. His thin lips press together. He stares at me. "Get out," Jeffrey Morison bellows. "Get out now, and I better not catch you sneaking around here again."

"I'm sorry," I say.

Then I run out of his office and down the stairs. My face is burning, flushed as red as his, though for different reasons. I'm embarrassed. I feel ashamed and dumb and wounded and outraged and afraid and confused; I feel physically ill. My rational self recognizes that my feelings are all out of proportion, but I feel them just the same.

In the pink bedroom, I shut the door and lie down on the floral bed. Then I do not move. Even my mind, my shark mind, is dead still. An hour drifts by. I lie there, do not move, do not sleep—or do I? Because suddenly there's my father; he's standing before me, his arms crossed over his chest, his head shaking. Then he asks, "What's wrong with you?"

So I must be sleeping. Because this has to be a dream.

But no matter how hard I try, I cannot wake myself up.

There's a knock on the door. I pry open my swollen eyes, scramble out of bed, and shuffle across the room. I bump into the edge of the dressing table and trip over the fluffy white rug. I fumble with the knob.

"Time for dinner," Ella says when I open the door at last.

"Oh," I croak. I clear my throat and try again. "Oh, yeah, sorry."

"It's okay. Are you ready?"

I am not ready. I doubt I'll ever be ready to see Jeffrey Morison again. But I say, in as cheerful a voice as I can manage, "Sure, let me just use the bathroom first."

I go wash my hands and face, and glance at my reflection. The girl in the mirror is red-eyed, blotchy skinned, hideous. I turn away and hurry back to the hallway.

We walk downstairs. I chatter the whole way there: about my swimming lessons, about the weather, about a book I want her to read. Ella doesn't say much in response, but she often doesn't say much, so I don't think she's necessarily noticed that I'm upset.

But when we reach the dining room, she pats my arm. "Don't worry," she says.

"I'll try not to." I smile at her, a small but real smile.

Then I stretch my smile wide as we step into the room. Everyone is already there, waiting, and I sense their impatience. "I'm so sorry!" I say, rotating my wide smile around the table. "I was taking a nap and somehow I overslept. You should have started without me."

"We'd never do that!" It's not Vanessa who says this, or Henry, or old Mr. Morison. It's Jeffrey. He says it with perfect pleasantness, and his accompanying grin shines.

"Thank you," I say. There's nothing else to say.

Vanessa peers at me. "Darling, you don't look so good. I hope you're not coming down with something." She leans back, as if my puffy red blotch might be contagious.

"Um. It might be a cold," I say.

"Drink lots of fluids and go to bed early," Jeffrey says. "You need to take care of yourself. What would we do around here without you? Ella would miss her lessons and my wife would be lost and Henry, well, I'm sure he'd be fine. He always seems to be, no matter what sort of trouble he gets into."

Henry grimaces. Apparently the fact that he passed his exam and is graduating did not improve their relationship.

Old Mr. Morison discharges a single sharp cough. "Is that the attitude you should be encouraging? You honestly believe nothing bad can happen to this family?"

Jeffrey smiles, revealing an astounding number of teeth. "Hasn't happened yet."

His father mutters something incomprehensible.

"Daddy!" Ella chirps. "How was work this week? I missed you."

"I missed you too, sweetie, but you know I'm working hard for you. On Wednesday I had ten meetings—can you imagine? I didn't even have time to comb my hair." Jeffrey pats his own nearly bald head, his eyes wide with alarm.

Ella and Vanessa laugh obligingly.

And I stop paying attention. I just can't do it anymore.

But the truth is that it doesn't matter. No one seems to notice whether I'm paying attention or not. They eat and they talk and I don't listen and it doesn't make a difference. Mrs. Tully comes in to clear the table. I don't thank her like I usually thank her, and she glowers at me anyway.

I spend the rest of the weekend avoiding Jeffrey Morison. It isn't hard. On Saturday the family goes out on the boat, and they don't return until late in the evening. On Sunday they have friends visiting and spend the day at the beach.

Vanessa and Henry both come by once to ask if I want to join them. Ella comes by twice. I thank them and say, no, sorry, no. I'm not feeling well. I'd better stay and rest up. Also, I might be contagious and I don't want anyone catching whatever I have. But have a great time!

Only Ella questions me. "You don't look sick," she says, scrunching her nose.

"Well, I feel terrible," I say. Which is the absolute truth.

Finally, it's Sunday evening. I'm in the pink bedroom getting ready for bed and thinking I've made it through safely—Jeffrey Morison will be leaving early the next morning—when someone knocks on the door. I open it a crack. I don't believe it.

"Are you feeling better?" Jeffrey Morison asks.

I nod. I don't trust myself to speak.

"Good," he says, twinkling his toothy smile at me. "I was hoping we could have a chat. I want to check in about my daughter's progress."

"Of course," I say. It would be unprofessional to refuse this request.

He glances inside my room. His smile withers as he looks at the flowers and ruffles and frills. "I always forget what my wife did in here. Shall we talk in the library?"

"Sure." I wonder if he makes the suggestion because it's more appropriate or because he wants to avoid the pinkness of the pink bedroom. Maybe both.

In the library, Jeffrey Morison relaxes on one of the large leather couches, his arms and legs flung outward. I sit in the chair across from him. It's awkward being alone with him, not only because of what happened the other day, but also because I barely know him—despite the fact that I am living in his house and I spend every day with his family; despite the fact that his family, especially his wife, talks frequently about him. We are still strangers. With almost nothing in common. I feel very small in my armchair.

"My wife tells me that my daughter has been making progress," he says.

"Yes, Ella has improved greatly in both her math and reading. Her long-division skills are especially strong. I'm very pleased with how well she's doing."

Jeffrey nods. "I know Ella can do the work. She's not stupid; I tell my wife that all the time. So I don't understand her underwhelming grades."

"Part of the problem is motivation. If Ella isn't interested or invested in the subject, she won't put in the effort," I say. In spite of everything, I'm happy to be having this conversation. I think it's important for parents to recognize their children's strengths and their weaknesses. Especially their weaknesses.

"Then how can we keep her motivated in a class setting?"

"If her teachers take the time and effort to build a genuine relationship with her, I think Ella will thrive."

"Considering the tuition costs at her school, I should hope her teachers take the time and effort to do that. I'll have to speak to them about it."

"That's a good idea."

"Well, I'm glad we had this talk. You're an insightful girl," he says with a smile. "Do I remember correctly—you mentioned you're interested in finance? Would you be interested in interning at my company next summer?"

"Yes," I say immediately. "Yes, I'd be very interested."

"We only take on a few interns each year, and it's a competitive process. But since I already know you and your abilities, we can bypass all that."

"Thank you! I really appreciate it."

"It's no trouble. Since I already know I can trust you." Jeffrey Morison stops smiling. His eyes harden; his mouth, his entire face. "Because I can trust you, can't I?"

"Of course," I say.

"So I can trust you not to tell anyone about anything you may have overheard in this house." He stares intently at me.

"I, uh . . ." I don't understand.

Then, all at once, I do.

He is talking about that phone conversation in his office. Phrases echo in my mind: "So he doesn't have any proof. . . . We should be safe then. . . . Lorry, sweetheart . . ." And I remember Vanessa watching her husband and Lorraine Chamberlain sitting together at the dinner table, talking and laughing as if no one else was there. I remember the heartbroken expression on Vanessa's face.

Then I understand what this is actually about. What Jeffrey Morison is really offering me, and what he expects in exchange. I don't know what to do. I don't know what to say. But he is staring at me, waiting for me to answer. I have to say no. Because how can I say yes when it means betraying Vanessa?

But how can I say no when he is giving me the opportunity

I want, the opportunity I need, the opportunity I've been secretly dreaming of ever since I got this job?

"Yes," I say. "You can trust me."

In my dream I'm lying in bed when a little girl comes to sit beside me. Not now, Ella, I say. I'm trying to sleep. I'm so tired.

I'm not Ella, snaps the girl.

Sorry. Of course you're not. I don't know how I could have confused them. Ella has dark hair, and this girl's hair is silver moonlight. Ella has a slight summer tan and this girl is so pale that her skin seems translucent. This girl is wearing a white dress, lacy and beaded and long, wedding-dress fancy. It's a dress Ella might wear because her mother picked it out, but Ella would never look comfortable in it. This girl looks comfortable.

I like your dress, I tell her.

She glances down at it, as if she has forgotten what she's wearing. It's all right, she says. But I have prettier ones that Father bought for me. You should see them.

Will you show them to me? I ask.

Not now, she says.

Why not?

You're not ready.

I'm ready.

No, says the little girl, you're not.

Please? Please show them to me, I beg. I know that seeing

her pretty dresses will change me, and I'm desperate to change.

Fine. But I warned you. She sighs as she slips down from my bed. Her white dress is too long; it trails on the floor behind her as she leads me to the mirrored wardrobe. Even though it's just across the room, it takes us a very long time to get there.

But that's my closet, I say.

We're sharing it, she says, and jerks open the door.

I leap back in horror. There are no pretty dresses inside, no clothing at all. Instead there are heads. Severed heads, chopped off at the neck. Lined up in a neat row. Blood dripping from the shelf. I stare at them. Drip, drip. They stare back at me. Drip, drip. They are all there: old Mr. Morison, Jeffrey, Vanessa, Henry, and Ella. Drip, drip. I want to scream, to cry, to run away. But I don't. It would be rude. Drip.

The little girl sighs again. See, I told you you weren't ready.

And then she starts screaming.

It's her screaming that wakes me. I jolt up and tell myself it was a dream, it's not real, it was a dream, just a dream. The problem is, I am now clearly awake and someone is still screaming. Loud and shrill and frantic.

At first I think it's Ella. But then I realize it couldn't possibly be Ella. Because the sound is coming from here, inside my bedroom, inside my bed. I lift my hand to my face. My mouth is closed. Yet as soon as my fingers cover my lips, the screaming stops.

For several minutes I sit there with my hand over my mouth, struggling to make sense of the situation. Then something—and I cannot describe what that something is—makes me turn my head to the left, toward the mirrored wardrobe across the room.

The door is open wide, revealing all the darkness within.

3

I SHOULDN'T DO IT. BUT I CAN'T HELP IT. "DID YOU HEAR ANY-thing last night?" I ask when we've finished our lessons for the day.

"Like what?" Ella says.

"Like, um, voices?"

"You mean the ghost? Eleanor? Did she talk to you? What did she say?"

"No. I don't know."

Ella shakes her head. "I didn't hear anything. What did you hear?"

"Nothing really. I think it was just a dream."

"A dream?" she says doubtfully.

"A dream," I say firmly. "Anyway, I have something for you. It's from a book about the Arrow family."

Ella eagerly takes the packet of papers from me and starts reading, her eyes rapidly scanning. The chapter is about Lionel Arrow and his five sons, but before the scandal and disap-pearance of four of the brothers and the tragic end of the fifth brother. It describes their childhood on the island, the pranks and hijinks and bonds and fun and fights. There is no mention of any daughter. No Eleanor.

Which is exactly my point: Eleanor didn't exist then. Eleanor doesn't exist now.

When Ella finishes reading, it's the first thing she points out. "I can't believe it."

"I'm sorry, but the truth is—"

"They left her out," she interrupts. "Poor Eleanor."

"No, Ella. If she existed," I say, "she would be in the book."

"Of course she existed. How could she be here now if she never existed?" Ella speaks so matter-of-factly that I'm almost convinced by her logic.

Almost. "But she's not here now. There is no ghost."

"If there's no ghost, who did you talk to last night?"

"I told you it was just a dream."

"Uh-huh. Okay." Ella gazes at me with wide, innocent eyes, but her mouth gives her away. Her lips twitch into a smirk, a very Henry-ish smirk.

I have no idea what to do. There seems to be no way to convince Ella that the ghost doesn't exist. Even worse, I now seem to be having trouble convincing myself.

Vanessa comes into the library waving a thick stack of envelopes. "Girls! Look at what came in the mail today. So many RSVP cards!"

"Great!" we say.

She glances at the photocopied papers on the table. "What are you reading?"

"We're doing some research on the history of Arrow Island." I smile at her. And feel rotten. Because my explanation is not the whole truth. Because there's something else I haven't told her. Something much worse.

"Fun!" Vanessa sits down at the table with us. "But if you're done . . . would you mind helping me sort these cards? It'll go so much faster."

"Sure," I say. Anything to relieve my guilt.

We make three piles: one for the yesses, one for the noes, and one for the ripped-open envelopes. Vanessa gives every yes a fond look and every no a slight frown.

Some of the names are vaguely familiar, names I recognize from the newspaper or fashion magazines. Then I come across a name I personally recognize: Joan Pritchett, my student Benny's mother, whose job offer I turned down for the Morisons'.

"The Pritchetts are coming," I say, more to myself than anyone else.

"You mean Benny? Benny's coming?" Ella asks.

"Yes, the whole family," I say.

"Good," says Ella.

Vanessa gives the card a fond look as I set it down into the yes pile. Then her fond look becomes a sly smile. "Joan was extremely annoyed I'd hired you away from her. But I knew she wouldn't be able to resist the party."

"It seems like most people can't resist the party." I gesture at the stacks. The yes pile is much taller than the no pile.

"It's Jeffrey. Everyone loves my husband."

I sit very still. I don't even breathe.

"It can be hard sharing him with everyone." Vanessa sighs.

I glance at Ella. She is watching her mother. When she notices me looking, her gaze shifts down to the envelope in her hand. She tears it open.

A moment later Ella announces, "Greg and Lorraine aren't coming."

There's a note scribbled on the other side. I read it—before it occurs to me that maybe I shouldn't read it. But it only says:

Sorry, V, it's the same weekend we're supposed to visit Greg's dad. Love, Lorraine.

Vanessa flips it over and studies the message, really studies it, as if there is more than a single simple sentence written there. Maybe there is. Then she tosses it down onto the no pile. She shrugs. "Who cares," she says.

Days pass and the secret festers inside me, growing more painful and more putrid with each passing second. I can barely think about anything else.

I have trouble sleeping. Every night I wake up two or three times, my heart beating so hard it hurts. It takes me hours to fall back asleep, if I can fall back asleep at all.

I have trouble eating. I'm only able to take a few bites of breakfast, lunch, or dinner before feeling as if I'm going to throw up. At home we always finish everything in our bowl, every last grain of rice; it would be wasteful not to. But now I start leaving half of my meal, or more. I tell myself it doesn't matter: in the Morison household, people don't always clear their plates. I feel guilty anyway.

It takes all my energy to keep up my tutoring sessions with Ella, to stay focused and engaged and cheerful during our lessons.

I spend time in the pink bedroom, curled on the pink bed, trying to strategize my way out of this mess. But there are too many pieces to the puzzle: the phone call, the internship offer, the surprise party, Vanessa's attachment to her husband, Jeffrey's busyness at work, Ella's obsession with Eleanor, Henry's rift with his father, Jeffrey breaking his office chair, Vanessa's competitive friendship with Joan Pritchett, old Mr. Morison's forecasts of disaster, my strange and unsettling dreams. . . .

The shark mind swims in sluggish circles, round and round, getting nowhere.

Suddenly I think of my mother. I need to call her, I realize; it's been days since I last called. I pick up my phone from the nightstand. Then I notice it's after midnight. I put my phone back down. But I'm still thinking about my mother. I'm thinking about how she would be peeling a potato and suddenly she would stop and her eyes would go empty and in that moment I would see her sorrow. And something shifts inside me.

I have to tell Vanessa about her husband and Lorraine.

Of course I have to tell her. No matter what Jeffrey Morison promised me. No matter how scared I am to do it. No matter what the consequences might be. I have to tell her and I will. She deserves to know.

And now that I've made my decision, I want to go to her room immediately and get it over with. But it's after midnight, so I'll tell her tomorrow. Or maybe . . . maybe I should wait until after the surprise party—it's in just over a week and it's Vanessa's pet project and she has invested so much time and money and energy into it. And she's so excited about it.

Yes, I decide, I'll tell her after the party.

Then I turn out the lights and lie down. It's such a relief to have finally figured out what I'm going to do. To have a plan. Maybe I'll be able to sleep now. . . . But for the first time in a long time, I feel wide awake. And extremely hungry.

I jump out of the pink bed and go downstairs. In the kitchen I open the enormous refrigerator and poke around for something that seems okay for me to take. Finally I grab a container of leftover spaghetti, turn around, and walk right into something warm and solid. Somebody.

I scream.

"Shh . . . it's just me," Henry says.

I stop screaming. "You scared me! What are you doing awake?"

"I never go to bed this early. Do you?"

"Yes. I have a job, you know."

"So what are you doing down here?"

"I'm hungry," I say. I hold up the container of spaghetti.

"You think it's okay if I eat this?"

"Yeah, if that's what you want. But I'm having apple cake with caramel ice cream for my midnight snack. Sure that's not what you want?"

I consider. "I want both," I say.

"Both?"

"I'm really hungry."

We sit at the counter. I eat the leftover pasta. And a huge slice of apple cake with caramel ice cream. And a smaller slice of apple cake. I scrape every crumb and fleck and drip into my mouth. Then I look up and find Henry watching me with amusement.

"I told you I was hungry," I say.

"I'm impressed," he says. "Was it homesickness?"

I frown. "What do you mean?"

"Whatever you've been going through lately. You've seemed kind of bummed. I figured you might be homesick."

"Not at all. I'm glad I'm not home," I say.

Then I realize what I've said and clamp my hand over my mouth.

Henry laughs. "The truth finally comes out."

I unclamp my mouth so that I can say, "No, no, no, I didn't mean that. It's just complicated there. My mom needs a lot from me. And my brother is a screw-up."

"In what way?" asks Henry.

"A couple of years ago, he dropped out of high school and got involved with gang stuff. We'd only hear from him when he needed something. Like money. Or when he got in trouble. He's been arrested a couple of times. Mostly for small things— vandalism, underage drinking, that kind of stuff. But once he and his friends held up a liquor store. My brother went to jail for that."

"Crazy." Henry looks shocked. I'm reminded of how different his world is from mine.

"Yeah . . . anyway, he's back. He moved home last month and is pretending to be all reformed. He got a job and is supposedly taking college classes in the fall."

"Maybe he is reformed."

"I doubt it," I say. "But my mom believes he is, so when he disappears again, I'm the one who's going to have to deal with it."

"Why you?"

"There's no one else."

"What about your dad?" asks Henry.

"My dad's not . . ." I stop. I stand up, collect our dirty plates and forks, and bring them to the sink. I turn on the water.

Henry comes over. I can feel him looking at me; I don't look at him. I'm afraid of what he's going to say. But he only says, "Hey, I'll wash the dishes."

"You know how to wash dishes?" It's supposed to be a joke, but I say it wrong. I sound mean, harsh, judgmental.

He laughs anyway. "Yes, allow me to demonstrate my awesome dishwashing skills."

I watch as Henry awkwardly swipes a soapy sponge across

the plates and forks. He scrubs cautiously and thoroughly. In the time it takes him to wash three plates and three forks, I could have washed a sink full of dishes. But I'm glad it takes him as long as it does. I need a moment to calm down.

I'm embarrassed to have told him so much about my family. I'm not sure why I did. Maybe it's the stress of the past week. Maybe it's the comfort from all the food I just ate. Or maybe it's this feeling of late night, how the darkness and stillness and quiet makes it seem as though we're the only two people in the world.

"Well?" Henry says when he's finally done washing the dishes.

I clap. He bows. I yawn.

"I should get to bed. It's way past my bedtime," I say.

"I'll walk you to your room."

"Thanks, but you don't have to."

"If I don't, who'll protect you from the ghost?"

"What?" I stare at him.

"Kidding!" He stares at me.

"Very funny." I walk out of the kitchen.

Henry follows. "You looked really scared. I better come with you."

"Are you sure you're not the one who's scared?"

"You found me out," he says.

We go up the stairs, down the hallway, and we stop in front of the door of the pink bedroom. I turn toward him to say good night. And suddenly my face is so close to his face that even in this dim lighting I can see the sheen of stubble on his chin, the faint freckles on his nose, the curl of his eyelashes. I notice he has extremely long lashes.

I take a step backward. "Good night," I say.

"Can I tell you something?" Henry says softly. "I missed our swimming lessons this week. As your swim coach, I'm really concerned about your progress."

I get it; it's a joke. But I don't laugh. And he doesn't laugh either. He doesn't even smirk. He leans toward me.

I think: He's going to kiss me.

I think: I want him to kiss me.

Yet I say: "What are you doing?"

He pauses. "Should I stop?"

"Yeah," I say. "Stop."

"Sorry, I thought . . ." Henry grimaces.

"Don't apologize. The thing is . . . I don't want to be unprofessional. I work for your family; I'm tutoring your little sister. It's not right," I say.

His expression relaxes. Then he actually grins. "That's why? It doesn't matter. No one in my family cares about that kind of stuff. Don't worry, you're not going to get fired or anything."

"You don't know that for sure."

He is still grinning. Then he actually laughs. "Relax. It's not such a big deal."

"Then why bother at all?" I say, annoyed. And a little hurt. I turn around and reach for the doorknob, and as I do, I remember Emma Rose telling me, "Henry's practically every girl's first boyfriend." I feel so dumb for falling for his tricks.

"No, sorry, I didn't mean it like that. It's just that you worry too much. About this, about your family, about everything. You shouldn't worry so much."

I let go of the doorknob and turn back toward him. I'm no longer annoyed or hurt. I'm furious. "Don't tell me not to worry. You have no idea what it's like for me, how hard it is. Everything I have I've had to work for. I've had to make sacrifices. I can't take anything for granted. You have no idea."

His face reddens. "Right. Because I do nothing, make no sacrifices, and don't work at all. And take everything for granted."

"I didn't say that."

"But that's what you meant."

"No," I say. "Though it's true, isn't it? You've had every opportunity in life, and what do you do? Mess around all day and barely graduate from high school."

Henry stares at me, his eyes cold and hard. "It's funny I ever thought you were nice. I'm glad I know the truth now," he says. Then he walks away.

4

WHEN I COME INTO THE LIBRARY THE NEXT MORNING, ELLA IS
already sitting at the table, doodling with the sparkly silver pen
I gave her as an attempt to bribe her into working hard my first
week here. It seems like years ago. I can't believe it was only a
month and a half ago.

"Good morning!" I say, and smile.

"Hi." She does not smile back. She looks tired.

"How'd you sleep?"

"Bad."

"Why?"

"Eleanor was so loud last night. I tried asking her why she
was so upset, but she wouldn't answer. You didn't hear her?"

"Nope. I didn't hear anything." I slept well, deeply and
dreamlessly, and woke up well rested for the first time in days.
It was surprising, considering . . .

"Really?" Ella looks incredulous.

"Let's get to work," I say.

"Wait," she says.

I wait. She doesn't continue. "Yes, Ella?" I prompt.

She frowns down at her workbook and mumbles, "I'm worried about the party. I think Eleanor is upset about the party."

"Why would she be upset? Is it because she isn't invited?" I ask, thinking of uninvited fairies wreaking terrible revenge in folk tales.

Ella snorts. "She doesn't care about that. Why would she want to go to the party?"

"Then why is she upset?"

"It's going to be so loud and crowded. Eleanor doesn't like that. She doesn't want all those strangers coming to her house."

"Yes, I can understand why **Eleanor** wouldn't like that."

"I'm scared she might do something."

"Like what?" I ask.

Ella shakes her head vigorously. I ask her again, but she still doesn't answer. It makes me nervous, but I just tell her to open her workbook and turn to page one hundred and twelve.

At noon we go downstairs for lunch, and I brace myself to see him. But then he's not there. And this makes me even angrier with Henry, irresponsible Henry Morison, who's always late for lunch—no, that's not true. Lunch is the one meal he's usually on time for, because it only takes him a minute to saunter from the swimming pool to the gazebo. So where is he?

I don't ask. I don't care. I smile and say hello to Vanessa and old Mr. Morison. They are sitting across from each other at the table but not talking to each other, or even looking at each other. I wonder if something happened before Ella and I arrived.

"Can you believe there's only a week to go before the party? I'm so excited," Vanessa chatters. She doesn't look well. Her face is flushed. Her golden hair is in a tangle. Her pretty purple dress has a jagged stain on the chest.

"One week," Mr. Morison grumbles. He doesn't look well. His complexion is chalky. His eyes are red. His hand trembles as he reaches for his water glass.

"What time is Daddy getting home today?" Ella asks.

"Oh, honey, he's not coming," Vanessa says.

"But it's Friday!"

"I know, Ellie, but he has so much work, he has to stay in the city this weekend. Hopefully he'll make it here next weekend. Otherwise we'll have to have his birthday party without him. Wouldn't that be hilarious?" Vanessa laughs. Haha. And keeps laughing. Hahahahahahahahaha.

"I'm sure he'll be here!" I say. I'm glad I decided to wait to tell her what I overheard. She already seems so close to breaking.

Vanessa stops laughing. She straightens her back and lifts her chin. She smiles broadly at us. Her eyes are bloodshot, so bloodshot that it seems impossible that she can actually see us. But then she says, "Ella, posture please."

Ella straightens her back and lifts her chin.

Mrs. Tully brings out lunch: grilled salmon and lemon pasta and salad with carrot-ginger dressing. They all start eating, so

I do too. Even though Henry still isn't here. And no one mentions his absence.

Perhaps because Vanessa only wants to talk about the party. She tells us about the gift bags she ordered for the guests. She tells us that there will be oysters served on an ice sculpture. She asks us how surprised we think Jeffrey Morison will be.

"Daddy's going to be so surprised!" Ella says. "I just hope that Eleanor—"

I look at Ella and raise an eyebrow. She looks at me. She clamps her lips together.

"Eleanor? You mean Eleanor, Fred and Minnie's daughter? Is she coming to the party? I thought they weren't bringing the kids. I'll have to check the list again later," Vanessa says.

"Enough! I can't take any more of this nonsense." Mr. Morison jumps up and hurries back into the house.

Vanessa watches him go with annoyance. Ella watches with concern.

"Is Granddad all right?" she asks.

"He probably has a stomachache. He has problems with his digestion, you know," Vanessa says scornfully. She takes out her cell phone and starts tapping at it.

"Maybe I should make him a get-well card," Ella says.

"That's a great idea," I tell her.

"Mom, do you want to help me?"

"Hmm? Help with what, sweetie?"

"The get-well card. For Granddad."

Vanessa blinks. "I'm sorry, honey. I have a hundred things
to check up on, like . . ."

"Never mind," says Ella.

"I can help you," I say. "If you want my help?"

"Thank you," she says softly.

Mrs. Tully comes back to clear the table. She picks up Mr.
Morison's half-eaten plate and looks at me accusingly, as if I
must be the reason he left before finishing his lunch.

I stand. "Come on, Ella, let's get back to work."

After we finish our lessons, Ella goes to her bedroom and
comes back with the most enormous box of colored pencils I've
ever seen—nearly a thousand pencils arranged by shade in lay-
ered metal trays. Her father gave them to her for her birthday,
she tells me.

I nod. "What can I help you with?"

"I don't know. Just stay here?"

"Sure."

While Ella makes her card, I review my lesson plans for the
next week. But I glance over every so often to check on what
she's doing. I don't see much. She has her arm curled protec-
tively around her paper.

"What are you drawing?" I finally ask.

"The beach," she says without looking up from her work.
"Granddad loves the beach. It's why he bought this house."

"Can I see it?"

"Um . . . when I'm finished. Maybe."

"Okay. You don't have to show me."

She keeps drawing. I keep reviewing my lesson plans.

"Does 'regards' have a u in it?" Ella asks after a while.

"Regards? Why are you writing regards?"

"I'm signing it 'Best regards, Ella.'"

"Are you sure you don't mean 'Love, Ella?'"

"I like 'Best regards, Ella,' and I think Granddad will too."

"You're probably right. Anyway, there's no u in 'regards.'"

"Best thanks," she says.

I laugh.

"Knock, knock!" Vanessa says as she walks into the room. She has changed into a clean dress, but her hair is still tangled, her face still flushed. "How are my girls doing in here? Let's see your card, Ellie-Belly."

"I'm not done yet," Ella says, tightening the protective circle of her arm.

Her mother reaches right down and picks the card right up.

I expect Ella to throw a tantrum, but she merely stiffens.

"What a beautiful drawing!" Vanessa says. "That's the beach, right? Granddad loves the beach. Oh, Ellie, you're such a wonderful artist. So talented." She sits down next to Ella— right next to Ella, on the same chair. Ella wiggles over to give her mother room. I watch them nervously. The chair is really too small for two people, even two very slender people.

"Best regards?" says Vanessa.

"Yes," says Ella.

Vanessa laughs and says, "You're such a funny girl." She curls her arm around her daughter's rigid shoulders and pulls her close. Ella resists, her body stick straight. Vanessa tightens her hold. Ella ducks away from her mother.

"I forgot my other markers. I have to get them," she says.

Vanessa watches her daughter scurry away. She continues watching, even after Ella is gone. Then she exhales heavily and covers her face with both of her hands. She makes a noise, a sob. "What am I going to do?"

I think: She knows about her husband and Lorraine.

I say: "About what?"

"Ella."

I'm startled. "What about Ella?"

"I love my daughter, of course I do. But sometimes . . . I don't understand her. She can be so cold. So withholding. Not like a little girl at all. I don't understand what's wrong with her." Vanessa sighs heavily.

And something inside me snaps.

"There's nothing wrong with her!" I say, my voice shrill in the quiet room. "She's not cold or withholding, she's shy. She's different from you, and her interests are different from yours. But that doesn't mean there's anything wrong with her."

"I know, I'm a bad mother, but—"

"Stop," I interrupt her. "You're not a bad mother. You're fine. If you just paid a little more attention to her, maybe spent some more time together, I think you'd be happier, and so would Ella. But stop trying to change her so much."

Vanessa stares at me. She inhales sharply.

Then I can't believe I interrupted her. I can't believe I spoke to her like that, and said what I said. I wonder if she's going to fire me. "I'm sorry," I say, "I shouldn't have—"

"No," she interrupts me now, with a tearful smile. "You're right. I'll try."

5

HENRY DOES NOT COME TO DINNER THAT NIGHT. NOR DOES HE appear at breakfast the next morning. A missed breakfast is not unusual for him, but at this point I've come to the conclusion that he's no longer here in this house on Arrow Island. So where is he?

I don't ask. I don't care. I smile and ask Vanessa what she has planned for the day.

"I was thinking about going into town," she says, and turns to her daughter. "Ella, would you like to come along? We can get our nails done."

"Okay." Ella smiles.

"And find you a new dress for the party."

Ella stops smiling.

"Or maybe a new book?" I suggest.

"Great idea! A book and a dress!" Vanessa says.

Ella looks at me. "Are you coming too?"

"No, you and your mom should have a special day together. Besides, I have some stuff to do here," I say. It's true: Ella and

Vanessa should spend some quality time together. It's true: I have to call my mother, email Doris, and fill out some medical forms for school.

However, I'm also feeling self-conscious about how inappropriate I was yesterday—chiding Vanessa, interrupting her—even if it turned out all right in the end. But I should be more professional from now on.

An hour later I'm at the spa, a place with soft lights and fragrant scents and plush chairs, getting my nails done with Vanessa and Ella. It's my first time at a spa, my first time getting my nails done, and it feels weird having a stranger crouched at my feet, scrubbing my toes. It tickles. I don't exactly like it, but I don't dislike it. And my nails look perfect when they're done—noticeably better than when I paint them myself.

Next we go to the bookstore, where Vanessa flips through style magazines while I browse the bestsellers and Ella scurries around in the kids' section. She emerges hugging a tall stack of books. The cashier says, "What a terrific reader your daughter is."

"Yes, she is," Vanessa replies proudly.

Ella blushes. But she looks pleased.

Ten minutes later, she looks much less pleased as she tangles with the dresses at a children's clothing store. Vanessa has picked out nearly a dozen for her try on; by the third one, Ella starts withdrawing.

"How about this one?" her mother asks.

She shrugs.

"Or this one?"

She shrugs.

Vanessa frowns.

Ella's gaze floats far away.

"Where's that yellow dress you were looking at?" I ask Vanessa. "I think it would be wonderful on her."

"Really? With her complexion?" she looks skeptical but goes to find it.

Then I quietly ask Ella, "Do you like any of them?"

She blinks. "What?"

"Of all the dresses in here," I say, "is there one you actually like? Or one you wouldn't mind wearing to your dad's party?"

Her eyes come into focus. She shuffles through flounce and lace and ribbon and sparkle, then pulls out a purple eyelet dress. "This one is okay," she says.

"Great," I say. "Now tell your mom."

"Tell me what?" Vanessa comes back into the fitting room.

Ella looks at me. I nod at her.

"I like this one," she says, pointing to the purple dress.

Vanessa looks befuddled—not because of the dress, I think, but because her daughter is expressing a preference for any dress. "All right. Do you want to try it on?"

Ella goes behind the curtain and comes out in purple.

"It's beautiful!" I tell her.

"Thanks," Ella says. But she looks at her mother.

Vanessa is studying the dress with dissatisfaction. It's the least fancy, least flashy, of all the ones she selected. I'm afraid of what she might say, but Ella speaks first.

"Mom, do I look okay?" she asks.

Vanessa shifts her gaze from the dress to her daughter. After a moment, her expression softens. "You're perfect," she says. "If that's the dress you want, that's the dress we'll get."

Our final stop is a women's boutique, where Ella and I sit in brocade armchairs while Vanessa tries on, seemingly, every dress in the store. Every time, she sashays out of the dressing room to ask what we think.

"I love it!" I say. Every time.

Ella says nothing because she is half asleep in her chair.

"This one also comes in red and a blue-green," the saleswoman says.

"Oh! Let's see the blue," says Vanessa.

The saleswoman brings it out with a flourish. It's a simple dress: sleeveless and scoop-necked and knee-length. The blue-green has an ocean shimmer.

"That color would look great on you," I tell Vanessa.

"No, it's your color. You have to try it on," she says.

"Me?" I say.

"You," she says.

"No, thanks," I say.

"Yes," says Vanessa.

"Yes," says the saleswoman.

"If you want," Ella murmurs sleepily.

I go into the dressing room. Then I look at the price tag. I can't believe it. I knew it would be expensive, but I didn't know it could be this expensive—more than the cost of everything in my closet combined. So very, very carefully, I slip into the dress. The fabric glides across my skin and clings softly to my body. I tell myself not to look in the mirror—this is not an item of clothing I could ever buy, so there's no point in looking in the mirror.

Of course I look.

A dress is not magic, I know. It can't transform you into another person. Yet I feel completely transformed. The girl in the mirror is not me; she's a fashionable girl, a confident girl, a sophisticated, stylish girl, a girl without a care in the world, a girl who would not, could not, be overlooked. For a moment I wish Henry Morison could see me in this dress.

Stupid thought. Stupid Henry. Stupider me.

"Come on out—let's see!" calls Vanessa.

Reluctantly, I pull back the curtain. Vanessa and the saleswoman ooh and ah. Vanessa tells me I look gorgeous. The saleswoman tells me I look stunning. The saleswoman turns to Vanessa and says, "That color's perfect on her, don't you think? Though I'd like to see her in the red. So exotic."

"No, the blue-green is the one for her," says Vanessa.

The saleswoman immediately agrees. "Oh, definitely."

"Um. Thanks." I hurry back into the fitting room, lift the dress over my head, and hang it back on the hanger. I return it to the saleswoman.

"Are you getting it? You have to get it," she says.

"You have to," says Vanessa.

"I don't think so," I say.

"It'll be perfect for the party," says Vanessa.

"It's perfect for any occasion," says the saleswoman.

"You're beautiful in it," says Vanessa.

"It fit perfectly," says the saleswoman. "Like it was made for you."

"Thanks, but I really can't buy it," I say softly.

Perhaps I say it too softly. The saleswoman brings the dress to the register. Vanessa walks with her, rambling about what color shoes would go best with it. "A soft gold, maybe, or what about coral?" she says.

I clear my throat. "I'm not going to buy the dress," I say loudly, clearly.

They whirl around. "What? Why not?"

"I can't afford it," I say.

Vanessa and the saleswoman stare at me. They are silent. I feel as if I've screamed some bad words or something. Maybe I have.

The silence seems to last forever. It probably lasts less than a minute. Then they all start talking at once. The saleswoman says, "Yes, well, that's understandable, dear." Vanessa says, "Sure, sure, that's fine, of course." Ella says, "Mom, is it time to go home yet?"

And I say, "I'm sorry."

We drive back to the house to find dinner is ready and

Mr. Morison is impatiently waiting in the dining room. After we eat, he and Ella go to watch a movie in the entertainment room. Vanessa goes to call her event planner with a new idea about hors d'oeuvres. I go to the pink bedroom and get ready for bed. Even though it's still early. Even though I'm not especially tired. But I don't know how else to get away from my embarrassment.

"Wake up! Wake up!" says the voice. A soft voice, a girlish voice.

I open my eyes. There is a shadow sitting at the side of the bed. I know I'm dreaming. I shut my eyes again and turn over, pulling the blanket up to my chin.

"Wake up!" the voice says, louder now.

I feel a weight on my arm, as if something—someone—is holding on to me, shaking me. A dream, I tell myself, it's only a dream. But I'm physically shaking. I turn back over, open my eyes again, and rub away the sleep. I squint through the darkness.

"Ella?" I say to the shadow.

She leans closer to me. "Are you awake?" she whispers.

"Yeah. Because you just woke me up."

"Oh. Sorry."

"Is something wrong?"

"Eleanor keeps bothering me. Can you hear her?"

I listen. All I hear is the sound of my breathing and her breathing. I shake my head.

Ella tilts her head to the side. She frowns. "She's being quiet now. But she's upset."

"Why is she upset?"

"I told you. The party."

"Right." I yawn. "Now that she's quiet, you should go back to sleep.

"As soon as I try to sleep, she's going to start bothering me again."

"How do you know?"

"I just know." Ella swings her legs up onto the bed. She wraps her arms around her knees. She looks very small, very young.

"Do you want to sleep in here?" I slide over to make room for her in the bed.

"Okay." She crawls under the floral blanket.

"Comfy?" I ask.

"Comfy," Ella says.

Almost immediately she starts snoring, breathy snorts that rattle the whole mattress, and I'm so startled that for a moment I think: Eleanor. But then I realize it's just Ella and I giggle into my pillow, and that's the last thing I remember before falling asleep. Neither of us wakes again until the morning.

6

MONDAY COMES. HENRY IS STILL GONE. THEN TUESDAY, THEN Wednesday, then Thursday. But I don't ask anyone where he is. I don't care. And yet . . . I find myself listening closely when Ella mentions her brother during lunch.

"Why isn't Henry back yet?" she asks.

"I guess his mom still needs him." Vanessa looks at her phone as she speaks. Her distraction is excusable, I suppose. There are only two more days until the big day.

"That woman never changes." Old Mr. Morison shakes his head.

"So when will Henry come home?" Ella asks.

"All I know is he'd better be back for the party," says Vanessa.

Ella sighs. "I wish he was here now."

I'm annoyed. Not at Ella—even though she has been waking me up every night to complain about Eleanor, then staying with me in the pink bedroom. I figure it'll stop after the party. I hope it will.

But no, I'm annoyed at Henry. Now that I know where he is, I'm annoyed at him for leaving. Though what else should I have expected? He's not grounded anymore. Of course he abandoned his family to go party with his friends in the city. Not that I care—it's only for Ella, who truly and deeply misses her brother, that I care. For myself, I'd be fine if Henry never came back.

Henry comes back that night. He walks into the dining room nonchalantly, as if he never left. "What's for dinner? It smells good in here," he says.

"Henry!" Ella leaps up from her chair.

"Ella!" Henry catches her in his arms.

"You were gone forever!"

"I know, I'm sorry. You must have been insanely bored here without me," he says. He smirks over his sister's shoulder. At me.

"No," says Ella. "We've been having fun. I got some new books."

I smirk back at Henry. But my smirk feels too close to a smile, so I turn away.

"How's your mother?" Vanessa asks.

"Fine. She's fine," Henry says. "Where's Granddad?"

"He was tired, so he went to bed early."

"Is he all right?"

"Yes, I think he has a cold."

"Another cold?"

"I made him a get-well card," Ella informs her brother.

"Then I bet he'll be better in no time." He grins.

Mrs. Tully comes into the dining room with a plate of food for Henry. He thanks her and tells her how much he missed her cooking. Then he turns to Vanessa. "How's everything going with the party?" he asks.

"Great! Everything's finally coming together," she says.

"It's going to be the best party ever. I can't wait!" Henry says.

Vanessa is smiling at him. Ella is smiling at him. Mrs. Tully is smiling at him.

And I am rolling my eyes, thoroughly disgusted.

When dinner is over, I wait several minutes after Henry leaves the dining room to leave the dining room. I linger in the hallways. I saunter leisurely around corners. I admire the art-work in the foyer. Yet somehow—how?—we meet on the stairs. And I angrily blurt out what I've wanted to say all through the meal: "I'm shocked you came back for the party."

"Of course I did. It's my dad's birthday," he says.

"But you don't care about stuff like that."

"That's not what I said."

"That's essentially what you said. Then you proved it by leaving."

Henry's face twists into a bitter smile, a smile uglier than any frown. "Have you been rehearsing this since I've been gone? Thinking how you were going to tell me off?"

"You're really conceited if you think I spent any time think-ing about you."

His bitter smile becomes a leer. "Maybe I am conceited, but that doesn't mean you weren't thinking about me. Admit it."

I flush. "Yeah, I thought about you, about how selfish you are."

Then Henry stops leering. He stares at me with no expres-sion at all, and this is somehow worse than his leer, his bitter smile, his perennial smirk. When he speaks, his voice is as empty as his face. "For your information," he says, "I left because my mom had a nervous breakdown. She was in the hospital for two days."

My anger abruptly shuts off.

"Henry, I'm so sorry," I say.

"Stop pretending," he says.

Henry leaps up the rest of the stairs, two at a time, rapidly rising above me. I stand there numbly until after he's gone, after the echo of his footsteps has faded to nothing. Only then do I walk slowly back to the pink bedroom. I shut the door behind me.

And I realize he's right. I'm not nice.

Wake up! Wake up! says the voice. A soft voice, a girlish voice.

I slide over in the bed without opening my eyes. I'm used to this now. "Get in, Ella. Go to sleep," I murmur.

But I'm not tired, she says. And I'm not Ella.

"No jokes now. I'm sleeping."

I never joke. Her voice abruptly deepens, so that it is no longer soft or girlish.

"Ella?" I roll over and look at her.

The shadow sitting at the side of the bed turns her face toward me. Her skin is grayish. Her eyes are black holes. Her dress is light pink with dark pink flowers. She is not Ella. She is not anyone I know. She is not human.

"I'm dreaming," I say.

You're not dreaming.

"Eleanor?" I say.

She smiles, her small teeth gleaming with moonlight.

"I'm going crazy," I say.

Going, going, gone. She gives a gurgling giggle.

"Very funny," I say. Strangely, I'm not scared at all. I don't get the sense that Eleanor means me any harm. Maybe she's a ghost, but she's also just a girl.

I need to talk to you, Eleanor says.

"Sure, what about?"

The party.

"Oh. Are you upset you're not invited?"

Of course not. It's going to be boring. That's what I want to talk to you about. I have an idea to make it much more exciting.

At this I feel a pang of worry. "I don't think we need to make it more exciting," I say. "It's already really exciting.

They're turning the swimming pool into a dance floor."

Eleanor rolls her eyes. Aren't you bored of being so boring?

"You sound like Henry now."

She snorts. That's ridiculous. I don't sound like a boy. I'm just tired of being well-behaved. Besides, it's the Morison family's last party, so we should make it a good one."

"What do you mean it's their last party?"

Eleanor shakes her head and smiles, small teeth gleaming, and I notice how sharp those small teeth are. Then I notice something else: her dress is not light pink with dark pink flowers; her dress is white and covered in bloodstains.

She sees me noticing. Something changes in her smile. Her black eyes seem to get blacker. Her teeth seem to sharpen. The blood on her dress, I notice, is fresh and blossoming.

And now I'm absolutely terrified.

"Eleanor, what are you going to do?" I say, my voice trembling.

I've changed my mind; I don't need your help. It'll be a wonderful surprise for you. You'll thank me after. She laughs, tipping back her head and opening her mouth wide so that the sound pours out like blood—a thick swell, a wave, and then there's an ocean of red on the bed, the floor, and I'm kicking my legs and waving my arms to try to stay afloat.

The blood fills my lungs, sinking me down and down and down.

* * *

I cough myself awake. It was a dream, only a dream, a nightmare, a terrible and meaningless nightmare. I open my eyes to reassure myself that I am alone in the pristine pink bedroom. And I am. I glance at the clock. It's almost five in the morning. The sky is beginning to lighten. I'm alone. Ella must have slept through the night.

I shut my eyes again and roll across the bed. Something stabs painfully into my back. I reach for it. My hand finds something small and cold and hard. I pull it out from under the blanket. It's the porcelain ballerina figurine that my father gave me for my sixth birthday.

How could that possibly be?

The figurine should be where I put it, in my suitcase in the mirrored wardrobe. It should be where I left it in my closet at home. It should be anywhere other than here in the bed with me.

I get up and drop the figurine into the wastebasket. Then immediately I stoop down and retrieve it. Even after everything that's happened, I can't bring myself to throw it away. I place the figurine on the dressing table and give her a nudge so that she makes a teetering twirl. I should get back to bed. But I can't bring myself to get back into that bed with its pretty floral quilt. In the gloom of early morning, the pink blossoms are the brown-red of drying blood.

So I go out into the hallway and tap on the door next door. When there is no answer, I tiptoe inside. Ella is curled up small on one side of her big bed, snoring. I lie down on the other side and quickly fall asleep.

When I wake up again, the sky is blue and the sun is dazzling and Ella is peering at me. "Was it Eleanor?" she asks. "Did she wake you up last night?"

And I must still be half asleep, because I simply answer "Yes."

7

THERE IS NO TAKING IT BACK. I TRY. AS SOON AS WE ARE SET-
tled in the library with our notebooks and workbooks, I tell
Ella it was actually a dream that woke me up, only a dream.
But she ignores my excuses. "What did Eleanor say about the
party?" she asks.

"Nothing," I say quickly, too quickly.

"Tell me exactly what she told you."

"She said the party was going to be boring."

"She said it'll be **boring**? What does that mean?"

"It doesn't mean anything. It was a dream," I say. "Now let's
get started. Open your book to page ninety-five."

"The party is tomorrow," she says.

"Page ninety-five," I say.

"What are we going to do?" she says.

"We're going to read page ninety-five," I say.

She huffs—very un-Ella-like—and opens her book.

Then we get to work. Sort of. We struggle through two sec-
tions, and Ella gets most of the questions wrong. She seems to

be making no effort at all.

"What's going on?" I ask.

Ella shrugs. She is gazing past me, but I know that if I turn to see what she's gazing at, I won't see anything. She is looking at something much farther away.

"Okay, let's move on to the next section," I say.

She gets nearly everything wrong in that section too.

I'm relieved when it's time for lunch. Relieved until we get downstairs and outside and I see Henry sitting at the table in his usual seat, in his usual neon swim trunks, with his usual smirk. My whole body tenses.

"Henry!" I say loudly, much too loudly. "Hi! How are you? Are you okay? Did you have a good morning? What's new?"

"Hey, Ella," he says. "Let's go to the beach when you get out of tutoring prison."

"Sure, the beach," Ella says absentmindedly as she slouches into her chair.

Henry looks quizzically at his sister. Usually when he asks her something, anything, she responds eagerly. Now she is as distracted with him as she is with everyone else.

"Ellie, posture, please," says Vanessa. "And what on earth are you wearing?"

Ella straightens. She is wearing a shirt with cartoon animals on the front. "Benny gave it to me for my birthday last year. Remember?"

"I remember." Vanessa grimaces.

"Well, I love your shirt, El," says Henry.

"All this foolishness about a shirt." Old Mr. Morison shakes his head.

Vanessa turns to me with a brittle smile. "I was thinking, perhaps you and Ella can take a break from tutoring this afternoon. I could really use your help with some party stuff," she says.

Mr. Morison frowns. "You can't possibly be serious."

"Lucky you, Ella! You're free!" Henry says.

"You don't mind, do you?" Vanessa asks me.

Ella gazes at her plate of food.

And I feel a sense of déjà vu. It's as if we are back to the beginning of the summer: Vanessa nitpicking her daughter. Henry needling his stepmother. Ella in a perpetual daydream. Mr. Morison criticizing his daughter-in-law. Henry provoking me. Vanessa asking me to do things outside my job description.

I don't like it, this feeling that we are going backward. It's uncomfortable and disorienting and slightly nauseating. Maybe that explains why I don't eat much at lunch. And maybe that explains the terrible mistake I make afterward.

Vanessa and I are in her office, compiling the final guest list for the party. While she dictates, I type. Then suddenly, out of nowhere, I blurt, "The other week I overheard this strange conversation on the phone between your husband and Lorraine."

"What?" She looks startled.

But I am more startled. I had a plan, and this is not it.

"What did you hear?" she asks.

"I, um . . . I was in his office because I was photocopying something for Ella—remember you said I could use the copier anytime? And your husband came in and he was on the phone with Lorraine, and she was upset about someone finding out about something, but he told her there was no proof and it would be all right." I speak quickly, confusedly, probably incoherently. Then I stop. I wait for her to respond with questions or anger or sadness. Or anything.

Vanessa stares at me, her face expressionless.

"It was probably nothing," I say.

She stares.

"I'm sorry," I say.

Then all at once Vanessa starts moving, talking, reacting. She stands up and says, "It's fine, don't worry, it was probably nothing." She laughs. She sits back down. She continues dictating the guest list to me.

And I realize that although there would never have been a painless way to tell her what I overheard—even if I'd done it according to my plan—I undoubtedly chose the worst moment of all to have this conversation: the day before the big party, a few hours before her husband is supposed to arrive.

What have I done?

* * *

This evening, Jeffrey Morison is very late for dinner.

"I'm sure he'll be here any second now," Vanessa says. She has changed for dinner, into a dark red dress that flows around her like wine. Her face is velvety with makeup. Her hair is freshly washed and dried and curled.

"Maybe he got caught in traffic," Ella says. She has also changed for dinner, into a lacy white dress. She looks itchy in it. She keeps scratching around the collar and under the sleeves.

"Maybe he forgot we exist," Henry mutters. He has also changed for dinner, into a collared shirt that is only slightly wrinkled.

"My son believes it's only his time that's valuable," old Mr. Morison grumbles. He has also changed for dinner, into freshly ironed attire, but even his neat clothes cannot disguise his tiredness. His skin is sallow, his lips pale, his eyes unfocused. He should be in bed.

"Sweetie, stop scratching," says Vanessa. "And sit up straight."

Ella drops her hands from around her neck and shudders up against her chair.

"Granddad, are you feeling all right?" Henry asks.

"I'm perfectly fine," snaps Mr. Morison.

Mrs. Tully comes in with a platter of salmon and a deep dish of creamy noodles, but Vanessa sends the food back to the kitchen, telling her to keep it warm until her husband arrives, that he should be here any second. There is a bowl of salad on the table, but no one seems to dare touch it, or even look at it.

Finally, there is the thud-thud-thud of footsteps in the hallway, and I feel the same déjà vu I felt this morning, but this time it's mixed with something else. Foreboding.

Jeffrey Morison enters the room.

"Daddy!" Ella gets up and hugs him.

"Jeffrey." Vanessa does not get up.

"Hello, my pretty girls!" he booms, his voice genial. But his expression is not. He looks annoyed. He looks tired. His hair looks sparse and greasy. His mouth is pinched. He sits down awkwardly, heavily, as if his body aches.

"Dad," says Jeffrey. "Are you well? You're looking a bit under the weather."

"I'm perfectly fine," Mr. Morison responds stiffly.

"Son," says Jeffrey. "I thought you were still in the city."

"Nope. I'm back," Henry mumbles.

"And you!" Jeffrey Morison directs a strained smile over to me. "You're still here!"

"Yes." I smile back at him. I try to make mine less strained, but I don't succeed.

"Yeah, she's still here," Henry says. He doesn't smirk.

Jeffrey Morison glances around at the blank plates on the table. "You haven't started eating yet? You shouldn't have waited for me. I'm famished. What are we having?"

Instantly, Mrs. Tully appears with the tomato soup, then a platter of salmon and dish of noodles. Then a leek frittata, sautéed vegetables, fried calamari, and a rosemary flatbread.

"Mrs. Tully, you've really outdone yourself," booms Jeffrey Morison.

"It's nothing." Mrs. Tully reddens and giggles.

"Daddy, how was your week?" Ella asks in her breathless chirp.

"Not too bad, sweetheart. Could be worse," says Jeffrey. "But things are very busy right now. I'm afraid I have to get back to the city tomorrow."

"Tomorrow?" Vanessa says. "Tomorrow?"

"Yes, dear. Tomorrow," he says.

Her face turns very pale. "Are you serious? We haven't seen you in two weeks and you're not even staying twenty-four hours?"

"There're some things I need to take care of."

"What things?"

"Important business." Jeffrey Morison jabs an enormous forkful of noodles into his mouth, so enormous that his cheeks swell as he chomps. Perhaps he thinks he can stop his wife from complaining if he crams his own mouth full.

But Vanessa cries, "Of course! Because business is always more important than family, isn't it? I made plans for us to celebrate your birthday this weekend."

He swallows his food. "We can celebrate next weekend."

"That's impossible."

"Why? My birthday isn't until Wednesday."

"Because . . . because . . ."

I glance around the table. Henry appears utterly focused on his food, attentively cutting and chewing. Old Mr. Morison is observing his son and daughter-in-law with curiosity. And Ella—once I look at Ella, I can't look away.

Ella is neither feigning interest in her food nor watching her parents. She is staring at the wall. No, she is staring through the wall. Her forehead is crinkled. Her eyes are dreamy. Her lips are fluttering. As if she is murmuring to someone. But no sound emerges from her mouth. And there is no one she could possibly be murmuring to.

"Because," Vanessa says, "I'm throwing you a surprise party tomorrow night. And you better be there. Or else. You bastard."

The dining room goes absolutely quiet.

Then Jeffrey says, "A surprise birthday party? What the hell are you thinking?"

"It's your birthday. You're my husband. What do you think I'm thinking?"

"How many people are coming? How much have you spent on this?"

"I do something nice for you, and this is how you react?"

"You know I don't like surprises!" Jeffrey shouts.

"No, I don't know that!" Vanessa shouts.

As they shout, Henry continues eating, Mr. Morison continues observing, and Ella continues doing whatever it is she is doing. I wish I understood what it is she's doing.

"Anyway," shouts Vanessa, "one person who is not coming

to the party is your friend Lorraine. I guess she knows that you hate surprises."

"Are you listening to yourself? Do you know how ridiculous you sound?" shouts Jeffrey.

"Don't call me ridiculous."

"Then don't be ridiculous."

"Fuck you, Jeffrey. Fuck. You."

I look at Ella and see her face freeze. Eyes shut tight. She is so still that it seems like she isn't breathing. She is so still that it frightens me. I am so focused on her stillness that it takes me a moment to register what happens next.

The bowl of tomato soup explodes.

Perhaps explodes is not the right word, but I can't think of a better one. The glass bowl shatters with a crash, shards scattering across the table. The red liquid blasts in every direction, splattering us all. We jump up from our chairs, shrieking with surprise.

Except Ella. She is motionless. Her eyes still shut. Soup bleeding down her cheek.

"What the hell just happened?" Jeffrey Morison bellows.

No one answers him. None of us can possibly answer him.

"Mrs. Tully!" Vanessa screams.

Mrs. Tully runs into the room, surveys the mess, and runs out. A minute later she returns with a garbage bag and paper towels and cleaning spray.

Henry gets up and starts picking up the broken glass. Old Mr. Morison dabs at the soup stains on his nice shirt; there is a particularly large splotch on his chest. Jeffrey and Vanessa stare wrathfully at each other, seemingly unaware of the activity around them. Ella is motionless.

I step carefully over shards and tomato and touch her shoulder. "Come on, Ella," I say quietly. "Let's go upstairs and get cleaned up."

She opens her eyes and nods.

I walk her to her room and tell her to take a shower. Then I take a shower too. My body feels very cold. I turn the water very hot, stand right under the spray, and watch the pink swirl slowly down the drain.

When I come out of the bathroom, Ella is waiting for me, sitting on the floral bed, in her pajamas. Her hair is dripping and her face is flushed. "It was Eleanor," she says.

I get a towel and drape it over her dripping hair. "What was Eleanor?"

"She did it." Ella shrugs and the towel slides off.

"What?" I pick up the towel again and wrap it around her head.

"Eleanor broke the bowl and threw the soup on us."

"No, it was just a freak accident."

"It was a warning," she says. "She's going to do something worse at the party."

"No, she isn't. Because Eleanor doesn't exist," I say.

Ella frowns. Her face is very small under her towel turban. Then she says, very, very, softly, "I'm scared."

"Oh no, Ella. Don't be scared. It's going to be fine. Everything is going to be fine." I pat her back reassuringly. I don't know what else to do or say.

Because the truth is: I'm scared too.

8

SEVERAL HOURS LATER, IT'S PAST MY BEDTIME AND I'M EX-
hausted, but I'm not in bed; I'm not even ready for bed. I am
sitting at the dressing table with my laptop, reading intently.
But every few minutes I get so overwhelmed, I have to get up
and take a lap around the pink room. Then I sit down again
and continue reading. I make some notes on a sheet of paper.
When I have all the information I need, I shut my computer. I
stare at my notes.

Should I actually do this?

I don't know what else to do.

So I run downstairs to the kitchen and get a few supplies.
Back in the pink bedroom I pick a pair of scissors from my pencil box. I pull a pillow out from its floral pillowcase and take the
pillowcase. From the bathroom, I grab the small metal trash
bin, take out the bag of trash, and put everything I've collected
inside the bin.

I carry it all to the door, place my hand on the knob. I stop.
There's something else I need. I turn back around. I see it. I

move slowly toward it, almost against my own will, as if hypnotized. I lift the porcelain ballerina figurine from the dressing table and gently place her at the bottom of the bin.

Then I walk next door, knock, and go inside the room. I sit on the bed, next to the small lump under the covers. "Ella?" I say softly. When she doesn't stir, I say her name slightly louder.

"Hmm?" She wiggles out from under the blanket and blinks sleepily at me. Her eyes are red and swollen, her face blotchy. She looks as if she cried herself to sleep.

"Sorry to wake you," I say.

"Is it Eleanor?" Her voice is raspy.

"No," I say automatically. Then I correct myself. "I mean, yes. Sort of."

"What do you mean?"

"We're going to set her free!" I announce.

I expect Ella to gasp or shout or bombard me with questions, but she nods calmly. "Good idea," she says.

"I brought everything we need." I show her the steel bin. "Ready?"

"Shouldn't we do it in your room? Since that's Eleanor's room?"

"Ella, you're a natural at this."

"I know."

In the pink bedroom, we sit on the floor, cross-legged and facing each other. I unfold the floral pillowcase and lay it flat between us. On top of it I place a candle in a glass jar I got from the kitchen. I take out my page of notes, the pair of scissors, a box of matches, a blank sheet of paper, and a black marker. Lastly, I take out the ballerina figurine and balance her next to the candle.

Ella watches me closely but says nothing.

I carefully use a match to light the candle. The flame sputters out instantly, and a twisting snake of smoke rises from the wick. I try again. It goes out again. I try once more, my hand trembling. This time, the flame catches and keeps burning.

"Weird," I say.

Ella says nothing.

"Okay, so on this piece of paper, let's write down all the things we wish for Eleanor. I'll start. Peace," I say, and use the black marker to write PEACE.

"Fun," says Ella.

"Good one." I write FUN.

"Not to be mad," she says.

"Not to be scared," she says.

"Not to feel bad," she says.

I write everything down. "Great."

To my surprise, Ella keeps going. I've never heard her say so much so quickly.

"Not to have to do things she doesn't want to do," she says.

"To have lots of friends," she says.

"No one is mean to her," she says.

"To do whatever she wants," she says.

"I want her to be happy," she says.

"Me too," I say. I write HAPPINESS. "Anything else?"

Ella shakes her head. The page is full. I set it down on the floral pillowcase.

"Now let's join hands," I say, reaching out my arms. Ella sets her palms on mine. Her fingers are cold. I look at my notes. "Now we have to say 'Eleanor Arrow, this is no longer your home.' We're going to chant it three times. Then we're going to say 'Eleanor Arrow, we set you free.' Also, three times. Ready?"

"Ready," Ella says solemnly.

"Eleanor Arrow, this is no longer your home," we chant three times.

"Eleanor Arrow, we set you free," we chant three times.

Shadows rise and sway around us, flickering with the candlelight. Despite myself, I feel uneasy. I am putting on this show for Ella's benefit—I want to relieve her fears. But all of a sudden it doesn't feel like a show anymore.

"Now we'll cut this paper into pieces and burn them," I say. I pause. I frown. "Under normal circumstances, we shouldn't be playing with fire like this. Fire can be really dangerous. I'll do the burning. You cut. Promise me you won't try this again, and never play with fire."

"I promise," Ella says.

I pass her the scissors, and she cuts the paper into strips. I dip each one into the fire. They burn fast. PEACE. Smoke swirling. FUN. The air bitter with burning. FRIENDS. Paper melting into ashes. HAPPINESS. Ashes dissolving into dust.

When the last strip vanishes, Ella and I rejoin hands.

"Now we're going to chant 'Good-bye, Eleanor.' Three times," I say. When I made up this routine, I worried it was too ridiculous, that I wouldn't be able to get through it without giggling. But my voice is serious. I am now completely serious.

"Good-bye, Eleanor. Good-bye, Eleanor. Good-bye, Eleanor!" we say.

Then something happens.

The flame flares up and doesn't go down. The candlelight fills the jar, expands past the jar, fills the whole room. The heat is fierce. The brightness is blinding. The air thickens and turns into something else, something solid. And hot.

"Ella!" I shout, but no sound comes from my mouth. I clutch her hands and try to pull her toward me. We have to get out of the pink room.

But Ella doesn't budge. And it feels purposeful—as if she could move if she wanted, but she doesn't want to move.

"Ella, come on!" I shout.

"No, it's okay. We just have to wait," she shouts back.

Yet neither of us makes a sound.

It makes no sense. How can I hear her if we're not actually speaking?

But I can hear her. So I wait. I hold on to Ella and wait.

After a minute, the fire begins sinking slowly but steadily, like water draining from a tub, until it's just a normal candle flame. Then, with a feeling like a sigh, the light goes out completely.

We sit silently in the dark. I'm not scared anymore. My body feels strangely light, as if I might float away. Suddenly I start laughing. As soon as I do, Ella laughs too. We laugh and we laugh, great big gusts of loud, wailing, joyous laughter. We laugh until we sob. Then we start laughing again.

The glaring overhead light comes on. I turn around, dazzled and disoriented by the abrupt brightness. There is a figure standing in the doorway.

"What's going on in here?" says the figure.

I blink hard to clear my vision. "Nothing," I say.

"We freed Eleanor!" says Ella.

"Who's Eleanor?" asks Henry.

I look at Ella. She looks at me. I sigh.

"You want to come in?" I say.

For a moment Henry merely stands there, and I think he's going to turn around and walk away. But then he does what I asked. Maybe because Ella is here. Maybe because he's too curious not to. He sits down on the floor with us.

"Eleanor is the ghost," says Ella.

"The ghost? We have a ghost?" He looks excited.

"Not anymore," I say. "We just set her free."

"She was the one who broke the bowl at dinner," says Ella.

"Huh, okay." Henry nods. "Tell me more."

Ella tells him everything: that Eleanor Arrow, forgotten daughter of Lionel, has been haunting us. That she was angry about the party, which is why she destroyed the bowl of tomato soup during dinner. But that we—she and I—have just set her free. And that the room filled with a bright light as Eleanor left.

"Great job, El," Henry says. "But I wish you had told me we were being haunted, so I could have helped. Or at least gotten a chance to meet her before you released her."

Ella looks at him apologetically. "Eleanor didn't like boys. Especially brothers."

"Hmm. Sounds like someone else we know." He looks at me.

I know he is talking about me and him. But I can't help thinking about my own brother. I stand up. "We should probably get to bed," I say. "Tomorrow's going to be a big day. Ella, want me to tuck you in?"

"No, I'll tuck her in," Henry says.

"You both can," she says magnanimously.

The three of us go to her room. Ella gets into bed. I sit on one side of her, and Henry sits on the other. "Good night," we say. I pat her shoulder. Henry kisses her cheek.

"Good night." Ella shuts her eyes and wriggles her face into the pillow. Her breathing slows and steadies. She seems to fall instantly asleep.

I look at Henry. He is looking at me. But as soon as my gaze meets his, he gets up and walks out of the room. I follow him into the hallway, carefully shutting Ella's door behind me.

"Henry," I say.

He keeps walking.

"Henry," I say again.

"Yeah?" He keeps walking.

"Can we talk? Please. Just for a minute," I say.

"There's nothing to talk about," Henry says. But he turns around.

I take a deep breath and say, "I want to apologize for yesterday. And last week. I'm sorry I called you selfish and self-centered. You're not. I just freaked out that night because . . . never mind. You were right. I'm not nice."

He frowns and my heart sinks and I tell myself that I did what I could—I apologized—and I can't force him to forgive me. But then he says, "No, you are nice. I only said you weren't because I was mad. I'm sorry."

"Don't do that," I say.

"Do what?" he says.

"Apologize when I'm apologizing. I'm the jerk here."

"But I shouldn't have told you not to worry so much about your family," he says. "You were right—I don't know what it's like for you."

"Yeah, but I don't know what it's like for you either. Though, stupidly, I thought I did."

"Okay, so now we're fighting about who's the biggest stupid jerk?"

"Yeah. Please let me win this one," I say.

"Never." Henry smirks. Or maybe it's a grin. Maybe it has always been a grin and I just never realized it. "Friends again?" he asks.

"Friends again," I say.

"How about a swimming lesson tomorrow?"

"It'll be too busy with the party and everything."

"Okay, swimming lesson the day after tomorrow?"

"Fine," I say with a sigh. "But the party . . . is it still on, you think?"

Henry grimaces. "Important question. No answer. It's pretty ironic that I've been dreading this event all summer, but now I'm worried about it **not** happening."

"What do you think will happen if it's canceled?"

"Vanessa will divorce my dad."

"Really?"

"It's possible. Ness has a way of overreacting."

"In this case, I don't necessarily think she'd be overreacting," I say, remembering the conversation I overheard. And how I told her about it at the worst possible time.

"Maybe not. But she definitely overreacted about Ella and the witchy stuff."

"What witchy stuff?"

"I told you, remember? Ella's falling-out with her friends?"

"You didn't say anything about witches," I say.

So Henry tells me the whole story. When Ella and her friends got in trouble for trashing the school bathroom, they hadn't been vandalizing for vandalizing's sake. They had been inspired by a movie about teenage witches, trying to cast a spell to see their future. So they drew hearts on the walls and draped toilet paper over the lights. They smeared lipstick on the sinks. Then they chanted magic words as they stared into the mirror, waiting to see what would become of them. And a teacher walked into the room.

"After that," he says, "Vanessa got rid of all of Ella's books and movies and toys that had anything to do with the supernatural. I think she was embarrassed that they all accused Ella of being the ringleader. Though . . . after hearing Ella talk about the ghost tonight, I can see how she might have been."

Then Henry lowers his voice, making it soft and spooky, and says, "Now will you please tell me more about this ghost? What's the deal?"

And because he lowers his voice, I have to lean closer in order to hear him. And because I lean closer, our faces are suddenly close together. Noses nearly touching. Lips almost aligned.

I quickly lean back. "I . . . I don't know."

"You actually think she was real?" Henry speaks normally again.

"Well, at first I thought Ella was making it up. Then I thought we were both making it up with our overactive imaginations or something. But what happened tonight felt really . . . real. Now I don't know what to think. It's all so weird and mysterious."

"Well, the world is a weird and mysterious place."

"I guess so," I say. "Anyway, I should get to bed. Tomorrow's going to be a big day."

"Hopefully," Henry says with an expression of wide-eyed panic that isn't all pretend.

We say good night. I go into the pink bedroom and clean

up the remains of our ceremony. I return the trash bin to the bathroom. I put the candle, matches, scissors, and paper on the dresser. I toss the floral pillowcase in with my dirty laundry. Then I'm about to get into bed when I realize there's something missing. I search on the floor, in the trash bin, on the dresser, under the rug.

The ballerina figurine is nowhere to be found.

It's strange. I've tried multiple times to get rid of the thing this summer, yet now that she's gone, I'm a little sad. And confused. **Where did she go?** I shake my head as I get into bed. The world is a weird and mysterious place.

But at least Henry and I are friends again. And—most important—the problem of Ella and the ghost has been solved. I hope.

9

THEN IT'S THE DAY OF THE PARTY. AS SOON AS I COME DOWN-
stairs, I can tell it hasn't been canceled. There is something
in the atmosphere, a buzzing apprehension. A sense of excite-
ment. Even though it's just Ella, Vanessa, and old Mr. Morison
sitting around the kitchen counter eating pancakes (Ella) and
drinking coffee (Vanessa and Mr. Morison), as usual.

But then Vanessa jumps up and exclaims, "What am I
doing? I have to go get ready. The event planners will be here
in an hour!"

Jeffrey Morison enters the kitchen. "Good morning!"

I freeze, and so does Ella, and so does Mr. Morison. Only
Vanessa turns to her husband. She walks right over to him
and clasps her arms around his neck and lays her head on his
chest. Jeffrey tips forward and kisses his wife's hair. A few
times.

"Morning, beautiful," he says.

"Good morning," she says.

I relax. Ella relaxes. Mr. Morison returns to his coffee,

looking faintly disgusted. The bags under his eyes are dark and
deep.

"Hi, Ellie. How's my pretty girl today?" asks Jeffrey.

"Good, Daddy!" Ella chirps. "Um, Daddy, can we go out on
the boat today?"

This was the original plan: Ella would distract her father
and get him out of the house, away from the party preparations
and arriving guests, until the magical moment of surprise.
Apparently Ella is still operating according to plan, even
though there can no longer be any surprise.

"Sure, Ellie. That's a great idea! Will you join us?" Jeffrey
asks his wife. As if he doesn't know about the party.

"I wish I could, but I have some chores to do around here,"
Vanessa says regretfully. As if she doesn't know that her husband knows about the party.

"We should see if Henry wants to come along." Jeffrey says
to his daughter.

"Yeah, I'll go ask him!" Ella hops off her stool, abandoning
her pancakes.

"Darling, will you make sure she finishes her breakfast
before you go? I'm going upstairs to get ready," Vanessa says.

"Of course, sweetheart," Jeffrey says.

They kiss.

I focus my attention on my pancakes. Banana. Walnuts.
Maple syrup. Delicious. I'm glad the Morisons made up.
Though I can't help wondering how they managed it. And I
can't help wondering if she told him that I told her about the

phone conversation I overheard.

But Jeffrey smiles at me when he comes over to sit at the counter. "Good morning," he says. "Oh, and before I forget— here's my HR manager's business card. Email her, and she'll arrange your internship for next summer."

"Thanks." I take the card he gives me and try to smile back.

"And how are you doing, Dad?" Jeffrey asks his father.

"If I were you," says Mr. Morison, "I would be more concerned with how you're doing."

"Everything is under control," snaps Jeffrey, and for a moment he is not Jeffrey Morison, rich and successful businessman, but a sulky kid annoyed at his father. He picks up the newspaper and starts reading, or pretends to.

I finish my pancakes and go upstairs to see if Vanessa needs any help. But she's not in her room. She's not in her office. She's not in the library. I go back to the pink bedroom and there she is, standing on the fluffy white rug, surveying the pink walls and ornate furniture.

"Oh! I was looking for you," I say.

She nods absently, still gazing at the floral and the frill. "I thought this room would be perfect for you. I wanted someone to enjoy it, especially after Ella refused to sleep here, but it is a bit over the top. The thing is . . . it's the bedroom I always wanted when I was a little girl. Or thought I did. I don't know. What do you think?"

"I think it's a beautiful room," I tell her.

Vanessa smiles. "So, you were looking for me?"

"I wanted to see if you needed any help today."

"I certainly do, which is why I came here to find you. Get ready. After lunch, you and I are going into town. We have an important appointment."

"What appointment?" I ask.

"You'll see."

Our very important appointment is at the hair salon.

"But I thought you needed my help with party stuff?" I say.

"No, no, no, of course not. That's what event planners are for. They bring staff. They set up everything. Our only job is to get pretty," Vanessa says, beaming, as if I had never helped her pick up invitations or type spreadsheets or stuff gift bags.

"Okay. Well, I'm happy to keep you company, but I don't need—"

"Two shampoos, deep-condition treatments, and blow-outs," Vanessa tells the receptionist.

We sit side by side as we get our hair washed and deeply conditioned and blown and styled. Vanessa tells her stylist she wants a twisted side braid bun. Then she debates with my stylist about what to do with my hair. The stylist wants to do waves and Vanessa wants it straight and I have no opinion at all.

"What are you going to wear?" the stylist asks me.

"A black dress," I say.

"What's the fit? The neckline? Does it have any embellishments?"

"Um. It's sleeveless and it dips a little in the front. It's just a plain black dress," I say. It's my graduation dress, the newest and nicest one I have.

"We should do waves to add texture," the stylist says.

"Do her hair straight," Vanessa says.

Ironed straight, my hair is a sleek curtain of black hanging all the way to my waist. I look . . . different. Older. Bolder. I'm not sure I like it. But Vanessa and the stylist coo and stroke and pat me like a pet.

"You were right," the stylist tells Vanessa.

"I know." She smiles.

The house already looks like a surprise when we return: tiny twinkling lights in the trees, tables swathed in linen, glittering glassware, attractive waiters in sleek uniforms. There is a bar made of ice, and a handsome bartender organizing bottles behind it. The swimming pool has been covered in frosted acrylic to create a glowing blue dance floor.

"It's perfect," Vanessa and I say at the same time.

Then she tells me she's going to her room to rest for a bit, and recommends I do the same. "Will you come up in an hour to help me zip up my dress?" she asks. "It's a little challenging to get into."

"Of course," I say.

I go upstairs to the pink bedroom. I want to take a nap, but I can't figure out how to lie down without creasing my hair.

Eventually I just pile all the pillows behind me so I can recline comfortably. Somewhat comfortably. I take out my laptop and check my email. There's a message from Ms. Baldwin.

Are you back in the city yet? I've gotten in touch with my friend Annabella Schultz, and she wants to talk to you. Let me know when you're available and we'll set something up. I don't want to get your hopes up, but things are looking good—fingers crossed!

I frown at the screen. I have no idea what Ms. Baldwin is talking about. What hopes? What looks good? Who is Annabella Schultz? That, at least, I can look up on the internet, so I do. Annabella Schultz, I discover, is the assistant director of admissions and financial aid at Waltman College.

Immediately, I shut my laptop. As if I'd seen something inappropriate, something I didn't want to see. But even with my computer closed, I still feel uneasy. I should probably email Ms. Baldwin back and thank her for her efforts, then tell her that I have no interest in going to Waltman College.

Instead I take out my phone and call my mother.

"Are you busy? Having dinner with Andy or something?" I ask when she answers.

"Wǒ zàijiā. Nǐ gēgē gēn tā de péngyǒu chūqù," she says. No, I'm home. Your brother is out with his friends.

"Which friends? Doris?"

I don't know. I don't think so.

"Oh. Okay. How are you?"

My mother tells me she's doing well. She tells me she is really looking forward to next week, when I come home. It'll be so nice for us all to be together again, she says, though this summer did pass quickly.

"It really did," I say, startled. I'd been so busy I'd barely noticed that the summer was almost over. I can't believe it. It seems too soon.

How are you? What have you been doing? she asks.

I tell her about the party. I describe the lights, the tablecloths, the waiters, the ice bar, the food, the band.

It sounds very beautiful, she says.

"Yes, it is," I say.

But so much money spent for one night.

"Yeah. . . ." I glance at the clock. "Mom, I have to go now."

When Vanessa opens her bedroom door, she is wearing a lacy silky something in white that I am almost certain is a bathrobe.

"I like your robe," I say to make sure. I don't know why it matters to me, but it does.

"Thank you, dear. It's an old one, but one of my favorites. I bought it for our honeymoon." Vanessa smiles dreamily. Her face is all made up. Skin smooth. Cheeks glowing. Eyelashes a long, thick sweep. Only her lips are still human: a little pale, a little dry, a little wrinkled. She has not yet applied her lipstick.

"You look so pretty," I say.

"So do you," she says.

"Thanks." I know she is being polite. I'm wearing my black dress. At graduation I felt sophisticated. Now I think I look like I'm going to a funeral. My flat black hair doesn't help.

"But I have a surprise for you." She goes into her walk-in closet and comes out with a dress on a hanger. It's the dress I tried on at the boutique last week, the beautiful green-blue dress that I could never afford. And now Vanessa is handing it to me, telling me it's mine.

"No, you shouldn't have; it's too much," I say, barely aware of what I'm saying. But then the beautiful dress is in my hands, the fine fabric flowing through my fingers.

"It's my pleasure," Vanessa says. "I wanted to thank you for everything you've done for us this summer. It's the least I could do. Ella is doing so well, and you've helped me so much too. So please, put on the dress."

"I can't," I say.

"You must," she says. "Oh, don't cry."

"I'm not crying," I say. And I'm not; it's just moisture welling in my eyes, just one tear slipping out. I wipe away that one tear and go into Vanessa's bathroom—an enormous marble room—and put on the dress.

Then Vanessa does my makeup; she insists. Her touch is light and nimble. It feels strangely calming to have her working on my face. She smells sweetly clean as the air after a good rain; she smells like her perfume; she smells like Vanessa.

"Ta-da!" she sings when she's done.

I open my eyes. I look at myself in the mirror. I look,

honestly, beautiful. In blue-green silk. With ironed-straight
hair. With shimmering eyelids and noticeable lashes and a
slight flush. With a glossy rosy mouth. I look beautiful and not
at all like myself.

"Thank you. Thank you so much," I say.

"You're very welcome." She gazes at me proudly, as if I am
something she made. In a way, I suppose I am.

"Um, Vanessa?"

"Yes?"

I know I should leave it alone. They seem happy; I should
be happy. But I can't stop myself from asking. "Did you tell
your husband I told you?"

"Did I tell him what?"

"About the phone call."

To my surprise, Vanessa laughs. "Oh, the phone call. Yes,
I told him."

"And he wasn't angry?"

"No, he was glad to explain. It was just a misunderstanding."

"A misunderstanding?" I ask. Hoping she will now explain.

"Yes, that's all it was."

"Oh. Okay. Good."

I nod. I zip Vanessa into her golden gown. She looks amazing, and I tell her so.

"Thank you, darling." She smiles at me. "One more thing.
You know those earrings I gave you? You have to put them on.
They'll be the perfect finishing touch."

Back in the pink bedroom, I hang my graduation dress in the mirrored wardrobe. Then I stare at myself, this beautiful version of myself, in the glass.

I'm confused by what Vanessa said: that she talked to her husband about the phone call and he wasn't angry. I'm confused by how Jeffrey Morison seems to have offered me an internship in exchange for my silence, and even though I broke my silence, he's still giving me the job. None of it makes sense. It feels wrong.

Though maybe it's just me. I'm not used to everything turning out fine. I don't believe in happily ever afters—I haven't for a long time. But maybe it is possible.

I go to the dressing table and take out the small white box in the top drawer. I look at the pretty earrings Vanessa gave me. Then I look at my ears in the mirror. I'm already wearing earrings: the tiny gold studs that my mother gave me that her mother gave her.

Slowly, I remove my mother's earrings from my ears.

Slowly, I put Vanessa's earrings into my ears.

She was right. They are the perfect finishing touch.

10

THE NOISE IS THUNDEROUS, SHAKING THE GROUND, VIBRATING through the air, filling the backyard with the sound of over a hundred people shouting and clapping and laughing as they scream, "Surprise! Happy birthday!"

Jeffrey Morison has his mouth opened wide. With one hand he covers his open mouth. His other hand he presses to his chest. His face is flushed. He looks genuinely surprised. Even I, who know he is not surprised at all, half believe that he is.

"What's all this?" Jeffrey says.

"Surprise! Happy birthday, my love!" Vanessa steps out from the crowd, shimmering in her gold dress, and wraps her arms around her husband. Ella and Henry join them, Ella snuggling between her parents and Henry standing at his father's side. A moment later, old Mr. Morison is there too, smiling.

Jeffrey beams. He appears too overcome to speak.

Really, he is incredibly convincing.

The party resumes. Guests approach the Morison family

to wish Jeffrey a happy birthday, to thank Vanessa for inviting them, to compliment their children, to tell Mr. Morison that he's looking well. Other guests continue drinking, eating, chatting. The band plays jazzy versions of classic rock songs. The sun is setting—the sky is softly red and orange and purple. It's all beautifully and exquisitely perfect.

But it's also kind of boring—for me, at least. After all, it's just a bunch of old people in fancy clothes gossiping and getting tipsy.

I wander toward the house and stand near the door, where I find something more interesting: every few minutes an attractive waiter emerges with an attractive tray of hors d'oeuvres. Over the next twenty minutes or so, I am offered a stuffed mushroom and a caramelized onion tartlet and a wasabi crab cake and an olive crostini and a prosciutto-wrapped scallop, and I accept them all.

As I chew my prosciutto-wrapped scallop, I see a familiar face near the bar. Although another attractive waiter is coming toward me with a tray of something that looks deliciously fried, I hurry toward the familiar face. It's Benny, one of my favorite students, and he's about to lick the ice bar.

"Benny," I say, pulling him back from the bar. "Don't do that. You'll get your tongue stuck, and when you unstick it, it'll really, really, really hurt. For days. Trust me."

He whirls around, tongue still poking from his mouth, and stares at me with shock. I love this about kids—how confused they get when they see you in an unexpected place. It takes him a moment, but then he grins. "Hi! What are you doing here?" Benny shouts.

"I'm tutoring Ella this summer."

"Oh!"

"How's your summer going?"

"Fun!"

"You're friends with Ella, right?"

"Right!"

"She's around somewhere. Should we go find her?"

"Yeah!" Benny laughs. He's such a cheerful kid, which is why he's one of my favorites.

"Where are your parents? Let's tell them you're going to play with Ella."

Benny gallops over to his father, who is chuckling with a bunch of old people in fancy clothes. "Dad! Dad! I'm going to play with Ella now!" he shouts.

"Okay, have fun!" his father shouts back.

Benny and I squeeze through the crowd to get to the Morison family. Henry has disappeared. But Ella is still there, held by her mother's hand on her shoulder.

I duck close and wave at her. "You want to play with Benny?" I ask.

Ella nods solemnly. And I realize that although she is not a particularly cheerful kid, she is now one of my favorites too.

"Come on," I say.

As Ella moves away, her mother pulls her back.

"Sweetie, where are you going?"

"I'm going to play. With Benny."

"But your father—"

I'm about to intervene, but Vanessa stops herself.

"Yes, Ellie, go play. Have fun. Be good." She lets her daughter go.

I smile at her, then I take the kids over to the dance floor, where no one is dancing yet. They giggle and whisper to each other, though even Benny's whisper is as loud as a shout. I see the waiter with the tray of fried somethings, and go get myself one. It turns out to be a fried risotto ball and as delicious as I imagined it would be. I eat it slowly while I watch the kids jump around.

"Well, well, well," a woman says.

I turn around. "Hi! How are you?"

"Certainly not as well as you." Joan Pritchett inspects me, from the smooth black crown of my head to my manicured toes. "Nice dress. Is it new?" she says.

"Uh, yes. I love your dress too. You look great," I say.

"This thing? I feel like a cow in it. Though I suppose you wouldn't understand. Doesn't Vanessa feed you? Probably not, since she barely feeds herself."

"Actually, the food here is really good," I say. It mystifies me how a child as cheerful as Benny could have a mother as negative as Joan. Maybe she's still annoyed at me for turning down her job offer this summer.

"Benny seems happy," I say. "He told me he's having a fun summer."

Joan shrugs. "How are things at the Morisons'?"

"Good."

"Really?"

"Yes, really good."

"I hear Lorraine Chamberlain came for a visit. How was that?" She smiles slyly.

I stiffen. "It was great. I think they all had a nice time together."

"I'm sure they did." Joan laughs as she walks away toward the bar.

I restrain myself from making a face and go get another fried risotto ball.

The sun sets. Conversations grow louder, the laughter more raucous, and people start swaying on the dance floor. Ella and Benny are playing freeze tag, which doesn't seem like the right game for only two players, but they're making it work. Jeffrey and Vanessa are surrounded by a crowd. Old Mr. Morison is deep in conversation with a man his own age. Henry is still nowhere to be seen.

I wonder if anyone would notice if I left. I doubt it.

After a few more hors d'oeuvres, I slip into the house, through the hallway, up the stairs, and into the pink bedroom. I shut the door and turn around. There's an unfamiliar girl standing there. My heart jolts.

But it's just me, just my beautiful reflection in the mirror.

Suddenly I'm overwhelmed with the need to get out of this dress and these earrings, to clean the makeup from my face, to wash this unnatural straightness from my hair. But before I can do any of these things, there's a knock on the door.

I guess someone did notice that I left.

"I knew I'd find you hiding in here," Henry says.

"I'm not hiding! I only left the party a minute ago. You disappeared hours ago."

"Not hours. One hour."

I shake my head disapprovingly.

"Uh-oh. You're not going to call me selfish again, are you?"

"Not out loud," I tell him, and he laughs.

Then, abruptly, he stops. "Hey," he says.

"What?"

"You look really nice."

I blush. "Um, thanks, uh. Would you like to come in?"

"No, no, it's too pink in there. Want to go for a walk?"

"A walk around the party?"

"Definitely not. Let's go down to the beach."

I hesitate. It's not that I'm afraid he'll try kissing me again—I'm sure he won't, not after the way I reacted last time. The truth is, I'm afraid that I might actually want him to try. . . . But I'm sure he won't and the summer is almost over and then who knows if I'll ever see Henry Morison again. So I might as well enjoy his company while I can.

"Sure," I say. "That sounds fun. Let me change first."

"Yeah, me too. Meet at the stairs in five?"

"Perfect."

I carefully remove the beautiful blue-green dress and the

delicate crystal earrings. I put on a pair of shorts and a shirt. I braid my hair. At the bathroom sink, I turn on equal parts hot and cold water and wash the makeup from my face. Then I look in the mirror and am relieved to see myself again. Though maybe also a little disappointed. But only a little.

As I walk down the hallway, I hear someone running behind me, then next to me, then past me. Henry races all the way to the staircase and shouts, "I win!"

"I've created a monster!" I yell. I do not change my pace.

Henry runs back over, turns around, and starts walking with me. He has changed into his swimming trunks and a shirt with a tear in the sleeve and a stain on the front. "You still look nice," he says.

"Thanks. You do too," I say.

We sneak out of the side of the house, whispering and giggling as we creep away from the party lights and noise and chatter. It's dark, but the moon is full and the sky is clear and the stars are bright, so although we stumble and wobble as we go down the winding path, we don't fall. And suddenly the ocean is luminous before us.

"Come on." Henry leads me across the sand.

"Where are you taking me?" I ask.

"It's a surprise."

"Another surprise?"

"Well, since the surprise party wasn't an actual surprise, we can make up for it now. My dad did act the part though, didn't he?"

"I was practically convinced, and I knew better."

"Sometimes knowing better isn't enough."

"Sad, but true. Are we going to the lighthouse?"

"I told you, it's a surprise."

Henry makes a sharp left, away from the water, into the brush. He takes out his phone to use as a flashlight. We follow a narrow trail up the hill to the lighthouse.

"I knew it!" I say. I stop and stare up at the tower. The paint is peeling, the wood decaying. It looks dangerously unstable. I move away.

"Nope, you're wrong." He grabs my elbow and pulls me forward, past the lighthouse and farther up the hill. His hand glides down my arm to find my hand. He hangs on to my hand. Probably so he can help me up some large rocks, which he does.

Friends, I remind myself.

But even after the rocky ground flattens into grass, he is still holding my hand.

In fact, I'm the one who lets go, pulling my fingers out from his grasp when I see where he's taken me. "Really?" I say. I use my freed hand to smack his shoulder.

"What? You don't enjoy a graveyard at midnight?" Henry says. Because now we are standing outside the Arrow family cemetery.

"First of all, it's not even close to midnight. Second of all, no."

"You're not afraid, are you?"

"Of course not," I say calmly. I'm really not. It's not too dark and I'm not alone and even though this is a cemetery, it isn't particularly scary. Mostly it's sad. Like the lighthouse, it hasn't been well maintained. The fence is a staggering square covered in rust and mold. The gravestones are stained and mossy and leaning in different directions. It feels like a long-forgotten place.

"Good. 'Cause we're going in." He swings open the gate. Or rather, he drags it open, very slowly and creakily. Then he walks to the far back corner. I pause for a moment, but I said I wasn't scared, and I'm not scared, so I force myself to follow him.

Henry crouches in front of a small, plain gravestone with a curved top. He holds up his phone to illuminate it. "I remembered right," he says. "Look."

I crouch next to him and squint to make out the carved letters. It reads:

ELEANOR

BELOVED DAUGHTER OF

LIONEL AND AGATHA ARROW

1911–1919

"Oh." I feel a soft breeze, like a cool breath, blow through my body. Even though the night is still, perfectly and completely, with no wind at all. But I'm still not afraid. In a way, this seems like the last piece of the puzzle. All this time, I had insisted that

I didn't believe in ghosts. And despite the unexplained noises, the bad dreams, the weird occurrences—I still don't.

But I believe in Eleanor Arrow.

It's a contradiction, yet somehow it's still true.

"Has Ella been here? Has she seen this?" I ask Henry.

"I don't think so. Everyone thinks the lighthouse is about to collapse, so we're technically not supposed to be around here," he says.

"Didn't stop you."

"I'm unstoppable."

"No kidding." I sigh. "Poor Eleanor. She didn't even get a mention in Family Cursed."

"Family what?"

"Family Cursed: A History of Arrow Island. It's a book about the Arrow family. I bought it for Ella to try to convince her that Eleanor Arrow didn't exist. But she was right all along. I wonder why they left her out."

"Maybe because she was so young when she died. Only eight."

"That doesn't make her unimportant," I say.

"Agreed," he says.

"We'll remember you, Eleanor. Hold on a second." I go over to the fence, where there is a cluster of small flowers on a thorny plant. I pick a few stems and lay them at the foot of her gravestone.

"You know those are weeds, right?" says Henry.

I scowl at him. "Doesn't matter. They're pretty."

"Right, sorry."

"Now apologize to Eleanor."

"Sorry, Eleanor."

"She forgives you."

"How do you know?"

"I know," I say.

We stay there long enough to get uncomfortable crouching, so we sit, long enough to get uncomfortable sitting, and so we lie down. Is it creepy that we're lying in the grass in a graveyard? Maybe. But it feels peaceful being here, watching for shooting stars as the moon drifts across the sky.

After a long moment of silence, I say, "I'm sorry."

"What for?"

"Calling you selfish."

"But I am," he says. "And you already apologized."

"I know. But the truth is, it wasn't really about you."

"Then what was it about?"

"Well . . ." I tell him about Waltman College, applying, getting accepted, and turning them down. "Even with the scholarship, I couldn't afford to go without taking out a bunch of loans, which is why I told my teacher I decided not to go. And that was true. But the real reason was that I can't leave my mother. So I was jealous of you. Of how you do whatever you want."

"Why can't you leave your mom?"

"She wouldn't get along without me. It's just . . . the two of us."

"Well, how's she doing without you this summer?"

"Fine, but it's only been a couple of months, and my brother is there too."

"Your bad brother? I thought you said he was making things worse."

"Yes. No. I don't know."

He doesn't say anything.

"Maybe it's also me," I admit, and start crying.

Henry rolls onto his side, props his head up on his arm, and gazes at me. He still doesn't say anything. He waits for me to explain. I've never thought of him as a particularly patient person, but now he looks at me as though he could wait forever.

So for a while I just cry. Then, when my tears eventually slow, I explain. "I guess I'm scared of leaving. Of letting my mom down. Of not being the perfect daughter. Of change. Of losing control. Of everything. Every single fucking thing. I'm just . . . so . . . scared."

As soon as I admit this to him—no, to myself—I start feeling better. I take a few deep breaths. I wipe my eyes. It has been a very, very, very long time since I've cried like that.

"You okay?" Henry asks.

"Yeah. Thanks for listening."

"It was worth it just to hear you curse. I've never heard you curse before."

I laugh. "Well, now you fucking have. So tell me your plans for after the summer."

"Well, I have orientation next week, so I have to figure out what classes I want to take and all that stuff. But I'll be back in the city after that—it's only a three-hour drive. So we can hang out then . . . if you're around and not tired of hanging out with me."

"Always around and never tired."

"Perfect." He smiles ruefully. "Now can I say something extremely selfish?"

"Yes, please!"

Henry lies back flat on the ground and stares at the sky. "I'm glad the reason you freaked out that night wasn't because I tried to, uh, kiss you or anything."

My whole body tenses. It would be easy just to agree. But if he's brave enough to tell me that, I want to be brave too. "Um, actually, it kind of was—not because I didn't want you to, because I did. But then I started thinking about how we're so different, our lives are so different, and I panicked."

"Okay," he says.

"Okay? You don't think I'm a total weirdo who worries too much?"

"The important part is you admitted you were dying to kiss me."

"That's not what I said!"

Henry smirks. "Why else would you panic?"

"Ugh, no, stop, let's talk about something else. How's your mom?"

"Much better. She and my stepdad went bowling yesterday, and she won two out of three games. They love bowling. Do you bowl? I can teach you."

"No! No more lessons!"

He laughs. I laugh. We keep talking as the night grows cooler, then cold; and I'm cold, I'm freezing, but I don't want to get up, I don't want to leave, I don't want this moment to end.

But eventually Henry sits up and asks, "Should we go back?"

"Never," I say.

"Your teeth are chattering."

"That's normal. My teeth always chatter. You haven't noticed?"

He laughs. "Come on. We don't want to miss birthday cake."

I immediately jump up. "Bye, Eleanor!" I say.

"Yeah, see you around, Ms. Arrow," Henry says.

We step through the gate and push it closed behind us. Our arms touch, brush, fingers tangle and twine. Then, hand in hand, we walk back to the house.

11

I WAKE UP IN MY FLORAL NEST OF BLANKETS, WITH THE SUN
streaming light and bright through the curtains, as the birds
chirp with wild cheerfulness outside the window. I smile.

Then I frown when I see what time it is. I've overslept.
Quickly, I brush my teeth and wash my face and change out of
my pajamas. I run downstairs to the kitchen, hoping I didn't
miss breakfast.

No one is there.

Furthermore, there is no lingering smell of butter or coffee or bacon. There are no dishes in the sink, no mugs on the
counter, not a single crust or crumb anywhere. I gingerly tap
the kettle on the stove. It's cold.

I check the living room, the dining room, the family
room. I go out on the deck at the side of the house and look in
every corner. I walk across the front lawn to the backyard and
around the swimming pool (which has been transformed back
from a dance floor). No one is there. Nor is there any sign of
last night's party, but that isn't surprising. Vanessa scheduled

a cleaning crew to come last night.

Maybe everyone is still sleeping—yesterday was a long and tiring day.

So I go back upstairs, knock on Ella's door, wait a minute, and go inside. She is not there. Her bed is unmade. Her closet door is open, and when I walk over to shut it, I see that most of her clothes are gone. I close her closet door. I make her bed. I notice that the books she usually keeps on her nightstand are also gone.

I take out my cell phone and call Vanessa. The line goes straight to voice mail. I call Henry. The line rings and rings; he doesn't answer. I walk downstairs to the kitchen again. I don't know what else to do. I'm hungry.

The refrigerator is full of food, as usual, and I'm relieved this much is normal. I make myself a sandwich and eat it quickly, standing over the sink.

"What are you doing?" someone asks.

I whirl around. It's Mrs. Tully. And I'm so happy to see someone, I smile at her. I swallow the food in my mouth. "Where is everyone?" I ask.

"What are you still doing here?" she asks.

"Why shouldn't I be here?" I stop smiling.

Mrs. Tully tilts her head, her expression thoughtful. Then she starts laughing. "Oh, they forgot about you, did they?"

"What?" Something twists in my stomach. I've probably eaten my sandwich too fast.

"The family went back to the city this morning," she says.

"They did? Why?"

"Mr. Morison wasn't feeling well, and they wanted to take him to his doctor. That's what Vanessa said, anyway." Mrs. Tully's face is set with glee. Spiteful glee. "How terrible that they forgot about you. But it's a good lesson, isn't it?"

My instinct is to politely excuse myself and go upstairs. Yet I don't do it.

Instead I look at her, not smiling, but not frowning either. My gaze is steady, and in a voice as steady as my gaze, I say, "Thank you for pointing out that lesson. In return, I think a lesson for you is that it's hurtful when you are rude to others."

I speak to her as if I'm speaking to one of my students. Gently, but firmly. Calmly disapproving. I speak to her as if she is half my age instead of three times my age.

"It's all right. I know you'll do better next time," I say.

Mrs. Tully glares at me, her eyes blazing, burning.

I politely excuse myself and go upstairs. And as soon as I'm upstairs, I start laughing. I can't believe I finally stood up to her. I'm so proud of myself.

But then I remember the Morisons and stop laughing. I call Vanessa again, and when the line goes to voice mail, I leave a message. "Hi, I heard about your father-in-law. I hope everything is okay. Please let me know if there's anything I can do to help."

I pace around the pink bedroom, clutching my phone in case she calls me back. I'm trying not to be hurt or offended. But . . . I'm a little hurt. A little offended.

Plus, I hate not knowing what to do next. Should I work on my lesson plans for next week? Or should I be packing my things and preparing to go home too? Since I don't know, I do both.

An hour later, there is a knock on my door. It's the woman who does the gardening for the Morisons. I barely know her—she works while I'm tutoring Ella—and I'm confused to find her here.

She looks confused too as she says, "Mrs. Tully asked me to tell you that she talked to Vanessa and the family isn't coming back, so we're going to close the house down for the season. She told me to tell you to go home. Today or tomorrow."

"Oh. Did she say anything about how Mr. Morison is doing?"

"No, but I hope the old guy is okay."

"Me too. Does Vanessa want me to call her?"

"Mrs. Tully didn't mention it. But she said that you'll have to drop off some stuff at the Morisons' apartment building in the city. She'll leave the suitcase for you downstairs. And she wants to know if you're going to go today or tomorrow."

I think it over. "I guess I'll leave early tomorrow morning."

"Great, I'll tell her." She smiles at me.

I try to smile back, but my face twists wrong, contorts, as if I've forgotten how. But this situation is so ridiculous: the gardener passing messages on to me from Mrs. Tully, who is passing messages on to me from Vanessa.

"Are you all right?" she asks.

"Yes, I'm fine," I say quickly.

After she leaves, I finish packing my clothes and shoes and books. I tidy up the bedroom. I tidy up the bathroom. I wait for the sky to darken and night to come, but the day seems to drag on. On and on and on. Finally the sun sets and I take a bath in the enormous tub. I put on my pajamas and crawl under the floral quilt. Then, for the last time, I go to sleep in the pink bedroom.

PART IV
THE CITY

1

TO TRAVEL FROM THE MORISONS' HOUSE ON ARROW ISLAND TO
their apartment in the city requires taking a taxi to the island
port, the ferry to the ferry terminal, the bus to the bus station,
and the subway to their building. The trip takes seven hectic,
stressful, sweaty hours. For me, it takes a few fewer minutes
because I take a cab from the bus station, though I never take
cabs. But I'm exhausted: from traveling all day, from sleeping
poorly the night before, from having to manage—in addition to
my bulky suitcase—a sleek suitcase filled with the things the
family forgot.

The cab turns on to a block of grand buildings and pulls
up in front of the grandest one. I try to straighten my wrinkled
clothes. The driver hauls the luggage out of the trunk. I pay
him and try not to fret over the cost.

As I approach the entrance, the concierge, a man in an
elaborate uniform and cap, opens the door. "Yes? Can I help
you?"

"I'm dropping this off for Vanessa Morison," I say.

"Let's see." He goes to his desk and picks up the phone.

I drag the two suitcases toward the elevator.

"Hey, come back. You have to wait here!" he shouts.

"Oh. Sorry." I drag the two suitcases to his desk.

He smiles—not at me, but into the telephone. "Good afternoon, Mrs. Morison. A girl is here with some suitcases, and she says they're for you?" He nods as he listens to her.

Then he stops nodding, stops smiling, tilts the phone away from his face, and tells me, "She says you should leave the luggage with me."

"What? I can't go up and see them?"

"Leave the luggage with me," he repeats.

I pause, then—

"I'm going up." I walk to the elevator and press the button. The door opens with a delicate chime. I step inside.

"Hey! Stop!" The man runs toward me.

The door closes. I am quickly and smoothly lifted up to the top floor. The hallway carpeting is plush and paisley, the walls shimmer like the inside of a seashell. I barely notice. I'm regretting my hastiness. I don't want to bother the family, especially if old Mr. Morison's condition is serious. So I decide to leave the sleek suitcase outside their apartment and go.

However, before I can do that, their front door opens. Maybe it's my own suitcase that gave me away—the plush carpeting softened but could not completely absorb the loud squeak of the wheels.

"I'm sorry," I say. "I didn't mean to disturb you."

Vanessa stares at me. Her hair is a snarled golden nest. Her eyes are red and wet. She is wearing a robe, but it couldn't possibly be her own robe—it's a dull purple plaid in unseasonable flannel, the fabric faded and pilled. It's something my own mother would wear.

"Are you okay? Is Mr. Morison all right?" I ask.

For a moment, she just continues staring at me. Then she says, in a sharp and unsteady voice, "I'll take the suitcase. Then you have to leave."

"What's wrong?" I ask.

"It's not a good time. Just go."

"But . . . can I at least say hello to Ella?"

"No, I don't think so."

"Why?"

"Joan told me about the spell."

"The spell? What are you talking about?"

"Ella told Benny, who told his mother, who told me that you and Ella were casting spells together. I don't want that kind of influence around my daughter. Especially now." Her voice cracks on the word "now." She wipes her wet red eyes.

"It wasn't like that—" There is a flash of movement behind Vanessa. I glance past her.

Ella is standing a few feet behind her mother. Her eyes are dark. Her cheeks pale. Her lips pinched into a line. She shakes her head nearly imperceptibly at me.

I look back at Vanessa. "Please let me explain."

"It's time for you to go." She takes the sleek suitcase and

pulls it into the apartment, leaving me in the hallway with my bulky suitcase.

As the door slowly swings shut, Ella lifts her hand.

Good-bye.

Then the door closes with a muffled thump. I feel it in my chest. Still, I stay there staring at the creamy-smooth surface of the closed door. Staring at nothing. Until the concierge comes to escort me out of the building.

He scolds me, but I'm not listening as I trip across the plush paisley carpeting, blur past the shimmering walls, and stumble to the elevator. He presses the button. The doors slide open. It's a smooth plunge down to the ground. I notice I'm not breathing. I remind myself to breathe. Inhale, exhale, inhale.

It's true that Henry said his stepmother has a way of over-reacting.

But this still doesn't make any sense. I've spent nearly two months living with the Morison family. Eating meals with them. Going into town together. Lounging by their pool. Talking and laughing. And now I'm being escorted out of their building.

Outside, the sun is blazing. The air is thick with humidity. Even on this clean, wide, tree-lined street, the heat is almost unbearable. Yet I just stand there in the middle of the sidewalk. A woman trips over my bulky suitcase and curses, rubbing her leg. She looks like she's in terrible pain. She yells something at me. I'm in such a daze it takes me a moment to understand what she yelled. She yelled, "Go back to your country."

"All right," I say, much too late. She is long gone.

* * *

When I walk into our tiny, dingy, thin-walled, stale-smelling old apartment, my mother stares at me in surprise. I failed to tell her I was coming back. Coming home. She steps out from the kitchen, where she is cooking dinner. She hugs me and asks what I'm doing here.

I mumble some explanation. "Where's Andy?" I ask.

She says he went to pick up something at the store. She looks at me with concern, but then she has to go back to the pans on the stove, where the hot oil is snapping.

The evening news is on in the living room, even though no one is watching. I go to turn off the television. My finger touches the button. Then I jolt backward, as if electric shocked. And my body feels as if I've been electric shocked. Because there, on the screen, is Jeffrey Morison.

He is coming out of an office building with two other men, one on each side of him, their hands clamped around his arms. He slouches forward, head down, face clammy, eyes on the ground—and for a moment I think that he must be the one who is ill, not his father. But as he walks past the camera, something flashes: the metal ringing his wrists.

Jeffrey Morison is in handcuffs.

The reporter is speaking, and I'm trying to listen, but I can't seem to put together the story. All I hear are certain words and phrases: fraud, scam, scandal, millions missing, a massive scheme, assets frozen, financial ruin, prison, years in prison, decades in prison, ruin, ruin, ruin. And I feel a throbbing pain in my stomach, my head, my heart.

The two men bring Jeffrey Morison to a police car and sweep him into the backseat. The car drives away. The camera pivots to the reporter at the scene, who is still talking, but my attention moves to the people standing behind him, a small crowd of observers. I stare numbly at a young girl in jean shorts and a tank top. She is clutching something in her hands. A doll, maybe—I can't quite tell; her fingers are in the way. The girl looks familiar. Maybe she was one of my campers at Sunshine Day. I can't remember. But I can't stop staring at her. Because she seems to be staring right back at me.

I know it's impossible. She can't possibly see me. And yet . . .

In a low and solemn voice, the reporter says, "The Morison family, the family that seemed to have it all, now appears to have lost everything."

Then the girl smiles, revealing a row of small, sharp teeth. Familiar teeth. My breath sticks in my throat. Fear creeps into my chest. It's Eleanor. And she's holding my missing ballerina figurine.

2

SEVERAL DAYS LATER, I AM LYING ON THE COUCH, STARING AT the TV, when the doorbell buzzes. I don't get up. My mother is at work. My brother is at work. It's early afternoon on a weekday. I cannot imagine who it could be. Nor do I care. But then there is a metallic clatter: the sound of a key rattling in the sticky lock. I jump up just as the door opens and my brother comes inside.

"What are you doing here? I thought you were working." I smooth back my hair and yank my pajamas into place. No one is supposed to see me like this. When my family comes home in the evening, I am always cleaned and combed and dressed. No one is supposed to know I spent all day doing nothing.

"I got out early. Why didn't you answer the door?" Andy says.

"I was busy," I say.

"Busy?" My brother glances pointedly from my disheveled hair to my disheveled pajamas to the disheveled couch to the soap opera on the television.

"Busy." I shut off the TV and move toward the bedroom.

"Where are you going?" He follows me.

"I'm going to read."

"What are you reading?"

"A book." I turn around to shut the door.

"Hey, don't be like that." He stands in the doorway so I can't shut the door.

"Like what?" I say.

"You haven't been yourself since you got back. What's going on?"

"Myself? What do you know about who I am? You've barely been around the past couple of years, so why do you think you know anything about me?"

"I'm your brother. I know exactly who you are, Little Miss Perfect. And this? This isn't you. So what's wrong with you?"

I stare at him.

And then I explode.

"What's wrong with me? What's wrong with you?" I say. "You think you can just come home and everything is forgiven? The favorite child, with your stupid job and your plans to go to school, and taking Mom out to dinner? Well, guess what. I see right through you. And when you disappear again, I know I'll have to pick up the pieces. Again. I'm used to it. But don't you dare think that I want it this way, that I only care about being a nice girl, a good daughter. I have to do these things because you're busy doing whatever you want. So while you're out in the world, you should remember that I'm stuck here, taking care of everything, because of you."

I'm shocked by what I'm saying, but I'm too angry to care, too angry to stop, too angry to look where I'm going, so I keep going—right into a ditch:

"Because you left," I say. "Just like Dad."

My brother flushes. His cheeks, his forehead, his nose, his chin, his whole face gets very red. I wait for him to lose his temper and scream at me. Once he's done screaming, he will stomp away. Then I can go into the bedroom, shut the door behind me, and be alone. All I want is to be alone.

But he doesn't scream at me. Instead he says, in a low voice, the last thing I expect him to say. "I'm sorry."

"What?" I'm certain I must have misheard.

Andy steps back from the doorway and goes over to the living-room couch.

I don't remember my brother ever apologizing to me before. Even when something was undeniably his fault, like when I was seven and he was ten and he dropped my thermos and the cover broke and he claimed the broken cover is what made him drop it in the first place. He never apologized.

So I'm flustered. That's why instead of going into the bedroom, I follow him to the couch. He sits down. I stand next to him, staring at him. "Andy?"

"Sit down or go away," he says. "Don't hover."

I sit down. "I didn't mean what I said."

"Sounded like you meant it."

"Okay, I meant some of it. But it's not your fault. For leaving."

"No?"

"No."

My brother shrugs, idly scratches his arm, still not looking at me.

And I realize he's hurt. I've actually hurt him. It's what I wanted to do, but I never thought it was possible—I never thought my brother cared enough about me to let anything I said or did bother him.

But maybe I was wrong. I've been wrong about so many things lately.

"Andy," I say, grabbing his scratching fingers. "It's not your fault. Things haven't been easy for you either. I know that. And anyway, you're not like him. You came back."

My brother pulls his hand from my hand. The physical contact seems to make him uncomfortable. But then he flops back into the couch cushions, visibly relaxing.

"Yeah, I guess so," he says.

"Anyway," he adds, a moment later, "what's your deal? Doris is worried about you. She said you've been ignoring her calls. She thinks you're depressed."

"Doris isn't a doctor yet. She shouldn't try to diagnose me."

"Whoa." Andy laughs. "I think I like this new mean you."

"It's not mean. I'm just being honest." I pause. Then I ask, carefully, casually, "What's going on with you and Doris, anyway?"

"Nothing. We're friends." His expression stiffens into expressionlessness, but his expressionlessness gives it away: my brother, like so many boys before him, has been kindly rejected by Doris Chang. I feel an unexpected pang of sympathy for him.

And so I change the subject. "Maybe I am kind of depressed," I admit.

"Because of what happened to the guy you worked for?"

"Yeah."

"But that guy's a crook. He stole millions from his investors and broke all sorts of other laws. He deserves to go to jail," says my brother, who has gone to jail.

I nod. It's true. Because even if it was Eleanor Arrow I saw on the television that day—and I can't help thinking it was, that she had returned to watch the family's downfall—the fact is that whatever Eleanor may or may not have done, it was ultimately Jeffrey Morison's actions that led to his ruin.

After reading numerous newspaper articles, I put the story together. Lorraine had been caught giving Jeffrey confidential information. That was what the phone conversation I overhead was actually about. Then once the authorities began investigating, they discovered evidence of fraud and the misappropriation of funds. That's why the family had rushed back to the city: not because of old Mr. Morison's health—which was, as far as I knew, fine—but because the police had shown up to take Jeffrey in for questioning.

"So why are you so upset?" my brother asks.

Yes, why have I spent the past few days on the couch while the television wailed with soap opera drama? Why haven't I answered Doris's calls or responded to Ms. Baldwin's recent email that said she had good news for me? Why have I been behaving so unlike myself?

"I feel bad for his family. They're losing everything," I say. The apartment, the cars, the jewelry, the house on Arrow Island—all of it would be sold to repay investors.

"Okay, so they're poor now. Welcome to the club."

"It's not just that. Their lives have been ruined."

My brother shrugs. "Not necessarily. Maybe they'll figure it out."

"I hope so." I think of Ella. I think of her as I last saw her, her face pale and sad and small, as their front door swung closed between us.

"Have you talked to them?"

I shake my head. "Vanessa thinks I'm a bad influence."

"Are you kidding? Is she crazy? Wait . . . are you crying?" Andy looks panicked.

"No. Maybe. A little. I'm sorry. I don't know what's wrong with me." I pull a tissue from the box on the table and dab my eyes, my nose.

"Nothing's wrong with you. But stop crying."

"A week ago I was with them in their house, doing everything together. And now it's like it never happened. This sounds so selfish, considering what they're going through, but I really thought my life was going to be different. Yet here I am, back at home, and nothing has changed. Nothing is ever going to change."

"No, things are always changing."

"Not for me. Unless I go . . ." I stop.

"Go where?" my brother asks.

My fingers clamp across my mouth. I hadn't realized I had been thinking about it, much less considering it. "Waltman College," I say, words muffled by my fingers.

"What are you talking about?"

I drop my hand and tell him about applying to Waltman, getting accepted, and turning down their offer. I tell him about Ms. Baldwin and her emails. Then I say, "But of course I can't go, no matter how much financial aid they give me. It's so far away and it's too short notice and even if it wasn't, I still couldn't go. I have to email Ms. Baldwin and tell her."

"You haven't emailed her back?"

"Not yet."

"You have to go."

"I know. I'll go email her right now." I stand and walk toward the bedroom.

"No. I mean you have to go to Waltman," he says.

I stop. I turn around. "I can't. What will Mom do?"

"I'm home now. I'll help out."

My first reaction is to not believe him. Then I decide to try something different. I decide to trust my brother. But . . . there are still too many obstacles. "I can't. I've got everything planned out for the fall. I've enrolled in classes and ordered textbooks and I have my tutoring students lined up," I say.

"If you don't go, you'll be the one keeping yourself stuck here."

"No, it's not that, it's—"

He cuts me off. "You're not like him either," he says. "You'll come back."

I stare at him. I keep staring even after he swivels around on the couch, picks up the remote control, and turns on the TV. He flips through the channels to a baseball game. He looks at me again. "Mèimei, you're wrong about nothing changing this summer," he says. "You've changed."

Then he turns back to the television. The batter swings and hits the baseball with a sharp crack. It flies high, then drops fast. Foul ball. My brother curses enthusiastically, punching his fist up in the air. And I laugh aloud.

He's right. I must have changed—if I'm actually thinking my brother is right about anything. And if that can happen, who knows what else is possible?

AFTER

SHE HAUNTS ME. SHE VISITS MY DREAMS AND I WAKE UP ANX-
ious. She slips into my thoughts and distracts me from my
work. She lingers in my memories. My shark mind keeps moving, searching for some kind of plan, any action I might take.
But I know there's nothing I can do to help her, at least for now.
For now, I can only hope that Ella is okay.

In the meantime, I keep busy with classes and friends and
a work-study job at the college library. Plus all the other every-
day stuff. Like checking my mail. "Hi! I have a package," I tell
the guy behind the desk.

He brings over a box. "Careful, it's much heavier than it
looks," he warns.

I'm not surprised. It's one of those flat-rate boxes that cost
the same price to send no matter how much it weighs—so I'm
sure my mother stuffed anything and everything she could fit
in there. The cardboard bulges in all directions. I haul it up to
my dorm room.

"What's that?" asks my roommate, Carly. She's an art

major from the Midwest. She has short bleached hair and wears lots of black and black eyeliner and looks terribly tough, but is extremely nice in a way that reminds me a little of Doris.

"My mom sent me a care package."

"All right! What's in it?"

"Let's see."

My mother was painstaking with the packing tape, so it requires a pair of scissors and some violent yanking to open the box. Then I take out the items, one by one, and show them to Carly. A carton of my favorite sesame cookies. A bag of loose tea. A vial of herbal medicine. A bottle of chili-garlic hot sauce. Socks. A new wool scarf. A pair of slippers. A pillowcase. Another pillowcase. A can of chicken soup. A can opener. Two sets of chopsticks. A fleece blanket. Some books I asked her to send. My sweatshirt I asked her to send. More socks. A tube of lotion. A pot of hand cream.

"Wow, how'd she fit all that in there?" asks Carly.

"My mom is a master of organization," I tell her.

"Nice." She puts on her coat and her backpack. "Okay, I'm off to class. I'll meet you at the library at four? Also, I heard there's a party on the third floor tonight."

"Perfect! See you later!" I smile at her as she goes.

Then I turn back to the box. At the very bottom, there's an envelope. I pull it out and examine it with curiosity. It's addressed to me—to my home address—and stamped and mailed, but there is no return address. The handwriting is unfamiliar: wide and angular, slightly sloppy.

I open the envelope. There are two sheets of paper inside: one large and folded, one small and torn. I look at the small torn one first. It's a note written in the same slightly sloppy handwriting as my address on the envelope.

Ella asked me to send this to you. I'm sorry I've been out of touch, but I've been busy. Maybe one day I'll be less busy. I really hope so. Anyway, I'm sure you're having fun and making trouble wherever you are. Swim safely.
—Henry

His note makes me so sad. Not because I care about him or miss him or wish things could have turned out differently— though I do care and miss and wish. But mostly I'm sad because I can sense his sadness in everything he wrote and everything he left out. Especially everything he left out.

I set the small torn paper down on my desk and pick up Ella's letter. For a moment I just hold the folded sheet like a prayer between my palms. Part of me doesn't even want to read what she wrote—I'm already so sad. But when I unfold the paper, I discover it isn't a letter at all. It's a drawing.

Ella and I are in the pink bedroom, a version of the pink bedroom that is actually more like a meadow than a room. The flowers on the quilt have spread to the floor and there's no wall behind us, just the blazing sun and a sky that's a beautiful shade of blue. But when I look closer, I see that it's actually not a single shade of blue, but many, maybe five, maybe ten, maybe a hundred, maybe all the blue shades in a thousand-pencil colored pencil set, maybe all the blue shades in the world, blended together on this one piece of paper, to make this one drawing of us. We're smiling. And I smile. In the corner is written: "Best regards, Ella."

ACKNOWLEDGMENTS

Many thanks to Kristen Pettit, Elizabeth Lynch, everyone who worked on this book at HarperTeen, and my agents, Sarah Burnes and Logan Garrison Savits. Thanks to Jonah Sirott, Maria Van Horn, Claire Stanford, Aurvi Sharma, and Sara Culver for all their help. My heartfelt gratitude to the MacDowell Colony, Playa, and the Virginia Center for the Creative Arts for taking such good care of me while I wrote and ate and wrote (and ate). And, as always, thank you to my family—I love you!